The Christmas Curmudgeon

A Christmas Story for Guys

James Cox

Copyright © 2007 by James Cox

All rights reserved. No part of this book shall be reproduced or transmitted in any form or by any means, electronic, mechanical, magnetic, photographic including photocopying, recording or by any information storage and retrieval system, without prior written permission of the publisher. No patent liability is assumed with respect to the use of the information contained herein. Although every precaution has been taken in the preparation of this book, the publisher and author assume no responsibility for errors or omissions. Neither is any liability assumed for damages resulting from the use of the information contained herein.

This is a work of fiction. Names, characters, places, and incidents either are the product of the author's imagination or are used fictitiously. Any resemblance to actual events or locales or persons, living or dead, is entirely coincidental.

ISBN 0-7414-4087-3

Cover design and art by James Cox.

Published by:

1094 New DeHaven Street, Suite 100
West Conshohocken, PA 19428-2713
Info@buybooksontheweb.com
www.buybooksontheweb.com
Toll-free (877) BUY BOOK
Local Phone (610) 941-9999
Fax (610) 941-9959

Printed in the United States of America
Printed on Recycled Paper
Published July 2007

"....the strange Child
Picked up by this overstuffed confidence man,
Affection's inverted thief, who climbs at night
Down chimneys, into dreams,
With this world's goods.
Bringing all the benevolence of money,
He teaches the innocent to want, thus keeps
Our fat world rolling. His prescribed costume,
White flannel beard, red belly of cotton waste,
Conceals the thinness of essential hunger,
An appetite that feeds on satisfaction,
Or, pregnant with possessions, he brings forth
Vanity and the void."

From "Santa Claus"
by Howard Nemerov

Dedication

For my Brother John

Acknowledgments

Deep bows of gratitude go to Bob Voorhees for his thorough editing of the book as well as for the hours he spent with me in discussion of the manuscript and for his insightful ideas regarding issues of content. I am also deeply grateful to Linda Brown for a second editing and thorough review of the book. Thanks to Steve Brady for the suggestion of including the poem by Howard Nemerov as an opening thought. He also offered useful comments on several chapters. My wife, Paulette, read all the revisions and offered insight and truth all along the way. Without her support, interest and thoughtful commentary I would be traveling a different road.

Prologue

I suppose my interest in the two-sided nature of the world goes back to childhood, to my first awareness that things are not always what they seem. This object of awareness, the duplicity of life, might start at a deeper layer, with trouble in my parents' lives, rooted in their middle class anxiety over constructing their contentment according to others' rules. Keeping up with the Joneses was the phrase for it in their day. There were appearances and there were realities; a full life in one way and emptiness in another. But, I don't see it clearly enough. I would like to go back into the roots of our family, into the lives of my immigrant grandparents who crossed over from Europe to America on a ship with a dream in their minds and found that the dream they imagined and the reality they experienced were not the same. I would like to study that, understand the opposition, the conflict, and its impact on them. The duplicity, that's the thing. The expectation and the disappointment. The ideal and the reality.

This disparity between the expected and the realized, the factual and the fantastic sticks in my gut like a swallowed failure. We try to achieve, to create a life full of successes. We buy so much to make the dream come true. We want our lives to be stupendous, but they always end up being ordinary. And Christmas condenses all of this into one incredible, twisted, gut-wrenching, calamitous and, above all, monetary orgasm. Christmas contains the intention to heal the crooked bone, but the exigencies of the treatment are too much a part of the illness.

This is what is at the core of what my brother Henry and I find most disturbing in our lives. And, though neither of us obsesses about such things, there exists a time each year in our lives that corners us like animals in the wild brought to bay by the relentless pressure of a pack of hounds. The hounds of money, consumerism, cultural conformity and debt. We are pushed to the edge of insanity and then over into drooling, wild-eyed madness. That is the Christmas season. And, we are the brothers Jenkins who made the news one year.

❖❖❖

My brother Henry started going bald in his mid-twenties. By the time he was married and the father of two adolescents, his head was like a ripe honeydew melon fringed with a row of fine brown fur. It looked like a hair hem had been sewn to his head from one ear to the other. He took it as a sign of diminishing youth, a loss of virility, even potency, views which he countered vigorously with weekends of wild feasting and drunkenness and virile, manly camping safaris into the remote regions of the Great Smoky Mountains, including nightly, almost nightly, romps with his lovely, slim wife, Janette, gyrating atop his 300 pound torso, bucking bronco style, her sandy, blond hair flying, one hand swinging in the air, (one can only imagine, of course; though Henry does have a tendency to be enthusiastic in the description), her gleeful shouts matching his grunts and howls, followed again by wild feasting and still more drunkenness. Thus, I have heard the sound of the beast and know the nature of its urgency, its love of life, its fear of death, its hunger.

Self doubt piles upon self doubt for Henry. Becoming bald, the humiliation of it, stirs the darkness in him, which for him, in the ordinary course of his life as a stockbroker, means finding ways to be mischievous, and, if feeling low and miserable, sometimes malicious. He likes to steal something from my house and then drop by and ask to borrow the very same thing. While I search for it with increasingly paranoid frantic anger wondering about the security of our home, digging through shelves, boxes and trunks of cars, cursing the neighborhood children, the neighbors, delivery men, my wife and my own children for thieves, he stands by sympathetically, assuring me that it doesn't matter, it's not that important, he can get one at the store.

"Relax", he says, "there's no point in losing your mind over it. Of course, I could use it ...that's why I came by to borrow it, but if you can't find it, don't worry about it. I'll just go waste some money and buy a new one. Then when yours shows up we'll have two. You know, after a while we can have a big garage sale, sell off the duplicates and go on a vacation with the proceeds."

Ha, ha. Henry is a funny guy. For some reason I never catch on. Maybe I'm becoming forgetful. In fact, it's true, as certain as recurring doubt. My wife Mary has mentioned it, too. Forgetting the last location of my car keys is a commonplace event. Of course, everyone does that, but I will even lock my keys in the car with the engine running. Mary suggested carrying a spare key in my wallet. It works.

I have put my pocket knife down and forgotten it, sure after several days that someone has stolen it only to happen upon it by chance weeks later in one room or another, on a table or on a shelf, not even able to remember how it got there in the first place. So here's the devil – doubt. It is through the offices of this forgetfulness that I am undone. Because I have learned to doubt my memory, I can't with certainty call Henry's bluff. And, accepting the role of fool rather than risking the disgrace of a false accusation has through practice made what was a role a reality.

There may be something deeper in the soul that roots this forgetfulness, something hidden, something itself forgotten. Oh, why not go the whole way and tell it all. My theory, which completely explains the problem, involves having a multiple personality including a secret subconscious character that operates beyond normal awareness who hides things just to cause torment and disorder in my life. Mary doesn't like this theory and won't offer it any support. It's too creepy for her.

    I am Henry's brother, Harry. My thick, dark brown hair extravagates from my head in unruly waves. The hairless one looks intently upon the fact that I'm not going bald with fire and ice as he stares at my head. Our blue eyes meet in stark opposition. Were we Titans, we would wrestle, but we have outgrown those times and now our competition has softened and corrupted into impolite verbal exchanges like those of politicians more interested in self-protection than winning. I smile knowingly. He accepts the truth but sneers.

    "Yeah, but I make more oodles of dough than you do with your noodle job, professor."

    "Yes, you do." My retort will surely irritate him. "I guess we can't all be corporate toads."

    "The whole country's a corporate toad. I just spread the wealth more evenly."

    "Hah! From those who haven't to those who have."

    Henry scours me with a jaundiced eye. "And you're a noodler, a writer of stories, not frequently published stories I might add and a professor of what? What is it, anyway?" *He knows very well what it is.* "English? Everybody speaks English, Harry. You profess what we already know."

    "Well, then, we're both just as useful as can be."

    "A couple of real donkeys, eh?" Henry's face lights up.

    "Reindeer without antlers pulling the cart."

    He clobbers me on the back with the flat of his huge fat hand. "Okay. Let's go have a beer."

    We've had this same conversation or some version of it many times. It's a ritual. We share a joke about being donkey-men, the basis for one of my failed stories. In the story I'm pulling a long wooden cart full of new toys. The traces squawk wretchedly under the weight. My mind grovels through thoughts

The Christmas Curmudgeon

of new debts, and the debts, like stones, weigh my head down to the ground. My nose sniffs the dirt of the road, and my tears fall, large round drops, burning, unnoticed. My family rides high on the bench seat, whipping me along as I pull the cart, and as I dig my hooves into the stony ground, straining with the effort, sweaty and tense, pulling as hard as I can, I think only of the pleasure it would give me, pleasure in the form of relief, just to make it over one more of life's many hills. Then, at the crest of the hill another donkey-man approaches from the other direction, pulling another cart just like mine, loaded with family and bags of toys, tears in his eyes and sweat on his brow. A look of beleaguered suffering casts a gloomy aura around his face.

"Merry Christmas," I say to him.

"Merry Christmas," he replies as he passes.

The two families in the carts wave to each other, all smiles and glad tidings. The whips crack and the donkey-men plod down the other side of the hill. All we can see is dirt and debt.

Maybe this present story, the one I'm writing now, is one of the central stories, maybe *the* central story, of our lives. It's the story of how we changed, how we came to terms with the truth and made our way to the next station: travelers, like all men are, on a journey of confusion and despair, folly and humor, through an ever-darkening darkness, brightened by the lights of family life, loving wives and our fierce friendship.

At the heart of this darkness, there is Christmas. How Christmas seems to galvanize all our dissatisfactions. How can we stand one more year of glut? Christmas, year after year, that symbol of self-indulgence and financial ruin. This veritable icon of American idiocy, denial, guilt, greed and consumption, brings us always to our knees, begging for relief. Will we get it? Will we get any relief? Will there be any respite from the ever turning wheel of work, consumption and debt? From the anxious burrowing into ourselves to find an answer? Oh, the crushing pressure of debt. Who knows? Christmas is only a day, after all. The rest of the year you may live reasonably, without fear, without being sucked into the dark hole of nothingness that Christmas creates, abandoned there to ruminate on your excesses. Or, you may not.

Chapter One

Every year about this time the tiredness comes. It settles in like an invisible fog. I inhale the damp, soporific vapor, close my eyes and reel with fatigue. Dazed, dull-witted and nearly demented, I stumble down the long hallway toward my office as energetic students fly past. Some greet me by name and I crinkle my eyes and grin falsely at their vigor. The gray marble floors and the light tan walls of this old building seem to absorb human energy. Perhaps, this place is an alien device surreptitiously planted here to drain us parasitically; a marble web for human flies. Apparently it can only victimize one person at a time. And, I'm the lucky one; the walls seem to hum with satisfaction. Maybe, the science fiction course I'm teaching has finally taken over my brain.

I swing through the door into the large reception area, which doubles as department conference room, where Sally sits in the center of her island fortress, imperious with wizardly secretarial knowledge of Windows, PowerPoint, Excel and even Photoshop. I cast a baleful, sinking look her way and lean wordless against the door to my inner sanctum, grateful for her presence, protection and understanding, then fall silently through, barely nudging the door closed behind me and, with three slow luxurious moves, stride, turnabout and splay in the ergonomic reclining chair behind my desk. My flab-enfolded bones fall helplessly into the embrace of the soft leather. My long legs straighten and stretch into the space beneath the desk. Comfort is an addiction. My belly rumbles. My eyes set in bags close, and my chin drops and doubles upon my narrow neck and Adam's apple. My mind lets go. The invisible fog descends.

When Christmas season arrives, for a minute or

two I try to shut down my mind then realize the futility. My brain goes into overdrive, hyper-stimulated by the stress hormones that the season releases. Every year, I promise my wife Mary that I'll be good. No explosions. No ranting and raving. I won't hide in the basement with a bottle of rum pretending to repair some broken household gear, a vacuum that won't suck, a toaster that won't pop, a piece of electronic crap. Make them work well enough to sell them cheap and be rid of them; that's how they were made in the first place.

The invisible fog. It doesn't provide the same smooth, clean, relaxed feeling that rum provides. Rum calms and cheers you. It's quieting. The fog fatigues. And the fog isn't silent. It whispers invidiously, "Christmas is coming, Christmas is coming." It beckons me to get going, attend to work, grade papers, think of gifts, read endless lines of sentences, call catalogues, make lists, plan wonders, rise from the dead. Something! Anything. No way. Not a chance. I'm not listening. I've caught the sleep too closely this time. The whispering fades. Slumber, sweet slumber, where is thy sting?

While I'm sleeping, it might be a good time to fill you in a little on the lives of Henry and me. He's a stockbroker, my brother, successful, and lives in a two story colonial house on an acre of land in the north end of the city where other upscale types like to live. Henry's fantasy is to buy a huge tract of land in the mountains a few miles west and live the lone eagle life, carrying on his business via the Internet, fax and telephone from the perch of a large deck overlooking the sea of trees that surrounds him. But his wife and children need the city proximate. Their youngest daughter, Viv, spends half her life at the library and Mel, the elder girl, gives real meaning to the term extracurricular. His wife Janette is at that busy age when social and school obligations engage her more than thought. And my wife Mary is her partner as much as possible, though Mary works part time.

The Christmas Curmudgeon

Ashton is a wonderful place to live, nestled in the mountains as it is, replete with natural wonders, fishing streams, parks, hiking trails and a stable economy. It's a small North Carolina city that contains the bounty of a much larger one. Arts, fairs, movies, theatre, fine restaurants and musical events abound. A low crime rate and a high rate of enthusiasm bless Ashton. And, there is beauty, natural beauty in the mountains, and all around, as far as the eye can see.

Mary and I live near the university, more toward the center of town than Henry and Janette. We've added two rooms to the back of our bungalow for the kids. The back yard harbors a grand maple tree, at least thirty years old, which turns gold and red when the weather changes in October. We picnic beneath its branches throughout the summer and fall. A euonymus hedge borders the front yard, split by the path to the front door, and a pair of Bartlett pear trees and a flowering red bud grace us each spring with sweet scent and beautiful blossoms. Mary gardens and I pretend to handiness, incarnating an adequate performance often enough. The house itself, vertical gray boards on the outside, sheet-rock painted neutral tones inside, takes in plenty of light through its wide windows, and doesn't creak or shudder in the wind.

With a friendly group of neighbors, a real old-fashioned neighborhood where most of us are acquainted, though a few have dispositions like iron grates, we're well satisfied. You would think I would have no complaints, and I don't really, not really. It's just that for as long as we've been here I've suffered the curse of this fatigue, a bone-weary tiredness. The sense of dreariness, the dull flower of displeasure that seems to scent each room I pass through with decay, delivers an aromatic decadence that saps my strength. It's Christmas and the smell of debt. I'm sure that I'm an escapist and sleep is my trap door.

So. I'm asleep, having a wonderful dream in which I'm the powerful and wise commander of the Star Cruiser Jules Verne. We're about to test for the very first time the new magnetic field engine which will enable star cruisers to travel at unheard of speeds using barely a wink of energy. Of course, there are risks. There's a chance the ship could polarize and split apart. I know this, but I can't tell you why. It's beyond my knowledge of the physics of space travel to understand the operation of the magnetic field engine. But, I understand that there are risks. I'm the commander after all.

While in my chamber aboard the ship, preparing my pre-test speech to the crew, a being from another dimension begins to materialize in front of my starboard window. For a moment, it's not certain whether she's inside or outside the ship. But then, as her body materializes completely and she begins to move, it becomes clear that she is, in fact, in my quarters. She's standing right in front of me.

She's wearing a liquid, skin-tight garment that delineates all the fine features of her magnificent physique. Those definitely aren't name brand clothes she's wearing. They are something better by far. I wonder where she got them. Her irises are amber and her thick brown hair shimmers with a thousand tiny lights. She incites in me the sudden urgency of all my needs and hungers. I remain in control, however, in order to further analyze her intentions. I'm used to this kind of experience, being the Commander and all ...powerful and wise. But, she takes me by surprise when she begins whispering in my mind telepathically.

"Commander." She speaks in a husky soft tone. "Commander. You have called and I have come."

"I didn't call you," I protest, somewhat annoyed by the violation of my mental space.

"I have a message." She tosses her hair with a swing of her head. Her luscious body throbs slightly.

I maintain control despite the fact that she rubs her hands down and up her sides then loosens the zipper at her throat. What if she gets unzipped? What will I do?

"Yes ..." She leans toward me, her full lips slightly parted. "Someone needs your help."

"Someone needs my help."

"Yes ..." Her face is next to mine, her hands on my head, my shoulders, caressing me. She kisses my neck, my ears and my face.

Suddenly, there's a harsh buzzing in the background. It's the Shipboard Intruder Alert. What's going on?

"Commander ...professor."

Professor?

The buzzing continues. I'm startled and disoriented.

"Professor. Professor Jenkins?"

Who? What?

"I know you're in there, professor. Come on now, wake up."

Still groggy, but able to open my eyes, I'm in my office at the university. Sally, my secretary, out in the reception area, is buzzing me on the inter-office intercom.

"What is it?" I say, not too happily.

"Your wife is on the phone."

A look at my watch tells me it's a quarter till five. I'm late for something. I feel sure of that, but I'm not able to remember what. "Well, put her on. No, no. Wait! How did she sound?"

"Like you're late."

I am late! I know it, but for what?

"Did she say for what?"

Sally laughs as she teases me. "She might have, but I'm not telling."

"Oh. ohh ...kay, Sally." *Okay for you.* A mock menace seeps into my words. "You will be sorry."

She says nothing then announces that she's leaving for the day.

What would I do without Sally? She's like a young mother to me, always anxious about my needs and I'm like an overgrown infant with food on my face wearing the hat of a professor. I'm forty-two years old and I can't even answer my own phone. I wouldn't know where my performances are scheduled from one day to the next if she didn't give me my platform, my pack of cards, my ball and my set of horns. I suppose I will have to buy her some sort of appreciative gift for Christmas. A gruesome prospect, but unavoidable.

I switch on the speakerphone and lean back in my chair.

"Harry?" My wife's familiar sweet slow speech starts at the click of the switch. "Did you forget Henry's dinner? You should be on your way by now."

So ...that's what it was.

"No, of course not. I've just been busy." She's patient with my blustering. "How could I forget my own brother's birthday dinner? I just got tied up here with some work."

"Mmmm, hmmm. Were you napping, Henry?"

What if I was?

"I was not napping."

"You were. I can tell."

"You have a woman's reason, Mary. What can I say?"

"Uh hunh, and do you remember where we're having dinner?"

Damn! She got me. "Alright." *I might as well eat the Dark Thing.* "Alright, I admit it. I've forgotten everything. I've done it again."

"You could get some of that Prozac."

"No."

"Go to a doctor."

"There's nothing wrong with me."

"You're a depressive narcoleptic."

"I am not. Sleep is natural. I'm a natural man."

"Okay, fine, Mr. Natural." Thankfully, she doesn't press the matter further. She smooches me over the phone. "Listen closely."

She's calling me from Gregg's Lands Away clothing shop where she works. What in the world will her co-workers think? Smooching. Maybe they all smooch over the phone. *They spend the day watching people change their clothes. Fat people, even ugly people, people with nothing better to do and no intention to buy. Who knows what that does to you.*

"If you leave now, you can pick up his hat at McCoy's. I know you know the one we picked out, but in case you forgot, I called the girl and had her put it aside. She'll be looking for you. Then you can drive over to the Olive Garden. God knows why Henry likes that restaurant, but that's...."

"He likes the Tiramisu."

"Oh, that's right." She returns to her agenda. "If you leave now you'll only be ten minutes late." She waits for me to respond, to announce my intention to follow her directions. But a voice from a deep hidden part of my psyche begins speaking, making a powerful suggestion. *Why don't we drive down to the coast for Christmas and spend a few days by the ocean?* It's startling. Yet, there's something awfully positive about the suggestion. I wonder if Mary would like the idea. We could go away. We could actually go. It feels like a good idea.

"Harry, are you still there?"

"Yes, yes, yes, of course, Mary. I'm on my way."

"Good then." She smooches again and I smooch her back.

I don't know when this phone smooching started. I really don't recall. And it hasn't been that long, either. No more than six months would be a fair guess. I don't remember what set it off. What got it going? No doubt, Mary would be disappointed if I didn't smooch her back. She thinks it's romantic, possibly a resurgence of our passion. I don't know what it means.

Struggling out of the ergonomic chair, which tilts back as you try to go forward, I almost master the correct maneuver for standing without looking like a diver practicing his jack-knife. Then the phone rings again. Sally should get the phone. But didn't she say she was leaving? I push the button and stand by.

"Professor Jenkins here."

"Harry!" The booming voice of my brother makes the phone cradle vibrate. "Did you pick up my hat yet?"

"I'm on the way."

He knows his birthday gift is a hat because for the past eight years since he moved here from Winston-Salem it has always been a hat. That's when he first erupted over going bald.

We were at a restaurant, without the kids, so it was a restaurant for adults, with soft music, soft lighting, white tablecloths and crystal wine glasses. There was no Formica, no ketchup dispensers, no disposal bins. The chairs were not attached to the floor. We were actually enjoying a relaxed evening meal. But, Henry fussed over his food, fuming and sputtering, obviously at his end over something. Janette eyed the ceiling then looked at Mary and me like Henry was a man she didn't know. Henry caught her.

"See. See. That's exactly what it's about. People begin to treat you like you're a moron or some old senile fool."

"What is what about?" I ventured.

"Going bald!" He looked up, incredulous. "Going bald is like dying. You hairy people don't understand. It's literally like dying. Your life is falling away. People look at you with sadness ...or with incomprehension, like you've been turned into an infant – bald, soft and pudgy, unable to think or speak. You're no longer yourself. It's terrible. It actually makes you feel feeble and unattractive. And worthless. You stop caring for yourself. You don't brush your hair because you don't have any. You just look at yourself in the mirror like some old person who has forgotten who they are. You stare at yourself. You don't brush your teeth. Nothing matters anymore. I'm telling you it's like dying."

That Christmas, as a joke, we got him an incredibly ugly hat, a WWI leather and cloth flight helmet with furry earflaps that covered his ears and straps that tied under his chin. We had an insignia of the grim reaper stitched onto the front. What a laugh. He loved it and he felt better.

"It's yellow." I'm anticipating his question regarding this year's hat.

"Yellow!? ...Ugh."

"But that's all I'm going to say."

"Oh, come off it, Mr. Christmas. Give me a break."

Mr. Christmas is code between us for you haven't sold out to the system, have you? You haven't defected to the women have you? It's an insult. We make it a point not to give in to any of the multitude of gift-giving rituals, not even for birthdays. No hints, no private list, no badgering for information regarding desires, needs or wants and no teasing secrecy. That's all part of the schematics that support the consumerism, the gluttony of Christmas.

"Okay, it's a hat."

"Oh, well big surprise. You know I know it's a hat. It's always a hat."

"Mary is on to the game, Henry. She told me not to tell or else."

"Or else? What does that mean?"

"I don't know and I'll need more time to find out. So, just know that whatever your gift might be, a hat or not a hat, it's ugly. There will be laughs."

There's a brief silence as we both recall the history of hats that Henry has received – a sombrero, a flowered watch cap, that Russian thing, a straw panama. What else? There were others. I know we both are imagining the same thing. It happens with brothers. It comes from childhood. You share the same life though you have different lives and sometimes, though you have different minds, you share the same thoughts.

Henry breaks the silence. "Harry, I can hardly wait. This year I can feel it. Santa Claus is going down this year. The corporate bastards are going to pay."

"A strange goal for a stockbroker, don't you think?"

"I hold no stock in retail, Harry, except drugs. We can't live without drugs."

"So it would seem."

"I'm putting up posters all over town. Amputate the Puppeteer! A picture of a marionette Santa. A pair of disembodied corporate hands above him holds the strings. Amputate the puppeteer! Get it?! It's gruesome, but good."

"What does Janette think about it?"

"Are you kidding? She'd kill me. If it weren't for Christmas she'd have no reason to live."

"Oooh."

"Oh, c'mon. Anyway, I want you to help me put them up."

"What?"

"The posters."

"I don't think so."

"Do think so! Think positively! Think fun!"

"Think two old fat guys in jail surrounded by drug-addled perverts," I say.

"No way!"

His exclamation reduces our conversation to silence. My blank response squats in the phone line like a protester in a college hallway.

"Let me think about it, Henry. Unlike you, I need to think about what I'm doing ...maybe if we're disguised and its night time."

"Okay, think. Think until you stink." I can tell by his tone that he remains cheerful despite my reticence. "See you ...don't forget my hat!" Henry hangs up.

November. The ashen sky, the dying ember, our steps through leaves toward dread December. For some the Christmas season is the season of joy, and for others the Christmas season is the season of dread. Some people sit before the warm glow of their televisions, their children gathered by their feet, and chuckle at their favorite special Christmas shows: 'The Grinch Who Stole Christmas' ...'Miracle on 34th Street' ...'Elf.' They laugh and they smile. They shop and they smile.

They smile and they smile. Goodness fills them. They give blessings to the misguided and unfortunate. They scatter coins to charities and the poor. They love the coldness of the snow when they are outside and the warmth of the fireplace when they return home. They are fools mesmerized by sleight of hand.

    I stand in the doorway, before leaving my office, and wait for a dizzy moment to pass. My mind swims. It's just the tiredness. A brush with the cold air, hatless, and a take-out cup of coffee in the car will revive my spirit. But, I'm tired to the bone and something unknown seeps through me. I swing forward boldly and face the open space of the departmental reception area. All the other doors are closed. The others are gone, professors and students all. None attends to this late hour. Perhaps, that's the cause of my fatigue.

    Of course, Sally is gone, too. So, the air is full of emptiness. Her island is spoiled with stacks of papers and a disarray of notes and letters. The whole room seems cluttered and the air dense with left over noise and this, along with the empty space, gives me a sense of sorrow and regret. Maybe I need some time off, a respite from the demands of work, the pressure and the people. But I know in my heart it's Christmas, the seasonal three D's: the dread, the debt, the depression. It hits me this way every year.

☙

Chapter Two

After picking up Henry's Do-Rag, I rush to the restaurant, arriving only fifteen minutes late. The hostess escorts me past several dividers and around two corners to a back section of the restaurant where Henry, Janette and Mary are seated at a corner table. Two windows overlooking the parking lot enhance the scene. Overhead, English ivy hangs from pots. The vines have crawled across the valances above the windows and tangles of leaves descend like tattered green curtains in front of the many glass panes. As we approach the table, a departing wine steward passes with a smug look of disdain on his face.

"I took the liberty of ordering wine," says Henry as we arrive. The hostess who brought me turns and leaves. Henry's cheeks are flushed and he's clearly feeling spirited. "We've sampled a few glasses and decided this Glen Ellen Cabernet is the best."

"Good," I take a seat next to Mary. She leans over and gives me a kiss.

"That's what we like," chuckles Henry. "A little affection."

"Happy birthday, Henry." I hand him the gift, which has been neatly boxed and wrapped by the girl at the store.

"Hey!" says Henry, smiling broadly, as he grabs the gift. "What is it?"

"It's a hat."

Mary shoves me in the side. "Don't tell him it's a hat."

"Why not?" I retort. "We've given him a hat every year for the past eight years. He knows it's a hat. He's prepared for it being a hat."

Janette and Mary give each other the lost wives look. They wonder from which planet their husbands

The Christmas Curmudgeon

were sent. My defense continues as prompted.

"Oh, yes. I see your look. But what kind of hat it will be is the question. That's the real excitement. Will it be a fedora or a sombrero ...a pink bowler, maybe? That's the real meaning of present-giving ...the thoughtfulness, the creativity that inspired the purchase."

We all watch Henry as he tears away the wrapping paper and opens the box.

"Wow!" He exclaims with obvious exaggeration. "It's a hat! But what kind of hat? That's the true excitement. Ha Hahhh!" He lifts it from the box and dangles the bright yellow cloth decorated with pirates and parrots in the air. The tie strings hang loose. He looks at me baffled, then nods appreciatively. "It's a bikini, by gosh! Won't I look good in this. Shall I put it on?"

Janette slaps Henry's arm. "It goes on your head not your bottom."

Mary sips her wine.

Henry ties the do-rag on his head and grins. The pirates and parrots stand out nicely. He looks odd but wonderful. Ooohs and aaahs all around.

"I'd wear that one all the time, Henry. It suits you."

"Arrr, me needs a hoop in me ear. Aye, and a sword, too."

"Yes, but can you still set sail, climb the rigging and fly with the wind?" Mary smirks.

"Maybe not ...but I can still steer me ship into the dock."

The food arrives and saves us from further insult. The dishes look surprisingly well-prepared for the restaurant known as the Hardees of Italian food. Lifting my glass for a toast draws everyone's attention and momentarily suspends animation.

"May the winds blow fair
And your skies be clear;
May your ship sail long
And every port be home."

"Well, I hope not," exclaims Janette.

" ...and your home port strong," I amend.

"Aye," goes Henry, swigging his full glass of wine. The rest of us take reasonable draughts.

"Bless you, Henry." Mary's sudden tenderness turns our faces toward her. We are touched and no one knows what else to say.

I refill the glasses and we drink all together again. The wine produces a pleasant calm.

Both Mary and Janette look lovely. Their faces glow and their smiles radiate good will, happiness and a comfortable state of well-being. They must use Oil of Olay. The fact that each of them has given birth to several children doesn't seem to have noticeably altered their figures, their physical features or their attractiveness. If anything, their beauty is deeper. Maturity and experience have enriched their presence. On the other hand, Henry is nine-tenths bald, has a huge belly and the beginnings of jowls. My drab sport coat sags on my shoulders, but hides my flab; my dress and appearance are generally disheveled. We look like a couple of Wal-Mart clerks who eat from the aisles and sleep in the employee lunchroom.

"Did you notice Janette's new hairdo?" Mary asks point-blank.

"Well, I was just going to mention it."

"I didn't notice either, Harry."

Henry tips his glass as I gaze intently upon Janette's hair. I don't see anything different.

"It looks great, Janette." *Go ahead. Take a stab.* "Did you have it tinted?"

Janette looks truly shocked. "Can you tell, really?"

Now, I'm not sure whether it's good to have noticed or not. It was just a guess, after all. Mary elbows me, but her elbow doesn't tell me which way to go on the issue. Does noticing mean I think Janette looks older and needs to look younger? Or, does it simply mean I think her hair is attractive? The truth is, I don't know. Yes, but, I haven't been around for forty-some years for nothing!

"I'd say you've been using Revitalique by Clairol, Janette. Your hair is infused with vibrancy, shine and vitality and I do think I detect a complex, yet optimistic, golden brown color that gives you a youthful and golden, likeable appearance."

"You're so full of baloney, Harry. You can't tell any difference, can you?"

Henry raises his wine glass silently, smiling at me. It's a toast to my failure. He knows and he laughs. I raise my glass and take a drink, but then sit up, shifting to a better position. Certain of having done well, I lift my chin and look at the others with superior conviction. "To hair and all that it means!" I raise my glass to the ladies in particular. Henry beams. Any two of us could spend an hour together and probably get along fine.

Our conversation moves around the events of the day to peculiar things seen in parking lots, mysterious car noises, strange billing practices, absurd comments made by people we don't really know and, of course, children. I discover that Willy, our eight year old, is dangerously close to becoming a skateboarder. Mary is nudging him toward a less urban, outdoorsier, short-haired, healthy mountain bike image of himself. I don't object. It seems to me that skateboarders, as a rule, do have a defiant sort of screw-you-I-don't-care attitude, despite all the defensive hollering and positive promotion they receive from activist adults with nothing better to do. Behavior speaks louder than words.

Henry discovers from Janette that Melanie, their sixteen year old, has a secret boyfriend – secret in the sense that Henry doesn't know about him. This coincides with a theory Henry has about mothers and daughters excluding men in order to form the path to womanhood. He's nonchalant, actually happy, about it. He doesn't want to know about boyfriends or anything having to do with boyfriends. He doesn't want to understand or talk about emerging sexuality or controlling your dates or, in fact, anything actually having to do with sex, impulses, female parts, vaginal devices, secretions, treatments, or upkeep.

We're a little woozy from the wine. The dinner plates are cleared and dessert and coffee are served – Tiramisu, of course. We're halfway into dessert when Henry perks up and goes into his I've-just-had-a-realization look.

"I'm surprised they haven't found a way to package this for Christmas," Henry announces, forking another large bite of Tiramisu into his mouth.

I nod my head, as do Mary and Janette. The three of us pass furtive glances at each other to check our expectations. Mary gives me the you-better-not-join-in-on-this look and Janette takes on a sort of trance-like but tolerant I've-been-there-too-often, pointedly numb face. I contain my delight, but give Henry a nod, a bad boy's sign, a secret permission.

Henry understands his position clearly. He has seen these faces before. It doesn't bother him. He's about to be transported to a higher plane.

"That's why this stuff is so damned good!" he exclaims. "Don't you see? They can't package it. What is it? Some kind of custard-like Italian cake concoction. You can't put it in a can. If you put it in a box, it would turn to rot, mold and stink inside of a day. If you froze it, you would ruin it. It would separate into equal parts of dry crumbly matter, yellow goo and that mysterious, thick, slimy, colorless liquid stuff that is the basis of all organic matter.

"Hah! Tiramisu has thwarted the Christmas pirates!"

"Christmas pirates?"

Henry points to his do-rag. "The gift inspires me, Mary."

Mary shakes her head.

"Think of it! There's hardly anything that hasn't been Christmas-ized." He looks down at his plate, childish glee on his face. "Some poor fellow in New

York is up right now burning his mind to ash trying to think of a way to put Tiramisu in a can for Christmas, but he can't. Ha! Haaahh! He can't come up with anything. He's so frustrated that he gnaws on a chicken bone from his take-out dinner. In a fury, he slams his desk with his fist." Henry demonstrates by way of pounding the table with the flat of his hand, all the time grinning and growling like a madman. The people at the next table look over at us, startled. "He realizes ...no, no ...he knows that he's going to be fired. The poor bastard is desperate. Hah! The poor fool."

"Oh, Come on, Henry. It's not that bad," says Janette, making a feeble attempt to settle him. To no avail. The whole scene makes me smile. The polite surface that supports the flotilla of tables and diners around us has been disturbed. We ride the swell from an underground eruption in a sea of quiet eaters.

"The guy realizes he's spent his entire adult life inventing ways to suck people into buying more and more stuff. Stuff they don't even need. Gnnnn gaaahh! The idiocy of it overwhelms him. He feels the horror of his hypocrisy. In actuality, he hates Christmas, just like any sane person, yet he sells it, day after day! Year after year! He has devoted his life to maintaining and promoting the commercial conspiracy. He lives off Christmas. It's too much. He can't stand it any longer! He writhes at his desk in an agony of self loathing." Henry nearly falls off his chair at this point as he twists and turns, alternately pulling at his cheeks and clutching his stomach to show how the man writhes.

"Stop it, Henry. You're annoying people."

The folks nearby shift in their seats and frown with displeasure. A hand raises and there's a nod to a waiter.

Henry rolls his head in an arc and turns to face them. "Sorry folks, don't mind me." He points to his head. "It's the hat."

The two men at the nearest table laugh. Their wives are mollified.

But Henry isn't finished. Thinking of the suffering of the imaginary Christmas marketeer gives him great pleasure. His laughter comes from a primitive, dark and communal depth that resonates in all men. We love to see one of our fellows captured in the amber of his folly. Henry's veins pop out on his forehead and temples and his face turns red with a swell of congested happiness, which triggers the same response in me. The laughter swells and surges; we're gasping for air. Our wives look upon our lunacy with a mixture of amusement, annoyance and contempt.

The waiter arrives and senses that we're just loudmouths having a good time. He asks our neighbors if they want to move to another table. Apparently, they will have to wait for a table to be cleared, and meanwhile, endure our lively offensiveness. They glare at us and whisper among themselves. For a few minutes, we self-consciously control ourselves and attend to our dessert.

When we have settled down, Janette questions Henry, "What is so funny?"

"You wouldn't understand," Henry feels the challenge in Janette's tone and shouts at her, unexpectedly angry. Now, the people at the adjacent table stop what they're doing, probably checking for the possibility of violence and considering avenues of escape. One of the women is bug-eyed; the other indignant.

One of the men leans over toward our table. "Take it down a notch, will you."

I nod repeatedly. But Janette feels stung and turns, red-faced, to Henry.

"Ohhh, and why is that? Am I so stupid? Is that it, Henry? Am I too stupid to understand?"

One of the men leaves to get the waiter.

"It doesn't have anything to do with your being stupid, Janette." He grins. "Your stupidity is beside the point." He smiles in a wide pumpkin-like fashion while rolling his head and eyes like a stooge just beaned by a brick. "You're a woman, Janette. This is

The Christmas Curmudgeon

not just a Christmas thing, it's a guy thing. Only guys understand what I'm saying here. Women are at the core of Christmas; they're inside it. They can't see it the way we do. Isn't that right Harry?"

I'm wary of speaking indiscreetly here. It's one thing to slander Christmas, quite another to cast women as somehow inside Christmas, actually fueling the fires of commercial insanity. Of course, we know this is true, so deeply, cruelly true. But it's a course that seems unwise. Still, I can't leave Henry hanging. Christmas *is* odious in too many ways.

"Well, it seems likely that women and men have different views of Christmas. Women and men see everything differently. They're both human but their minds are twisted by diffcrent terrors. Traditionally, men have felt a greater share of the economic responsibility in a family – they're conditioned to feel this way – and, as a result, they tend to be more alert to things that target their ...uhhh, financial security – scams, come-ons, lies, cons, deceptions, false claims, advertising exaggerations, that sort of thing. Women have had their perception altered by sugar plum ballerinas. You see..."

"You boys have altered perceptions," Janette says, lacing her comment with acid, "because it's so hard to see clearly with your heads so far up your butts your stomachs flutter when you sneeze."

Two waiters approach and stand beside our table.

"I just see the absurdity." Henry speaks as much to the waiters as to anyone else. He smiles and wipes tears from his eyes.

"We're going to have to ask you to leave if you don't quiet down."

Henry muffles a snort.

"It's simple enough to see the absurdity," Mary leans forward and whispers, ignoring the waiters, "but to see the totality, the total reality, that's another story."

We stop to consider the point. The waiters decide to leave.

Janette breaks into a beautiful, relaxed grin. She may see something beyond her annoyance. She may have just had too much wine. She smiles magnificently – a Crest toothpaste smile. Then we all smile and continue smiling, like idiots, and laugh with the awareness of our predictable, quite human, family behaviors.

The conversation smoothes and settles like a river at the end of a run of rapids. We're in a deeply peaceful wine-induced calm. We share a sense of loving one another. We silently toast our neighbors as they prepare to leave. It's a New Age kind of moment. *Maybe we should light a candle and exchange home made beaded necklaces.* I'm careful not to share this thought with the others. The wives might take offense and Henry might start ranting again. Besides, to him, loving is a practical activity. Sex, talking, hugging, arguing it out, thinking ahead, planning and doing the right thing – that's love. I might even agree. *Beads are for bozos; candles for storms.*

Minutes pass in silence. Then we begin the gathering up, the paying of the bill. Our final remarks, like a simple song learned long ago, pass from our lips drunkenly.

Mary smiles as she looks around the restaurant. "It's a beautiful life."

"So it is," I raise my nearly empty glass for a toast. "To the beauty of life and to beautiful wives."

"Hear, hear." Henry assents affably.

We drain the last few drops in our glasses and go.

◆◆◆◆

"Posters?" inquires Henry, before we separate to go to our cars.

"Oh, alright," I say. "Posters."

On the way home, Mary scolds me for supporting Henry. I know what she's after and try to explain that Henry, like all men, reacts to the financial obligation that Christmas entails with a fury that he tries to joke away.

She snorts. "How do you feel about it, Harry?"

Well ..." *Don't do it you fool. Don't say a word.* "For most men, Christmas is a kind of indentured servitude. It puts you permanently in debt. You can't escape. It comes every year, and every year you're buried in that hole. By the time you dig your way out, what's the first thing you see? It's Christmas again. There it is waiting for you like an evil gnome, its sharp-toothed grin wide with delight, just waiting to gnash, then tear another chunk of flesh from your body. You develop a dread."

Mary is silent, considering my remarks. She will file them away for future lessons, yet unknown to her, or me, where I will be corrected, shown the error of my thinking and put to shame.

Chapter Three

We got our dog two years ago, almost two years ago to the day. I remember the day well and reflect upon it often. It was then that I realized that the literary musings of a famous French woman, an alcoholic and celebrated author, might be right. The man of the house has the same status as the children; no matter if he is a modern man who washes the dishes, dusts and helps with the laundry. The woman still considers him a child. The house is her domain. No matter if she is a modern woman who has a job in the workaday world. She manages the house, writes the checks and, like a fairy godmother or Glinda, good witch of the north, she casts spells on all within her realm, making for them a charm, delivering unto them a boon, healing and saving and asking only fealty in return, belief in the wisdom of her way, no complaints about her cooking and cooperation with the dictates of her system. I abide within.

Willy had been frightened by some older boys Halloween night that year. They were just teasing him, but he didn't feel safe. He was but a bit of a boy. Tom, our older boy, feeling aggressive at age fourteen, was all for chasing down each one of them and punching him in the face. I decided we would talk about the problem and work out some civilized strategy, which turned out to be talking about the problem and making sure Willy kept us informed if anything else happened. That's what I thought anyway. Then Mary came home from work one day, about two weeks later, with one of those happy cat-just-ate-the-bird looks on her face. This is how it went.

"What's up?" Suspicion comes naturally as a response to Mary's mood.

She cakes her teeth and shakes her fists up and down with excitement. She can be like a kid that way. Sometimes I like it and sometimes I feel impatient, or worse, old and dull. "I've got a surprise."

Oh, no. She's traded in her car again.

"I can't wait." My mouth tastes of salt.

"Come out to the car." *Oh God, she has. There was nothing wrong with her old car. It was almost paid for.* She twirls around in a complete circle and a half and heads back toward the front door, glancing back over her shoulder. "C'mon."

Her car, the same five year-old Honda Accord is lightly bouncing in the driveway. The engine is off. Then I see it, the large baggy face of a dog, her paws up and down on and off the passenger side window. Mary runs to the car, opens the door and the beast lunges out. In two leaps she's at me, up on her hind legs with her enormous paws on my chest. Well, she's friendly, at least.

"Now, before you say anything ...just look at her. Isn't she cute? Isn't she the greatest?"

"Mary, she's gigantic."

"And she's just a pup!"

"Wow. Let's go inside."

"No, no, the kids need this. It will be great for Willy."

"Look, I like dogs ...nobody can say I don't like dogs ...but ..."

"No buts ...Let's go inside and let me explain."

"I understand why you got the dog, but this ...this is more like a lion. Look how big it is. We're looking at Gargantua here, Mary."

"He that has patience may compass anything. Remember?"

Stunned to silence, no argument remains.

Once inside, the dog settles down to roaming the house. We sit at the kitchen table. The dog shuffles in and out and in again, panting, puts her paws up on Mary's lap, then hears a noise, bounds out of the kitchen, slides through the doorway into the hall knocking a chair off its feet, barking low and deep, each woof separated from the last by several seconds as if she has to think about whether to woof again or not.

"Here's what," Mary begins. "Dixie down at the office had a Great Pyrenees, just a beautiful dog. She brought it in sometimes and, anyway, it got free early last spring and, wouldn't you know..."

"Ho, Whoa, gal." I hold up my hand. "Slow down. And, just an aside here. Who in the world is Dixie?" Mary has never mentioned a Dixie before and now she's talking about her like she's one of the old friends we used to have. "Does she come from deeply hillbilly Confederate stock?"

"What?"

"How do you get a name like Dixie?"

"It's not so strange. She named her own daughter Texas and calls her Tex."

"That's what I mean."

"Well, Mr. Brainy. In case you haven't noticed, we now live in the South. Women here have names like Dixie, Sue Ellen and Georgia, and men have names like Jeb, Jessie, Gudger and Buddy. It's how it is."

"Okay, I forget. I still think about the civilized world a lot ...where monster truck rally has the same appeal as Confederate flag underwear and pickled hog brains."

"We've been here ten years, Harry."

"One of my students spits tobacco juice in an orange plastic Hot Spot gas station cup during class."

"Poor baby." She pats my cheek. I nod my head. *Okay for you, baby. I'll send him down to your shop for a fitting.* The huge dog returns and sits at our feet by the table, apparently listening.

"Anyway," Mary throws her right palm up like she is suddenly carrying a tray, "Dixie's dog got free and got pregnant ...the Newfoundland next door to her she thinks is the culprit. Imagine that. So General Grant, that's Dixie's dog – now that is funny isn't it?" I nod appreciatively. "She had four pups, well five, but one didn't make it. And, oh my God, the mother ate the head of the dead one, so Dixie put the rest of them aside and had to feed them until the mother settled down. Then the mother died. Apparently, she ruptured something or had some complication they didn't know about. Anyway, she died. Dixie was heartbroken and cried for a week. She couldn't bear to part with the pups after that and kept them at home for the last seven months. But, look at her ...can you imagine four of those in your house? So, she asked me if I wanted one."

"And, of course, you said yes."

"Who wouldn't? Look at that big goofy thing. And ..." She's looking at the dog. She grabs the huge head of the dog, rubs it and tugs it around this way and that. "She's sooo sweet. She'll be great."

"Well, I can see it's not up for discussion. So what now?"

"Nothing now. It's all done. I just got back from the vet on Maple Street. She's wonderful, and the dog has shots and tags. We're good to go. Can you wait to see the look on the kids' faces? It will be soooo fantastic."

The reason we don't have a dog is because we have kids, Mary. It's sooo stupid. "The children feed it and walk it." I'm stern.

"It?" Putting her hand to her mouth. "Oh, you're right."

She's ignoring me. Issues like responsibility are already clear in her mind. Agreement is inconsequential. I'm certain she doesn't see the kids feeding and walking the dog. She sees them playing with the dog, rolling around the floor with the dog, throwing balls and Frisbees for the dog to catch and lying about with the dog in front of the television.

"Here you are calling the dog IT like it was a thing, and I realized you're right. She doesn't have a name. Dixie never named any of them. Won't it be fun?"

"Won't what be fun?"
"Naming the dog."
"We can call her Fiasco, Fifi for short."
"Family meeting after dinner. We'll name the dog all together."
"Well, then, it's decided." I stand up. "I guess I'll go back to my duties as shareholder of the corporation."
"Poop."
"That's right ...and don't call me Mr. Brainy. I don't like it."

♦♦♦♦

Working in the den with the door closed all afternoon grading student papers makes me more inclined to like the dog. She'll be good for going for walks and, no doubt, for the kids. There may come a day when we'll all go for a walk together as we did when the children were small. Maybe when they're grown and flown from home and their own children are small, Mary and I will come to visit, and then we'll all walk their dog. *Maybe when Mary is dead and I'm old and lonely, we'll all go for walks. God, what a thought.*

There are no great student writers this quarter, and the grading is going slowly. It's hard to differentiate between bad and not quite so bad. Usually, one or two students stand out, and that affects the whole class and the teaching. It's like putting Miracle-Gro on your plants. All the students prosper because of the great ones.

Anyway, I'm sitting in the den when an outrageous screech flies in from the front of the house. Melanie, Henry's oldest daughter is back. She visits regularly and stays for a day or two – something to do with babysitting Willy and spending time with her friend from next door, Mrs. Farucci's daughter, Laura. Mel has dyed her hair orange and Laura has dyed hers maroon. Both have pierced ears and are contemplating more piercings. They slick their lips with weird-colored lipstick. They look ugly but they're cool. Go figure.

But Laura causes no harm, she's actually quite sweet. Still, her mother reminds me of the horror movie that Tom thought would be great for me to see – "Hostel." In this movie, wealthy sadistic people actually pay to torture and kill unsuspecting guests, mostly young, attractive college students, staying at a hostel somewhere in Bulgaria. But, I digress. Laura's sweetness, and her appearance, must simply be born of decisiveness, an active clarity about how she does not want to be.

Sauntering down the hall, I'm certain that Mel's trauma doesn't match the scream; certainly nothing as in "Hostel," probably comparable to the time Tom barged in on her in the bathroom. A stubbed toe at worst. My approach gives her a chance to reconsider the seriousness of whatever happened. Mary runs past me, frowning. I arrive shortly thereafter. Melanie stands in shock and disgust, her bag strapped to her shoulder, with one sandaled foot in the air as though ready to stomp a bug, balancing wobbly on her other foot. She emits another growling screech, clenching her fists in front of her face.

"What is it, Melanie?"

"Uncle Haaarrry ...." Melanie flings her hands down to her sides with a look of incredulity. Her bag strap slips, but she catches it with her hand. "Looook!"

I looook. Under the uplifted foot oozes the large sloppy mess of dog vomit she has stepped in. Vomit still drips from her upraised sandal.

"Let me take your shoe off, Mel." Mary's attempt to be helpful doesn't appear practical. She's going to get vomit on her hands. Why doesn't Mel just back up and sit down? Mary steps around to where Melanie can hang on to her shoulder for balance.

Then, just at the right time, our younger son Willy flings the front door open and, as Willy will, lunges forward blindly, never concerned that anyone might be in the way. He stops just short of knocking Melanie off her feet. As it is, she has to put her toe down for balance taking the back of Mary's practical hand with it into the goo.

"Oooohhh, yuck. Did you step in it?"

"What do you think, Sherlock?"

"Ha, ha," Willy sees the potential. "Melanie, why did you barf on the floor and then step in it?" He laughs and laughs.

Melanie punches him in the arm, stepping back into the vomit a third time to give her punch meaningful thrust. Mary, still squatting, loses her balance as a result of the sudden movement and falls, sliding her arm through the vomit, then rolls back upright and sits. She looks at her arm sadly. She looks at me as though I'm to blame.

Mel leaves her foot in the goo in order to grab Willie's neck and says, "I'm gonna put your face in it, turkey."

Willy twists and turns, but Mel has a strong grip. She practices karate. Her strength and her moves are effective, especially when peeved. Gradually, Willie's face lowers inch by inch toward the vomit.

"Let him go." A tone of authoritative threat tinges my voice. She looks to see if I mean it. She lets go.

Mary eyeballs me sideways from her position on the floor.

"Willy, go to the bathroom and get a towel for this mess. No, get two towels," I say. Willy hesitates, then looks at me while rubbing his neck. "Do it now."

"Let me get your shoe off, Mel." Mary, eyes me indulgently, as though she thinks I might actually have been helpful. "She must have eaten something bad."

"Who? Mel?" I smile, dumb.

"The dog, Harry."

"Just - kid - ding." *Where is the dog, anyway?*

Willy brings the towels and Mary wipes her hand and arm and Mel's foot, then puts the towel over the mess. Willy and I stand across from each other. I pinch my nose and he grins.

"She probably ate something rotten. Who knows what," says Mary.

"There was mold on those rotten leftovers in the fridge," I say, realizing that the one who found them should have thrown them out. *But, nobody gave the dog rotten vegetables. Nobody would do that.*

"Did you eat those Mel?" Hand over mouth, Willy stifles a laugh.

"No, Willy, I didn't." Mel sneers. "I was saving them for you." She looks at me. "Did you get a dog?"

This one I take for my turn. "Yes, we did. It's Tom's and Willy's dog, but you can help when you're here." Willy's mouth opens in amazement and silent joy. "Young people will be responsible for the dog."

"Really?" Despite being sixteen and oh so cool, Mel claps her hands and jumps up and down on her toes with excitement.

"Really." I smile and Mary laughs.

I wad up the first towel then place the second towel on top of the vomit and let it lay there to absorb what it can.

♦♦♦♦

After dinner we sit at the table. Mel has opted to stay over and will do homework with Laura. *They will stay up to all hours of the night, giggling and whispering. You will not sleep until daybreak.* Mary passes out numerous slips of paper.

Mary says, "everybody writes down the name they want for the dog. Fold your paper in half, then we put them together and give them to dad. Any questions?"

No questions.

"Good." She continues. "Dad will read the names and then we'll write the name we like best on the next slip of paper. If no name is eliminated on the first round, the name with the fewest votes is eliminated."

"What if two have the same fewest votes," asks Tom.

"They both go." No one realizes that if two have the fewest votes then one will have to have three votes and the ballot will be over.

She looks around the table. No one objects. Everyone is thinking of names, and each wants the name he or she creates to be the best. I've got my own plan. My name will be so bad it will be eliminated right away.

"Okay," says Mary. "When we get down to two names we vote one last time and the majority rules."

"Can we have dessert first?"

"There is no dessert, Willy. Go get a banana."

The first round goes well. I'm ready to read the names. Willy eats his banana. Melanie taps her fingers. Tom pretends he couldn't care less, twiddles his thumbs, whistles nonchalantly, then pats the dog's head under the table. Time passes slowly.

"Henry, are you going to read the names?"

"Sure, sure. I'll read them." I sip my coffee and smile. Everyone stares at me. At last, they're finally annoyed. Mary presses her lips together. She plans to wait me out.

"Oh, all right. Here goes." Everyone comes to attention.

"Dumbo, because she's dumb and huge."

Groans from everyone.

"Tiny ...Lucy ...Sushi ...Shazaam."

The votes are cast. I vote for Tiny, sure that this is Willy's creation. The dog resides among us largely because of him. This will be Willy's dog. Willy will love and feed her, especially if she gets his name. *A theory, no doubt, but we must have theories or growth will not occur, knowledge will harden and newness will never reach nowness. By golly, I'm becoming a Buddhist.*

"Here we go." I unfold the papers and make the tally. "It's Tiny with four votes! Sushi gets a mention."

"Yeeeeha," goes Willy.

Tom laughs and even Melanie looks pleased. Mary smiles.

"I see no reason for another vote. Is everyone in agreement?"

Mary cocks her head, surprised. The young ones cheer and start calling out, "Tiny, Tiny, Tiny, Tiny." Tom drags her out from under the table. Willy runs around the table yelling, "yes, yes, yes." Tiny gets excited and runs after Willy, knocks him over and sits on him. She starts licking his face. Melanie shrieks with laughter. It's a good thing, a really good time. Everyone laughs. Secretly smiling, Mary and I look at each other, for the first time in a while, with peace and love in our eyes.

◆◆◆◆

In the evening now, back in the more recent past where this story actually takes place, I sit with my son, Willy, on the living room couch and show him a set of pictures taken by my grandparents. There's a light on beside us. The windows are dark and the house is quiet. Willy is at the age when he's interested in family origins. Wondering where he came from has always intrigued him and none of the usual answers seems to satisfy him. He has many questions, a practice that I, hopefully, encourage by showing an interest and by being honest in my responses to him.

The cover of my grandparents' photo album doubles as a frame for a picture of the two of them. It's one of those formal, posed pictures with grandma seated, wearing a flowing white lace-trimmed dress, her hair in a bun, and grandpa standing beside the chair a little to the rear in a plain black suit and string tie. Decorations made of sequins, old buttons and fake leaves festoon the cover bordering the picture.

"This is my grandma and grandpa on my mother's side ...your Grandma Jenkins' mother and father."

"What kind of camera did they use?"

"That's a good one. I believe it was called a box camera. Yes, that was it. They had a Brownie box camera. You had to stand a certain distance to get a good picture. You looked through a little window at the top left at the back of the camera and framed your shot. The film rolled out against the back of the camera inside and the pictures were all black and white like this one."

"Grayscale."

"Yes, like that."

Willy holds in his hands one of the few books of photos we have of his great-grandparents. They had taken photographs on their first vacation. After working hard for many years to make a home in their new country, they had decided to take off for a long-awaited and well-deserved two week rest.

"They left the old country with enough money to start a small business in New York in furniture repair. They made most of their money re-caning old rocking chairs and tables. Did you know you were named after Grandma Wilomena?"

"Yeah, Mom told me. Why'd they leave the old country?"

"They were from France. Grandpa served in WW I in the infantry; he was wounded in the leg. Afterwards, after the war, he said that whenever he went around in his home town or anywhere in that region of France, he saw the faces of dead men. He thought coming to America would help him forget."

"Did it?"

"I think it did. When I knew him, I was a little younger than you. He smiled and laughed plenty. He told good stories, too, but not often. He was a nice man."

Willy opens the book to the first page. The photograph there pictures a cover of a stylishly printed brochure. At the top, in ornate calligraphy, we read "Birch Bay Cabins." The bottom third provides information about the place: AAA rated; Rustic Relaxation; 30 acres of woodland with streams and a beach on the shores of Lake Champlain. Proprietors – Ed and Nan Burdine. The center includes an artist's rendering of a lovely cabin surrounded by shrubs and flowers and backed by woods overlooking the curving shoreline of a beautiful bay on the lake. A series of similar cabins recede into the distance along the shore, none of them situated too close to the others. There would be privacy and community, the opportunity to make friends with other folks on vacation. Perhaps they thought to establish a place to return to again and again, to rejoin their newly-made friends and make a pattern in their life together.

I know from previous viewings that the pages of the photo book are embellished with Grandma's tiny script. She wrote in readable English, a feat Grandpa never achieved. Along with the photos, the corners of which are stuck in slots cut at angles into the heavy tan paper are her comments, written in the borders and at the bottoms of the pages. They illuminate the pictures.

The remaining pictures are all shot on location, at the site of the promised vacation wonderland. First, the cabin itself, with the dilapidated front porch, the cracked front window, the broken slats in the exterior wall, unpainted wood no doubt weathered gray and coming apart, and the weedy field mustard, goldenrod and thistle around the entrance and off to the side. "What a surprise," reads Grandma's comment, "but after nine hours on the road we are so happy to be here we don't care. The bed at least is comfy and the stove works! We had tea and napped. Tomorrow we will swim."

Another photo reveals a naked man in flight – leaping into the woods – hairy-legged, hairy-backed, hairy all over, chasing a naked woman mostly obscured by a birch tree, her rotund rear end and the end of one leg visible, nothing else. "Our first sight of soon to be good friends Walter and Veronica Jankowski on their honeymoon. Frisky! How delightful they are, so young and fresh. And, so funny! After we

The Christmas Curmudgeon

had met in person, Walter said he wants to make a big copy of the picture I took to put in a frame above his mantle."

Willy laughs a lot at this picture.

"Hah! What's he doing!?"

"What's it look like?"

"He's running out there naked!"

"Yes, he is."

"What an idea."

"Well, young people who have just married do that kind of thing. They're wild and full of crazy ideas."

Then, we view a picture of a huge fat man lying on the lakeside beach, head pointed toward the water, feet toward the trail that meanders down from the cabins. He's dressed in a black t-shirt and black pants, the clothing soaked wet so that the shirt shines in the light. The man's face looks swollen and has bristles, gray and black whiskers. He's not dead. He's dead drunk, fallen down, and looks for all the world like a beached walrus with fat pink human arms attached to the body just below the neck. There is a circle drawn in ink around his left foot. "You can't see it well, but Mr. O'Reilly broke his ankle on a rock. It was purple and quite swollen. What a time we had hauling him up to his cabin and then to the local doctor. After his foot was cast, he and Charlie tied one on. Charlie, O'Reilly, and young Jankowski went fishing every day after that. The girls including Mrs. Burdine played euchre. Wonderful! If men weren't already such fools, we'd have to invent ways to make them so."

Next, a photo of Grandma in dark shorts and a striped top standing by the lakeshore, holding a large 2 or 3 gallon can in the air dripping with weeds and muck. The shore line rolls away from her feet, thick with reeds, cattails and a small-leafed, prolific water lily. A pile of trash and a few half-deflated tire tubes can be seen on her right, part way up the slope of the beach. Grandma herself had slipped in the muck. She poses with the back of her free hand pressed against her forehead, looking away from the hideous can, her mouth opened in a circle of shock. The dark tendrils of the lilies are in her hair and hang from her arms and neck. The caption reads: "The fishing is great!"

There follows several group shots, one of the men holding up stringers of fish, great pride on their beaming faces, one of the women sitting near the beach and one of everyone, apparently taken by Mr. Burdine who's not in the shot.

Another picture shows the front of Frank's Fish House, a rambling wood building in three sections with the sign stuck on posts over the central section; a big wooden torso and head of a fisherman, cap on head, a great trout cradled in his hands with "Franks Fish House" carved large in an arc over the man. An oversized mug of beer painted on another sign hangs from the eave over the railing of the front porch. Apparently, this is where they gathered at night to socialize, eat fish fry, laugh and sing. No comments from Grandma here.

There it is: the dream and the reality so different as to be absurd. The pictures attempt to and do capture the absurdity. My grandparents had a great sense of humor. They laughed painfully from the depths when they shared these pictures with my brother Henry and me, so many years ago. Each of the twelve pictures captures some aspect of the beautiful ugliness of their vacation. Their experiences, like pies in the face and pratfalls, made them clowns who had escaped, for the time, the hard tasks that held them.

Then we look at the last of the pictures. A close-up of the two of them, grinning, the two sunburned faces at odd angles, his face topped by a blue porkpie hat, her blond hair stringy wet. A wiggly arrow is drawn to the side of her face where a swollen lump is visible. The marginal note says, "Stung by a bee! A yellowjacket."

"I wonder if they had a good time."

"They said they did."

"Grandpa's one leg was pretty skinny."

"Yes, he usually walked with a cane. It ached him a lot, sometimes."

"Well," Willy sighs, "that was cool."

"I'm glad you liked it. Okay, it's time for bed."

When he's on his way up the stairs, I call to him.

"Willy."

"Yeah, dad."

"How old are you now?"

"Eight."

"I remember being eight. Good night, Willy."

"Good night, Dad."

What a fine boy is Willy, my younger son.

Chapter Four

Henry's birthday dinner has sent a warning that Christmas is on its way. A sign lights up in my mind like a garish window display featuring Santa and seven elves, their eyes blinking red and green, surrounded by skyscrapers of gifts stuffed in boxes, beribboned with bands of satin, shiny and glowing, surrounded by strings of multi-colored twinkling lights. Harry has given his first Christmas oratory. Janette brings over cookies, the first of many bakings. Mary is Christmas alert. Shopping lists are being created in the subterranean refuges of her mind. I can see the debts accumulating. I can hear the screams of joy, the shopping gabble and the sharp-witted calculation. Fatigue with a twist of tension settles into my bones. Rum with a twist of lime calls me to the basement.

  Another day goes by. I look to Tiny for solace and what passes for companionship. Essaying on lengthy evening strolls we discover wordless, nameless things beneath the bushes. It seems I have taken charge of Tiny's constitutionals. What a surprise. No one else did and after one outing she started sitting next to me, eyes expectant, nudging my leg with her huge face. Nothing stops her. She nudges harder and woofs, upping the pressure every twenty seconds or so, yelping and whining insistently.

  Once again, it's plain as popcorn, the way to get on with my duly appointed duties is to take care of someone else's business first. Out we go, two hands on the leash as she pulls me down the sidewalk. We pick up speed and I have to jog to keep up. I pull back and dig in and then have to leap forward to keep from being toppled. She sees a squirrel, starts barking and goes full out. No fool, that squirrel heads for the oak

The Christmas Curmudgeon

tree on the corner. I run to keep up, but it's no use. The dog lunges ahead as the squirrel starts climbing and in one smooth, flying dive I'm in the air and then just as quickly flat on the ground, scraping through the grass and weeds, headed for the tree. Fortunately, Tiny can't climb trees, so I come to rest a leash length from the trunk.

Back on my feet, I give her a lesson, "I'm the master and you're the dog. When we go for a walk, you're supposed to behave. Running free is for when you are free. Now, get over here and SIT until I say it's time to go." She comes and sits obediently, almost as though she knows what I'm saying.

The rest of the walk goes pretty well except that thoughts about Christmas advance with every step. My childhood memories betray me. They say that Christmas isn't what it's supposed to be. *Christmas isn't what it used to be.* What can I do? I stop for the dog to sniff the rotting carcass of a bird and listen to the story unfolding in my mind.

The first time I remember disliking Christmas was the first time I remember disliking myself. I was seven years old. I had received an alphabet toy consisting of letters printed on small grooved wooden tiles that you could slide around and rearrange on a track on a wooden board. I believe the toy was called an Alphagram.

The toy was truly a surprise and I loved it. For that reason, all the joy and wonder of the moment as I opened the package to see the toy was transparently revealed on my seven-year-old face. Someone, no doubt a real entrepreneur of the Christmas spirit, seeing the opportunity to "capture the moment" for all time and thereby encapsulate for posterity the true joy of Christmas so resplendently presented on my face, took a photograph the very second I looked up to acknowledge my privilege and to see if anyone was watching me.

I will neither forget the look that I know was on my face nor ever forget the way I was looked at by the adults present on that Christmas day. For the first time in my life, as I sat on the floor beneath the tree, I felt that element of human exchange where what you are is taken as an object for the interest and pleasure of another; my self as a commodity. The instant the flashbulb popped and the camera captured a moment of my soul for future distribution as a photographic delight, I experienced myself as a thing.

I didn't know it at the time, of course. Arriving at an understanding of such an experience occurs later, through the kind of philosophical analysis you might make as an adult. So, as a pajama-clad child, seated among the wise men and women, all in robes, drinking their coffee, I didn't know, but that doesn't change the fact that the experience was intensely visceral and psychological. Looking back on the event, it's clear that I felt myself being turned into a thing by their staring eyes. It was an awful moment of a presence transformed into an object with a concomitant, albeit transitory, tearing of the consciousness.

You might imagine a momentary flit of disembodiment, an astral projection so brief as to be invisible to the naked eye, and the body there observed by the hovering spirit, the body of a seven-year-old seated at the base of the Christmas tree, illuminated by a flash of light, his face looking into the distance at the people in the room, the fabulous toy held in his hands; this body experiences several seconds of death.

In that instant, when the light flashed outside my body, the light inside my body blinked. And in that moment of escaped consciousness and collapsed life energy, my soul was punctured and a psychic vortex formed into which was sucked the whirling essence of shame and despair that is at the heart of Christmas. This horrid load was injected into my self, into the soul of a child.

Now that I'm older, I can describe the experience I could only feel back then. But, I remember quite well coming across the photograph of myself (my joy exposed) in the family photo album, along with several extra copies tucked away in the back of the album, some years later. I took a pair of scissors and cut my head out of all the pictures. In fact, in a truly inspired few minutes of dark passion, as the memory resurrected, and the desire not to exist as such an object became strong and was fortified by a mad impulse to punish those who had so objectified my being and distributed my happiness as a photographic commodity, I went ahead and cut my head off in as many pictures of any kind that I could find.

My mother was horrified when she found the album with the mutilated pictures. She confronted me and I baldly admitted to the crime. She was absolutely dumbfounded. I couldn't explain myself at the time, nor did I try. I was quietly satisfied and resolved to keep my feelings to myself.

"I think he's deranged," my mother said.

My father made no comment on the matter, and the whole incident was swept away and forgotten.

Yes, this is the essence of Christmas. It's not merely the commercialization of a day designated as the birth of Christ. Hah! What spiritual boondogglery! What a masterful transmogrification of a special time meant to be revered (as time in general should be) into a gaudy spectacle of ever-expanding greed and exploitation. What a hoax! What treachery! The essence of Christmas is not merely this, this yearly scheduled programming of the Christmas buying season. But it is, in fact, and most direly so, the commodification – if I can be so rude as to invent such a term – the commodification of the human soul: the introduction of children, all children everywhere, to their self as a thing. Oh lost! Oh shame! Oh despair!

You might liken it to a weird experiment being performed by aliens. The aliens, all of them, of course, would be adults, most of them parents. They would be traveling the universe to find something they had lost in their culture many eons ago. Greetings, Earth children! Christmas greetings. We are soul dead and want your joy. We're going to turn you into us. No, it won't make us feel better, but it will demonstrate our power. And the exercise of power is the only thing that suffuses us with anything like pleasure – not joy, no, no, nothing of the sort, but a kind of hand-wringing satisfaction that is almost life-like. Better than being the old workaday zombie, wouldn't you say?

Chapter Five

For several weeks, life goes by so rapidly that even my dreams are blurred. Clandestine gatherings occur regularly between Mary and the children, but I can't stop to eavesdrop for clues as to the direction of their plans. What I know for sure is that secret Christmas bargaining is going on, pleas and quiet arguments, deliberations, machinations, schemes, manipulations, what have you. My sons, Willy and Tom, negotiate strategies quietly in either of their bedrooms. My niece Melanie helps Mary make horrible decorative things, which then make appearances throughout the house – ugly little wreathes surrounding candles, boxes wrapped in festive colors with Christmas collages pasted on the sides and hideous wall hangings. I dig into work at the university and cover my head at home.

Before I know it, the week of Thanksgiving has arrived. I feel like I've been entombed in my office. I have term papers to read. It's a course devoted to science fiction and fantasy. *Maybe that's why I'm having these weird dreams.* The students were to write on a topic of their own choice, the object being for them to get into the spirit of creativity, liberate their imaginations and write with freedom. They loved it. Thirty students. An average of fifteen pages each. That makes four hundred fifty pages and three days left before Thanksgiving and a four-day weekend.

Sally, my secretary, is organizing the material for the English Department website I'm setting up and I have two lectures to prepare. I feel tight and tense all over. My mouth is dry. I'm constipated. I'm developing a painful pimple next to my left nostril. I'm coming down with a cold. *I must need some Alka Seltzer Plus!* I haven't slept well one night out of the month. *Nytol!*

The Christmas Curmudgeon

I have too many things to do. *Xanax, give me Xanax!* Note to self; stock the basement with extra bottles of rum.

Henry calls and Sally puts him through to my office. She doesn't try to intercept Henry even to determine the purpose of the call. She knows better. She thinks Henry is a maniac. Henry knows this and he likes to play it out. He makes a point of addressing her as "long tall Sally" and saying that he's Bill Busy Guy looking to talk to Dr. Highbottom or maybe Dr. Lahdedah. I pick up the phone.

"Harry! Harry! You've got to come over. I've got something to show you."

"I'm grading papers, Henry. I can't come over."

"Just give them all A's, Harry. By this time next year you're going to be on the brink of wealth. I've been working hard, Harry ...these past couple of weeks. This one's a winner!"

"Sure, Henry. We're going to co-host our own radio show. Henry and Harry's best stock picks. It will be like that show, "Car Talk," with the two brothers. We'll use financial terms to parody people's sex lives. We'll support the corporate hegemony."

Let me explain at this point that Henry has been a stockbroker for nearly fifteen years. He has an established clientele. He rises each morning, not to an alarm clock, but when his body decides it has had enough sleep. He moseys down to his office, takes his calls, makes a few trades, peruses the market news, then sits back and stares out the window; then he may go out, depending on his mood, to have a coffee, a muffin and a relaxing read.

Henry invents a new scheme to make a million dollars two or three times a year. A few years ago it was investing in TelMex (the stock name for the telephone company of Mexico). No sooner than we had each bought three hundred shares that were *guaranteed* to skyrocket the Mexican President's brother was linked to a drug cartel and a nasty political upheaval ensued. The Mexican people were disturbed from their hundred year siesta. The country was on the edge of a revolution, the economy on the verge of collapse. Massive fear and suffering spread throughout the land, which affected the entire geographical neighborhood, a situation that could only be countered by enormous loans from the U.S. and an exponential increase in the export of illegal drugs. The stock plummeted twenty-five points and never recovered.

Another winning Henry scheme was Mail Order Pet Wear. People want to dress their dogs up in costumes, tuxedos and formal gowns, Superman and Yoda outfits, devils and delivery men. Don't ask me why. We actually made a little money on that, but then decided to sell it to the two women who did the sewing. Henry got bored. It took up too much free time. Mary and the kids had a welcome home party for me when that venture was put to rest.

After formal pet wear came the mountain top jazz festival – fun, but a financial loser. People in the South, outside of New Orleans, don't know jazz. If it ain't cloggin' music, bluegrass, or old time gospel it's probably anti-American; it may in fact be insidious, a dangerous creeping northern influence like bagels and lox, Yankee magazine or raised garden beds. Mary has been patient with me over the years. She knows I love Henry and I suspect there's a part of her, just as there's a part of me, that thinks Henry's wild scheming will someday bear a giant, ripe and juicy fruit.

"Wrong!" says Henry, sounding slightly offended. "Most people's sex lives are already a parody, of what, who knows. Besides, when have I ever led you astray?" He chuckles maliciously.

"Look, Henry..."

"Say no more, Harry. If you don't want to hear about it, I understand."

"Henry, you know I am always interested..."

"No, no, no, don't worry."

"Look! I'm grading papers. Do you want to come by the office right now?"

"I'm in no hurry, Henry. I understand that you

have better things to do. It can wait."

"Well, fine. Why didn't you say so?" I'm not going to let him make me feel bad about putting him off.

"Say, I've got an idea." His voice is benevolent and smooth. "Why don't we get together the day after Thanksgiving? The wives will be out shopping and we can get together without the kids. We can relax. We'll have plenty of time. And, you know, that would be a great day for the posters."

I had forgotten about the posters. Maybe I had hoped he had forgotten about the posters. A promise is a promise, however, even among madmen. "Okay," I laugh. "Sounds good. Okay."

"See you Harry. You're a real brother. You've always been a real brother."

We hang up. That stinker. That dirty rotten stinker. I know he's up to something that's going to cost me through the nose. I'm no longer worried about the posters; now, there's another plan. The smell of a scheme of large proportions infiltrates the vestiges of his communication. Something awful, something ludicrous and unreal, perhaps something dangerous with lunacy and weird unprofitability lurks near the horizon. There's no use pretending that I'm going to escape getting sucked into Henry's plan. I can't escape. His enthusiasm is contagious. He always finds a way to convince me that it will be worth the time, the money and the heart.

I'm already tired, anticipating the entanglement, the preposterous and convoluted arguments we will have, the eventual decline and failure or abandonment of the venture. My office is warm and the afternoon sky is turning gray. I lean back in my chair, fatigue overtaking me. I consider calling home, chatting with the kids. No, school's not out yet. Maybe a stretch of the legs will revive me.

When I step out into the reception area, Sally bounces out of her chair.

"I've got the website almost ready."

"Great." I yawn.

Sally takes no offense. "You need a walk out in the fresh air."

"That's the plan."

"Look, uh, Professor Jenkins, can I leave early today?"

"Why not?"

"Oh, the others don't want me to go. Professor Brott is being ...well, you know, especially anal."

"Go ahead. I'll take the heat."

"Oooh!" She jumps at me unexpectedly to kiss me on the cheek and, surprised, I turn my head enough so that she makes contact near the side of my mouth. I blush, but Sally laughs, bends to the side and puts a hand over her mouth. "Uh oh, professor. What will people say?"

"Nothing, I hope." She laughs again.

I look to her desk for a tissue to wipe away any telltale lipstick.

"Okay. Got to go. Thanks bundles." She grabs her purse and a big bag from under her desk and heads for the door, waving her hand over her head as she goes. "See you tomorrow. And, thanks again. You're the best."

She leaves me in a daze. I haven't had my walk, but I'm not sure now I want one. I stand there confused. *I know what you're thinking. I'm not thinking anything. Oh, yes you are ...you've got a dirty thought. I do not. You do. I can see it there in your imagination. What? That's crazy. I'm in a daze. I'm not imagining anything. What about that image of her in her underwear ...lifting up her dress so you can see? Her light pink underwear. Lacy edges, slightly transparent crotch so you can just detect a hint of her curly hairs. I am not imagining her in her underwear. Ah ha ha haha. I think you were.*

"I am not imagining her in her underwear!"

Wouldn't you know it, just at this moment, as I'm inadvertently protesting my innocence out loud, Hedler pops his head through the door. Hedler is Professor of American Thought and Literature – Emerson, Thoreau, Hawthorne, Melville, Adam Smith, Veblen etc. Great speeches of great Americans. Oratory. Lincoln, Martin Luther King. He loves it. Recent, author of a celebrated text, he has taken on an illustrious, noble demeanor. But, praise has made him humble, though his deep satisfaction at everyone's envy belies another side. The pretense of humility is the highest form of arrogance. Still, he's my closest ally and friend in the department.

"At it again, eh, Harry?"

"Not a chance ...and never was."

"Will there be a departmental scandal?"

"Get off it."

"100 bucks and I don't say a word."

"See me in the alley."

He scratches his face by the side of his mouth lightly with a finger. "Got a little lipstick there, Harry." His tongue hangs out.

"You're a real pal, Hedler. How about a hike? I'm falling asleep."

"Can't do it. I was just looking in to see about the website."

"She says it's almost done."

"Good. Seeya." He retrieves his head and the door shuts silently.

Forget about the walk. It's too dangerous to go anywhere. I might run into someone, have to talk, think of things to say. It's too daunting. I return to my office and settle in for a nap. Naps are beneficial; better than walks.

In the dream, I'm the commander again, but no longer in outer space. It seems I'm on vacation, on leave from my duties. I'm in a bar having a beer. I'm sitting on a stool watching an overhead television at the end of the bar. It's a football game and I'm not particularly interested. The place is dim and smoky. The football players run and collide. One man's uniform splits open when he's hit. It looks like his body has split open and he's stuffed with cloth. He falls to the ground, acting like he's hurt. He rolls from side to side clutching himself as piles of the cloth stuffing flow from him and fly around him. It's strange and disturbing.

Then, the bartender passes. I glance at him. His knuckles are twisted and gnarled from arthritis. He has a protruding lower lip that hangs away from his teeth slightly. His suspenders vibrate and make a snapping noise. This bizarre, almost alien aberration makes me look away.

I sense the approach of the woman before I see her. She comes forward from the far end of the bar where misty clouds and darkness seem to muffle the sounds of people's voices and make their bodies indistinct. This is like a dream – I think this in the dream. It's the same woman from the other dream. This time she's wearing a black leather micro-mini skirt. Her black boots come to her knees. Her thighs are white as porcelain, soft as powder. Her hair is teased out. It shimmers and surrounds her shoulders. She could have stepped from the pages of a punk surreal Calvin Klein advertisement from "Elle" or "W." She walks forward slowly and sidles up next to me. Placing a hand on my shoulder, she leans over and whispers in my ear.

"You can have anything you want, Harry. You can have everything you want." I can hardly believe it. A surge of excitement spirals through my body. She backs away, her mouth opens, smiling, and as it does her face begins to change. She whispers again. "And if you can't have what you want, you can have something you don't want."

The smile changes quickly then and suddenly she's transformed. Her face sags with deep set folds of blotchy spotted oily skin. Large pimples with yellow pustules protrude from her cheeks and forehead. Her eyes are rimmed red and the whites writhe with tiny red veins. Her teeth are brown and rotten. She leans in toward my face leering hideously. Gahhh! I wake up with a start, feeling a jolt of fear hit my chest. My heart pounds wildly. Sit up. Breathe in gulps of air.

The Christmas Curmudgeon

Bend over. Dizzy. Not able to think clearly. What's happening? I invoke the name of Jesus in this moment of fear and confusion. Nothing happens. Eventually, my heart rate slows down and I can see again. I vow to bury myself in work.

The schoolwork gets completed at last. Another two days have passed with plenty of late night hours. Late nights and lipstick are not a good combination. I've got nothing to hide, but sometimes it's best to roll past Go and collect your two hundred dollars without landing on anyone's property. Stay on the board, move along, take a train ride, contribute to the community chest and stay out of jail.

Tired doesn't say it. I stumble home like a man beaten. I sleep through an afternoon, a night and into another morning. Groggy but ready for real life, I emerge from the bedroom to find Tiny waiting in the utility room and everyone else gone. Tiny has left a pile in the corner by the door. She sits quietly, seeming to smile as I clean it up. I understand the satisfaction she feels, the pride at having made a statement.

There's a note on the table telling me they have all gone to the grocery store to find a good turkey and the rest of the Thanksgiving fixings. Tomorrow, it turns out, is Thanksgiving Day. How this is possible, I have no idea. In the bathroom, I check my face and shirt for lipstick stains. There's a slight pink tinge on my shirt collar. I scrub it with soap, scrub my hands and face, forego shaving and the shower. At home you don't have to be perfectly clean.

Tiny and I head down the street, my arms stretched out in front of me. I stumble forward as she pulls me down the sidewalk. She jerks me from side to side, switching from tree to tree. I look like a blind dowser using a dog instead of a forked stick. During this wild stiff-armed tango, still dazed from too much sleep and disoriented for time, I'm talking away to Tiny trying to get her to pay some attention to my state of mind.

"What happened, Tiny? Where did the time go?

Wasn't it just yesterday we were out in the park taking a summer snooze? What happened to Halloween? Did we have Halloween? Am I losing my mind? Am I having some sort of middle-aged crisis? What the heck is going on? Answer me, Tiny. At least bark, will you? You know I'll understand. The words don't matter, Tiny. It's the acknowledgment that counts."

No dice. Tiny is intent on finding some hidden treasure. She doesn't even know what it is she's looking for, but find it she will, whether it's a smelly old sock, a rotting scrap of meat or a limp french fry dropped from some kid's paper sack. But the walk does work. I wake up, still disturbed by the slippery disappearance of so much time from my life, but ready to accept that Thanksgiving is about to bloom. I'm ready to eat myself into a state of torpor.

Ahh, Thanksgiving.

Chapter Six

Thanksgiving is the official beginning of the Christmas season. A passing nod is given to whatever historical event the day celebrates. Other than elementary school teachers and their students, no one really remembers anything about Thanksgiving except, of course, that it's the first feast day of the season of feasts. Thanksgiving isn't Thanksgiving anymore. It's Turkey Day.

Before Christmas completely encroached on and took over Thanksgiving there was a transitional period when Thanksgiving Day retained at least some of its identity as a holiday. Its dignity as a day for a family gathering remained intact. Despite everyone's tacit acknowledgment that it was the first day of the Christmas season, there was a sense of purpose hidden in the togetherness, the grace and the meal. During those transitional years, the greatest thing about Thanksgiving was that it was the one day you could still enjoy the company of your family in true holiday fashion without any effort. All you had to do was eat, clean up a little, watch some television, sit around and talk, maybe play a game or go for a walk with the kids. It was a good day, a day of simple pleasures even if we didn't know for what we were supposed to be thankful.

This year we're gathered at our house. Henry and Janette arrive early so that Janette can help Mary with the food. Henry and I have to make sauces and toppings for our magnificent desserts. The kids gather in the family room, taking turns at "Doom" on the computer.

The spread of the feast is nothing less than awesome. The turkey is gigantic, crisp, brown and aromatic. Mashed potatoes and gravy, greens and

The Christmas Curmudgeon

beans and cranberries. Dressing with scallions, nuts and sausage stuffs the bird. Henry and Janette have brought a glazed ham, sweet potatoes and Henry's famous steaming multi-grain bread pudding with brandy crème sauce. I have contributed the equally celebrated Harry's deluxe crumb crust pumpkin cheesecake.

Henry and I fancy ourselves two famous European dessert chefs. He does the haughty English accent; I do the snooty French. Christmas Day we do a repeat performance with our presentation of eggs Benedict and crepes Suzette. Our desserts and gourmet specialties are received with accolades. The whole European posture with the fake accents, the chef hats and the grandiose descriptions of our offerings and our sufferings during the food preparation is a conceit and a mockery, too.

All the children gather around the table. My boys, Will and Tom, are at my left with Viv in the middle. Melanie, claiming status as a woman for the first time, sits with Janette and Mary on the other side. Henry sits at the other end. As usual, the children are up to something. Willy can hardly contain himself. He keeps rubbing his flat-top haircut, which is what he does when he's nervous and worked up.

Mary has loaned him her old Minolta 35mm camera. Apparently he has in mind becoming a photographer; something to do with grandma's photo album. Over the past year, he has perused the album repeatedly, marveling at the message it carries from the past. Now, he prowls for pictures, seeking to capture some mystery about his family and his life. He's an investigator and explorer.

Tom grins at Melanie, but they're both in control. Viv looks around at the others, bursts into giggles, then stops and does it all over again. Melanie kicks her under the table. Tom pulls one of Viv's braids. Surprisingly, she doesn't get angry. She smiles at Will and pokes him in the ear. Willy rubs his flat-top, then reaches around Viv and pinches Tom's arm.

The Christmas Curmudgeon

Tom kicks Melanie under the table. On an on it goes, like the Three Stooges.

"Okay," says Henry. "What's up?"

"There's nothing up," says Melanie in a tone as false as the jet black streak in her orange hair.

"Tom?" I say.

"Hi dad," says Tom with exaggerated maturity.

Non-sequiturs. *Denials.* There's definitely something going on.

"Willy?"

Willy rubs his head. "I'm hungry. When can we start?"

Viv bursts out in a fit of giggles. A riot of laughter erupts from the children. The parents look at each other and decide that the children are idiots.

Henry and I, sitting at opposing heads of the table, command the distribution of the food. Tiny sits squarely-centered in the doorway between the kitchen and the dining room, squirms and jerks, pawing the floor as she growls and yelps in an agitated conflict between eagerness and disciplined self control. She knows she's about to receive great bounty, scraps from the hand of every person seated at the table.

We eat and then we eat more. More turkey and ham. Dressing. Cranberries. Arms reach and pass. Salt and pepper. Butter and rolls. It's as though we're making trades. An historically developed harmony in our movements minimizes the need for talk. People nod and indicate what they want. Everyone takes turns saying "thanks."

It is while the mashed potatoes are passed around for second helpings that a tense, anticipatory silence develops among the children. Henry spoons a plentiful glob onto his plate. He takes the serving spoon and digs into his potatoes.

"What's this?!" he says. He digs again.

Willy, beside himself with anticipation, squirms in his seat. Viv breaks out laughing. Then all of them are laughing. Henry puts two fingers into his potatoes and pulls out a jelly-like substance. He wipes some potatoes off it. He puts it in his mouth and sucks off the rest of the mashed potato making loud, disgusting, slurpy sounds, then pulls the object slowly from his mouth, growling with disgust as he does. Something long and brown stretches from his teeth, an imitation worm made of brown jelly. He picks it from his mouth and holds it in the air. Willy snatches his camera from the floor and takes a shot.

"What is it? A worm? God! I hate it when those things get in the mashed potatoes!"

"Eat it!" shouts Willy, laughing maniacally.

"Eat a worm!" goes Henry. "You don't know me, do you? I've eaten many a worm. They're good …an excellent source of protein." He sucks it back into his mouth and makes a show of chewing it up. Henry's cooperation has made all the kids happy. You can tell they're completely satisfied that it was a commendable trick. There's nothing more awesome than eating a worm. Everybody digs through their potatoes looking for worms. There are several more. The kids eat their worms greedily. The excitement agitates Tiny beyond endurance. She woofs and paws the floor madly. Henry gathers worms from the adults and hands them down to her.

"Don't worry, Tiny." He leans over and pats her on the head. "There's more where that came from."

The kids are boisterous and talkative throughout the meal and the adults join in heartily. Only Mary maintains a reserved attitude. Tight-lipped and quiet, she speaks calmly now and then, but in the simplest, most contained manner. Janette raises an eyebrow at me, tilting her head toward Mary. I shrug innocence and shake my head in ignorance.

Mary and Janette clear the dinner dishes and pile them in the kitchen while Henry and I ready the desserts. When we finally sit down to savor the delicacies, I notice that my fork is missing.

"Don't start eating your dessert." I speak to a unanimous, quizzical rising of heads. "Where's my fork?"

The Christmas Curmudgeon

Everyone looks across the table at me, not a sign of guilt on their faces.

"Everyone else has a fork. Where's mine?"

"Did you look under your napkin?" Mary can be so helpful.

"My fork isn't there. Who took my fork?"

"No one took your fork, Harry," says Mary.

"Maybe it fell on the floor," offers Henry.

"Maybe it sprouted wings and flew out the window." My sarcasm falls flat.

"It's not on top of your head." Janette sets off a round of laughter with that.

"For Pete's sake, get another one." Henry rises from his seat. "You want me to go get you one?"

"No, I want the fork I had."

"Aren't we being a little silly?" Mary always enjoys talking to me like I was a child, but I won't blow up at her and spoil the dinner.

"Okay, okay." I throw up my hands. "You're right. Sit down, Henry. I'll get my own fork. Go ahead. Start dessert. I'll be back in a second."

I go into the kitchen and just as I'm pulling out the utensil drawer, it hits me. *What in the world. What is wrong with you? You put the fork into your pocket.* I pat my pocket, and, sure enough, there it is. The thing of it is, I can't remember how the fork got into my pocket. Sure, I must have put it there, but why and when? The truth hits me again. *You sneaky bastard. I know who you are. Go on. Fool. Try to remember. You never will.*

Here's where the multiple personality theory enters. I can't elaborate on it now, because I've got to go back and eat dessert with the others, pretending, of course, that I got a new fork rather than discovered the fork in my pocket. Suffice it to say that it's the Hidey-Guy – that's what I call him – a part of my self literally unknown to me that operates in my life outside of or inside but next door to my awareness. He hides things. That's the sole purpose of his existence. It's the only realistic explanation. If I hid them or misplaced them, I'd remember at least some of the time, but no, I don't remember. In fact, it's like having blank spots in my life that I'm not aware are there, periods of time that don't exist. That's when the Hidey-guy does his thing.

We eat dessert, making sure to sample both offerings. I believe my crumb crust pumpkin cheesecake is superior to Henry's multi-grain bread pudding, even with his brandy crème sauce, which is undoubtedly superb. No one wants to take a vote on which dessert is best, but we force them to vote anyway. Nobody wins because everybody keeps changing their minds. Then we drink coffee and groan about how much we ate. We don't think at all about the people starving in Bosnia, Rwanda or Bangladesh or any other weird country on the other side of the world. We're Americans. It's an American celebration. Unfettered eating, slurping, grunting and sighing with satisfaction denote the day. We eat with no conscience. We're stuffed. Two of the adult males present burp.

The kids and Tiny go back to the family room to loaf, watch television and whisper among themselves. After clearing the dessert dishes, we sit around the table with tiny glasses of brandy.

Mary says to me, "Harry, why don't you be in charge of the Christmas drawing this year?"

Why don't I hang myself in the bedroom?

"Why don't we skip the name drawing?" I ask.

Mary gives me the look that means "don't even start giving me a hard time, Harry."

I know it's useless, but the need to protest is insistent. *Some other person, somewhere, must understand the absurdity of the Christmas drawing. Please.* I wish in vain that it could be my wife. *So, give it a shot, anyway.*

"The purpose of the Christmas drawing is to reduce the cost of everybody buying everybody a present, even though you usually get a present that you don't even want," I say.

"That's right." Mary is calm. She will wait for

my difficulty to pass.

"But, the fact is, we end up buying everybody presents anyway. So, why have a drawing to eliminate buying everybody a present?" *Idiot, do the Christmas drawing and get it over with. Nothing will change what happens.*

"Will it make you happy if we stick to the Christmas drawing?"

"Sure. The idea itself is a good idea. What could be better than cutting the cost of Christmas?"

"Well, we've talked it over and we've agreed to stick to it this year ...except for the kids."

"Who is we? I don't remember talking it over."

"Janette and I have talked it over."

"Oh. Well. Then, it's been ratified by the board of directors!"

"Ha ha! That's a good one!" Henry interjects.

"That's right, Harry. We're going to give the Unified Male Workers Front a break."

"Except for the kids?"

The kids get extra presents. That's always a fact. Everyone knows this, and the knowledge seems like it ought to undermine the whole idea of the Christmas drawing, but it doesn't. Why, you ask? Because the Christmas drawing is a sham. It's a token appeasement to the old, crusty, niggardly fathers, Harry and Henry. We're supposed to feel that our concerns about cost and commercialism have been acknowledged and truly integrated into the Christmas scheme. Not a fart's chance in a hurricane. No way. The damn thing actually adds expense to Christmas.

"We always get the kids more than one present ...and Loretta and Ellen (the spinster sisters of Janette and Mary) will want to buy the kids something."

"Fine," I speak with a tone of warm concession. "Christmas is for kids. I will do the Christmas drawing."

Sucker. It's not going to work. It never does.

"I always like to see who I'm going to get," says Henry. "I always hope it's one of the kids. I like to see

The Christmas Curmudgeon

the look on his or her face when he or she actually gets a ten dollar present. It's priceless."

So it begins. Thanksgiving Day has been suborned. Let the serious Christmas planning begin. The first round of negotiations has passed. *Fool. There has been no negotiation.* Now, each of us must write on a piece of paper our name and what it is we want more than anything else that costs less than twenty dollars. *Hah!* The kids are called back and I distribute slips of paper. We all write it down. Sure, no one has thought ahead. We sit around forever suppressing burps and farts and writing. *This is probably someone's version of hell.* Finally, each person draws a name. We must then some day go to town with this mission: buy that one gift that Mary, Janette, Henry or Harry, Viv, Melanie, Tom, or Will each desires, realize you can't find it, then get them something else close enough to the desire to create a fissure, into which you may look, down, down, down to the bottom of your soul and seek there a way to hide your disappointment.

For my own part, I already know that there is absolutely nothing I desire that costs less than twenty dollars. Also, history reveals that all of us will fail to get exactly what the person whose name we have drawn had in mind. It's inevitable that on Christmas day we will sit together amidst a pile of unwanted junk, smiling or pretending to smile, depending on our ability to not take anything personally. Only Henry and I will maintain a perspective that permits seeing the drawing and the gift-giving for the stupidity it represents. Of course, not to worry, the adults will compensate for the failure of the Christmas drawing by buying everything everyone really wants in addition to the stuff they never wanted in the first place. It's truly mind-boggling.

☙

Chapter Seven

Henry and I have established our own Thanksgiving Day tradition. It's called The Turkey Day Hot Wheels Drag Race Preliminaries. This stupendous competition is the precursor to the even more fantastic Christmas Eve Hot Wheels All Out Spectacular Drag Race Finale. Both races are well attended by the children. Henry and I are proud. Even Melanie, who is sixteen, still enjoys racing her Hot Wheels cars.

The old guys, that's Henry and me, carefully set up the track with no gaps between sections and with exact parallels in the slopes of both sides of track. The two orange plastic runways shoot down from the top shelf of the living room bookshelf, cross the living room floor, curve around and down three steps to the garage, negotiate a banked U-turn, climb a ramp back up the steps and finish with a long slow straightaway back across the living room floor to the finish line.

Each person picks three Hot Wheels cars for the run off. Henry tallies a win-loss graduated point system for the players and their cars on a fantastic program he has loaded into my state-of-the-art eight year old Dell computer. Prizes go to the top three winners. Also there's a booby prize, which one of the old guys wins every year. We pick only one car and deliberately pick a loser. It's not hard. We have a box of several hundred Hot Wheels cars, and we can pick a loser as easily as the kids choose winners.

The game goes on for hours and the competition is intense. We let the kids scream their brains out rooting for their cars and arguing about the speed and fairness of the track. The old guys join in and scream and argue, too.

Henry has donned for this occasion a classic sports enthusiast's cap with a blue bill and a dome of alternating white and blue triangular sections. His car, a futuristic idea that failed, has exhaust pipes like Medusa's hair curling from its engine.

"Look at that, will you. It's ready to fall over." My scorn doesn't faze him.

"Speed?" Henry points at my replica of a Peterbilt truck. "If that thing makes it to the garage, I'll eat my hat."

"I'll have it fixed and back on the track before your junk tubular space thing takes the turn to return."

"We'll see about that, you turkey. My ride may be ugly but it can GO!"

"No doubt it will GO to the junkyard after I whip it clean off the track."

He smacks my back. As role models, we are sure to teach our children the basics of competitive superiority: mockery and a cocky attitude. It's our duty as fathers.

The old guys are eliminated early. We cap a couple of beers and sit back and watch, both of us drifting in and out of food fatigue, a somnambulant state of wakefulness that is conducive to daydreams and near-total loss of reason. Mary and Janette clean up in the kitchen, which they don't mind because we've got the kids and they can talk and plan to their hearts' content. Something's up with Mary; that's for sure. She hasn't been this furtive since she traded the big screen television in on a new washer and dryer. A thought abruptly arrives from the dark side of my mind and then just as abruptly flees. I see an image of Mary walking down a hallway, a shadow moving behind her. It could be anything or anyone. It's mildly disturbing. I sit up to the sound of the races, all the kids screaming as Tom eliminates Willy's car in their final run.

"Damn you, Tom!" Willy instantly covers his mouth and looks at Henry and me. Everyone laughs.

My boy Tom and Henry's Viv are into the finals. It's a five race run off between the two fastest cars –

The Christmas Curmudgeon

Viv's 1992 Malaysian casting of the Dodge Viper with metalflake green finish and gold wheel hubs and Tom's 1980 (can you believe it?) Hong Kong casting of a '36 Ford hot rod, chopped, channeled and raked. The stakes are high. First prize gets a night out with three friends, two pizzas and a theatre movie. Second place gets the night out with one friend, a pizza and the movie. Third place gets a movie or a pizza with a friend. In the name of peace and for the sake of sanity the old guys are recruited to man the release lever that starts the cars down the track.

"I'm going to run you and that sissy girl car off the track," says Tom, age fourteen, with appropriate viciousness.

"Oh yeah," says Viv. "My car goes so fast it makes yours look like it's going backwards."

Tom is hard-pressed to come up with a response as scientifically erudite as that of a fifteen-year-old girl. He gets red in the face then recovers. Meanwhile, Willy loads his camera, having decided that, if he can't race, he may as well take pictures.

"You're so dumb, you'll probably blow your car up trying to shift the gears."

"Oh, right," says Viv. "Like I'm going to be actually driving the car." She puts her car on the track behind the starting gate on top of the bookshelf.

Tom is really peeved now. "Yeah, well, your brain could fit in it."

Viv looks at him like he is soooo dumb for saying that, pointing to the car and to her head to demonstrate that her car is, no doubt, too small for the brain in her head.

"Your twerpy hot rod even has the flames going backwards," says Viv. "Look ...they're climbing up the rear end on the trunk instead of flying off the front."

Willy takes a photo of Tom and Viv arguing for posterity. Tom puts his car on the track, aligning it perfectly for the take off. "That's the reflection of your car bursting into flames as the engine blows and flips it off the track." Tom sneers at Viv smugly. He wastes no more time on petty banter. He's ready for the race, hands on knees, eyes level with the cars.

Viv smiles and stands beside her car on her side of the track.

"Ready, set, go," says Henry.

He pushes the lever that releases the cars and they blast down the track amidst the roar of screaming fans. At the end, the flag drops on Tom's side indicating that he has won this race. Viv can't believe it. She hasn't lost a race all day with the Dodge Viper and Tom's hot rod has lost two in the course of the eliminations.

Viv wins the next two and Tom looks worried. Tense silence fills the family room as preparations are made for the next race. Tom blows on the wheels of the Ford hot rod, clearing any dust. He works the wheels up and down a little and checks their spin. Viv watches him with amused disdain. She has learned the cool distant look from her mother. Henry wiggles a finger at her.

Tom wins the next race and they are two and two; an exciting final match is guaranteed. Tom gives his car another overhaul, all the while chanting magic incantations aimed at influencing the outcome. Viv even blows on the wheels of her car and spins them, with a look of self-ridicule as she does.

"What in the world is this supposed to do?" she asks.

"You don't stand a chance, Vivvy," says Tom. "You don't know what you're doing." I half hope that Viv wins the race. She really wants the pizza movie combo and Tom could use an attitude realignment.

They put their cars up on the track and the final race is on.

It's Henry's turn to push the lever. Everyone agrees we dads have done a fair job of setting up the track and pushing the lever. Not excellent, but fair. There's a momentary pause as Tom and Viv check the alignment of their cars on the track. They're both satisfied that they are set for the perfect run.

The Christmas Curmudgeon

Henry pushes the lever. The cars burn off the top shelf and roar down the track. They are wheel to wheel all the way down the first slope, into the garage and around the U-turn. You can't tell which is in the lead. Tom gains a little on the uphill return but loses some on the long run to the finish. They remain side-by-side, not a sliver of advantage to either car as they roll down the home stretch. It looks like a tie. The cars shoot toward the gate aided by the roaring of everybody in the room.

"Yes, yes, yes, yes!!!" yells Tom.

"Come on, come on, come on," pleads Viv.

The cars hit the gate. The flag drops. Tom screams, jumps into the air, and whips his arms up and down as though flagging the win himself. He runs in a circle, yelling, "Yes, yes. Yes!! I win! I am the champion!! Yes!!" He then runs off to the kitchen to proclaim his victory to the moms.

Henry completes the computer calculations. He grins sardonically. I have won the booby prize with my orange and silver Hong Kong casting of a Peterbilt construction tank truck. The booby prize every year is having to install above your front door the giant plastic head of a Santa that says, "Ho, Ho, Ho, and Merry Christmas," amidst the tinkling of chimes when anyone opens the door.

Despite his two early losses, Tom has indeed won the prize. He returns triumphantly clucking. Sour and pitiful Viv has the composure to shake his hand. She'll recover. Melanie watches television in the corner, impervious to the goings-on. Third-place-Willy is unhappy that the racing is over. He's chanting, "Let's do it again, do it again, do it again." Henry and I have to stop the commotion for awhile. Gad. We need a rest. Willy gets to stay up and watch a DVD.

The Christmas season is underway!

Chapter Eight

The night is restless. A thick haze drifts head high in the purple air making it difficult to see. We move forward slowly, myself and four others. Fifty yards out, we stop behind a rim of trees that borders the parking lot. Three employees squat against the front wall smoking cigarettes, their red vests festooned with colorful buttons of varied sizes. From this distance I can't read them, but I know the messages they display. Employee of the Month. No Whining. Yellow smiley faces. Brand names and logos. Damn, it's going to be a brutal night.

Henry and his team will be at the rear loading docks by now, ready for action. We wait for the explosion, everything clockwork and ready to go. The charges had been placed in the morning, undetectable. All of us had gone shopping; a few even made purchases: a quart of oil, some photographic film, a dish towel. Nothing big, just the odd items. It made Earth shopping familiar again, calmed us and kept us on track.

I jerk and twitch when the C-5 plastique blows out the side walls of the building. The force tears inward, blasting five or six aisles of commodities to bits creating frag from packaging and shelving that slices and shreds the bodies of the people in there. Razor thin jolts of tension cut through my brain. The rest of the crowd, mostly employees at this hour, fly screaming and bloody out the front doors. The Big-Box structure has been brought to life and is spewing its guts. Henry and his commando team chew the backs of the fleeing figures with laser bullets. My muscles jump and I rock-and-roll as we mow 'em down out front the old-fashioned way. They lurch and stagger, then their bodies fall. The blood sprays. Side teams have already gassed the floors. We light it up and the explosive boom roars as we run for cover. My heart pounds in the darkness of the night. Eight minutes and counting. We're finished and it feels good. Even with all the guts and goo, you can't beat a vengeful slaughter. The steady crew, back on the star cruiser, awaits our return.

Then, out of nowhere, four of the Big-Box store employees jump one of my men. They go for his gun, and the rest of us dive in to stop them. Wild and ferocious fighting ensues. A crazed woman reels toward me swinging a pink high-heeled shoe, its price tag dangling. I brace myself for the hit. "Yaaaahhh!" she screams, the heel in my face.

Jerking awake, I nearly fall off the bed. The sound of chatter in the kitchen, punctuated by frightening shrieks coming from the back yard, tortures my sluggish brain.

"Keeeyiiii! Unh! Unh! Unh!"

I sit up on the edge of the bed. Melanie performs karate in the back yard early mornings. I forgot she stayed overnight. She used to stay only on nights she babysat for Willie or when she studied late with Laura, but recently it has been other times for no apparent reason. Mary says she just does it to get out on her own occasionally. I don't mind. What do I care? She's a good kid. Soon enough, she'll really be on her own. Too soon.

Henry's breakfast is scheduled for this morning; his latest money-making scheme, no doubt, mapped out in detail. I wonder what it will cost. Part of me wants to tell Henry that I'm no longer willing to participate in his lunacy. Can't do it. I can't afford it. Part of me looks forward to this new adventure, the fun we will have, the win or lose atmosphere of the actual execution of the plan, Henry's wild enthusiasm, his comic rages, his gleeful outbursts and my own restrained excitement and sober, more existential appreciation of our brotherhood in action.

The noise outside continues to batter my brain.

Melanie reaches some fearful exercise crescendo.

"Keeyaahh!!! Ka!! Unh!!"

God.

I peer through the Caribbean style Hunter Douglas window blinds. Melanie does katas. She goes through another round of punches and kicks. Finally, she stops and lays out flat on her back in the yard, catching her breath before moving on to the next set. Melanie is into physical fitness. She takes aerobics, lifts weights, takes Tae Kwon Do and practices combat moves with incredible intensity. She wants to be a martial arts movie star. Her crew cut hair, serially pierced ears, single nostril ring and tattoo of a hawk on her shoulder give her that special Sigourney Weaver gone punk, up-against-the-wall, kick-ass sexuality that only boys destined to be sociopaths find attractive. She's considering upgrading to an orange spiked hairdo and a piercing of her left eyebrow.

Melanie's silence allows other sounds to penetrate. There's a crack and a thud from the front of the house. There's woman talk in the kitchen. Then, there's the unmistakable jingling sing song "Ho, Ho, Ho and Merry Christmas" of the giant Santa head. It penetrates the house like a wicked native spear of sound, a veritable Christmas missile. Two more times it resounds – "Ho, Ho, Ho, and Merry Christmas." I clutch my pajama shirt as though in pain; I twist the cotton cloth and grimace. *Relax. Don't let it bother you. Take a deep breath. Repeat after me – Christmas is for kids, Christmas is for kids. Unh.*

Tiny has sensed the change in my consciousness and knows that I'm awake. She's snuffling at the bedroom door. I let her in while I shower, shave and get dressed. Looking around for my wallet and keys signals Tiny that we're ready to go. She chases herself around in circles and we head for the front of the house, stopping by the kitchen to see who's up and what plans are stewing in the witches' pot.

Mary and Janette are seated at the kitchen table drinking coffee and eating Pepperidge Farms

Chesapeake cookies. They each have their own bag. I can tell by their manic mood that they will be gone shopping all day. The cookies are just the beginning of their loss of self-control, Christmas impaired judgment having taken charge. Massive cookie consumption is a bad omen. Apparently, Melanie will be going with them. An apprentice woman, she must learn The Way of shopping. *Will Melanie discover a connection between the Tao of shopping and Tae Kwon Do?* Perhaps, she will buy more aggressively. *Perhaps, she will karate kick her creditors in the teeth when they come calling.*

"Good morning."

Mary and Janette greet me in unison. "Good morning." Mary adds cheerily, "There's a present for you in the utility room."

"A present? Really? Who's it from?"

"It's from Tiny." Mary smiles at Janette. A single sudden burst of laughter issues from Janette's mouth, spewing cookie crumbs across the kitchen table.

Tom steps in at just this time, a rosy look of cheer upon his face. "Ho, ho, ho..." He sounds like a robot. "And Merry Christmas!" He, no doubt, enjoys the horror of the giant Santa head. He's just busting with pleasure and pride at having completed the installation correctly.

Tiny, now hooked to her leash, pulls me around in a circle. We head into the utility room. She sits quietly to the side, eyes downcast. She looks away from me, clearly feeling bad. There's dignity in her humility.

Reentering the kitchen, I unhook Tiny and hand the leash to Mary. "Why take her for a walk if she's already done her job?"

Mary pats Tiny on the head. Janette's laughter continues, corrupted into a series of horsy snorts, blurts, spurts and coughs by her efforts at self-containment. Tom grabs a can of soda from the refrigerator and disappears. I watch him go realizing I should have congratulated him on a job well done.

"You need the exercise."

I don't really know why I walk the dog. It's a task that has fallen to me. The consequences of not getting the dog outside in time are therefore also my responsibility. I don't know how this logic settled on me or how the responsibilities were initially sorted. Some kind of evil deity may be involved. A faint memory calls to say that it goes back to my childhood. My father – I stop to stand and see it clearly, as vivid a picture as memory can portray. I see his face; he enjoyed giving me dirty little dog clean up tasks. I'm not going to pass his mean little game on to my children. *But the dog isn't even your dog!* That's right. It's not even my dog!

I used to contend that the dog is the children's dog. They are the ones who enjoy her. I didn't want a dog at all. I know what dogs do. Dog do. Everywhere. Whenever they get the chance. I especially don't want a big hairy dog with no manners. A dog that drools. A dog that chews things up. My things. How come it's always my stuff? My shoes! My best shoes. A dog that licks her twat and anus in public. A dog that humps things, visitors, armchairs, little children who have fallen down. I thought it was only male dogs that did that.

Mary feeds the dog. I walk the dog. The children hug the dog and lay around on the floor with the dog watching television. The dog loves the children. The dog loves Mary. The dog looks down on me. I'm sure of it. I'm the one who cleans up her messes. I'm the one who puts the chain around her neck and pulls against the very essence of her desire to be free and roam at large in the world, crapping and pissing on anything that takes her fancy, eating garbage of every kind, even animal waste. The dog eats turds! Rabbit turds mostly, but any dry chewy turd will do. What's up with that?

I return to the utility room. Tiny follows, apparently to make sure I perform the clean up correctly. Melanie comes in through the back door, rubbing her shoulders. Her face is red and she's breathing hard.

"Peeiou," she squinches her nose at Tiny and makes an icky face. Melanie smiles at me.

"Hi."

"Hello, Melanie. You look flushed."

"I love it." She beams with youthful energy. "You should try it, Uncle Harry. Tae Kwon Do!" Suddenly I feel extra tired.

"Ohhh." I nod agreeably. "I already practice."

"Really!" Melanie is an enthusiastic person. "What do you do?"

"I practice No Kan Do."

She gives me a well-practiced mom look and passes into the kitchen.

"Hi moms!" Melanie shuts me into the utility room.

Turning to the task at hand, surrealism strikes.

"What is this, Tiny?" These aren't normal, even for a really big dog like Tiny. They're enormous – subway cars, zeppelins. "These are gargantuan, Tiny. What'd you do, eat a restaurant? Geez."

Tiny sits on her hind legs, wide-eyed and friendly, seeming to smile. Now, the monster shows no remorse. Fortunately, we have a special plastic shovel designed for the job. Deftly, I slip the shovel under one dog doo then the other; a pair of solid firm ones that come up clean from the linoleum floor. I'm thankful for that, at least, though the smell is still something egregious. I bag the poop and spray the spot with Pine Sol and wipe the floor clean. *Why don't you bring these babies into the kitchen for the mommies to see? Go ahead. Do it.* I decide against it. After all, the master of the house should behave maturely. *What does that mean? Master of the house.* The plastic bag goes into the trash. I return to the kitchen.

"You moms shouldn't eat so many of these." Melanie points to the cookies, picks up the nearest bag and shakes it. Melanie has also perfected the parental tone. Someday she will be someone's mother.

"Yes," Mary shows Melanie a fake smile. "Come and tell me that after you've had several children."

"I'm not going to let having children interfere with my fitness." Melanie stands like a cowboy at the edge of a dangerous shootout.

Though it seems a plausible assertion, both Mary and Janette break into a guttural laugh that ascends to shrieks of hilarity. Apparently, Melanie's attitude is naive to the point of being ludicrous.

Melanie stomps off.

Mary hands me the leash.

"I would like a Chesapeake cookie."

For some reason this sends Mary and Janette into another fit of laughter. Mary hands me her bag. There are no cookies left.

"Woof!"

Returning from the walk with Tiny, which isn't really a walk – more of a sniff and jerk – I see the three women coming out of the front door. Mary and Janette are putting on their jackets. They step down elegantly from the porch. The two of them are wearing environmentally correct Deva Lifewear garments. Melanie has taken a shower and her hair is wet, but she's dressed like the moms in an attractive Deva dress, along with a sweater and jacket. She's ready to learn The Way of Shopping. They parade forward to pet the dog and give me instructions.

"Don't forget." Janette speaks in a kindly tone. "Henry is waiting for you. He's cooking a big breakfast, too. I've never seen him so excited."

"He's come up with a new scheme."

Mary raises her eyebrows, but there isn't time to pursue it. Melanie is eager to get underway.

"Let's go."

Dressed the way she is, I realize that she's practicing to be a mom. Is she aware that this outfit she wears is mom clothes? Perhaps it's something in her attitude, too, the sort of calm confidence that only the knowledge that you are about to spend a pile of dough can bring.

The Christmas Curmudgeon

Henry has noticed this change in Melanie before. He says that probably this year she will be lost forever, gone into woman world. She already reads "Cosmopolitan." She plans her life on the phone. She courts, not only the look of urban defiance, but the look of mystery. He amazes me by telling me that very soon, for all practical purposes, I will never see or speak to Melanie again or, at least, not for a long, long time. But that's how it is when girls make the leap. How Henry knows this is a mystery. Maybe he sneaks "Cosmopolitan" into the bathroom to discover the truth about women.

Looking at it objectively, I can see that Henry is right. Melanie has grown up and travels on a different plane. Every so often I see her among a group of her friends, all dressed in wild costumes, waiting for the boys to make the necessary adjustments and advance. She is cloistered in gang membership, unable to see beyond herself except to wave a greeting to a passing uncle she once comfortably sought out with confidences and little surprise objects held carefully in her hands, a tiny tree frog, a perfect flower, a grasshopper, a pretty stone.

Even though she's not my daughter, as the oldest of our combined families, I feel she's a harbinger of separations to come. Every one of the children, Tom and Will and Henry's Viv, will join a school of other brightly-colored fish and swim away off into the vast ocean of the world. I can't help feeling a deep sadness about it. For a moment, I wish that Tiny could be a better listener.

The car takes off down the street. Some serious shopping will soon be underway. I stand at the door and think fitfully about credit card bills, until a mild panic seizes me. I pat my pockets for a cigarette. That's another bad omen. I turn to go indoors. Fastened to the front door, the giant head of Santa leers with a wide, toothful plastic grin. Two teeth on the left side of his face are broken and black triangles form gaps that lend the head a slightly vampirish air.

The Christmas Curmudgeon

Opening the door to go back inside, the Santa head speaks, "Ho, Ho, Ho and Merry Christmas." Suddenly, I feel strangely anxious, dreadful. Almost insane.

Chapter Nine

Henry's Breakfast consists of poached farm fresh eggs, pancakes with real butter and real maple syrup, thick sliced hickory smoked bacon, Hillshire Farms Italian sausage cut into lengths, orange juice, grits, gravy, cinnamon rolls, grapefruit and orange sections, honey nut bread toast with Dickinson's 'Old English' style blackberry jam, Starbuck's coffee and half and half.

"Henry, what can you be thinking? Wasn't it just yesterday that we ate turkey and dressing, mashed potatoes, cranberry sauce, glazed ham, two desserts and more until we nearly exploded?"

"The more you eat, the more you can eat. It's a Christmas axiom."

"You're kidding."

"Answer me this," Henry pulls out a chair for me. He splays his right hand out, inviting me to sit. I sit down. "Are you hungry?"

He's got you there. You are hungry.

"Well ...just a little," I say.

"You could eat then?"

"Sure, Henry. It's ten o'clock. I'm used to having breakfast at six-thirty."

"Then let's eat. Eat as much as you want."

He's up to something.

"What's the point, Henry?"

"Ah hah!" He slams his hand on the table. "You see it, don't you?"

"Whaat?!" I don't see anything but plates piled with food.

"Something has to be done, Harry. It's time someone spoke out."

We are headed somewhere but I'm not sure where. Henry stabs a sausage with his fork, picks the whole thing up, it's about six inches long and as big around as a half dollar. He holds it in the air, twirls it, examines it, then shoves one end in his mouth and bites off about one third. Juices drip down his chin. He chews and swallows.

"Does this have something to do with your latest idea, Henry?"

His mouth widens into a grotesque parody of a smile.

"Think about it, Harry. It's true, isn't it? The more you eat, the more you can eat. In fact, the more you want to eat. It's true, isn't it?"

I don't have to think about it. Though it's absurd, what he's saying is true. I nod wisely, as though Henry has made a profound statement. It seems to be what he wants. Henry pours me a cup of coffee. I decide on a small portion of pancakes and bacon.

"Is that all you're going to have? I spent a lot of money on this breakfast. I took a long time to prepare it, too. The least you could do is eat something."

"I am eating, Henry. Look." I put a forkful of pancakes into my mouth. Henry chomps off another big bite of sausage. We chew. He's still smiling at me with the crazy face.

"Now that's the Christmas spirit. Wouldn't you say so, Harry? Consume more and more. And if you don't do what is expected and feel ridiculously happy about it, you are made to feel guilty."

"Consume vast quantities."

"Correct," says Henry. "That's my point. Any alien could see that we're conditioned from birth to consume. It's deep in our culture. We are totally immersed in messages telling us in one way or another to consume day in and day out. It's so deep it has actually affected not only our way of seeing and thinking but also our physiological drives. We're hungry beyond the actual needs of our bodies. The more we eat, the more we can and want to eat. Isn't that unnatural?"

"Okay. It's unnatural. The more we eat the less

we should want to eat. Therefore, the more we have the less we should want." *But appetite comes with eating. So said Rabelais.*

"That's right! Now you're on the right track."

Henry is agitated. He can't sit at the table and eat his breakfast like a normal person. He paces around the kitchen, waving another forked sausage in the air with one hand and with the other hand he takes turns, either taking bites from a cinnamon roll or slurps of coffee. He wipes his mouth with his sleeve and starts in on his real message.

"I can't stand it anymore, Harry. This Christmas madness, it's driving me nuts. Just griping about it isn't enough. Janette is no help. She just laughs. She calls my 'little upsets' Christmas seasoning, like paprika for God's sake!"

"Or Tabasco sauce," I offer.

"Exactly," says Henry, calmer. "Well, I've come up with an idea. It's time to fight back."

"How, Henry? Christmas is a many-headed monster, a Hydra, anything you try to do will only make it worse." *It might even be the beast with seven heads, come from the depths.*

Henry holds his hand up, points at me. "Anti-Christmas cards."

"Anti-Christmas cards?"

"Yess! I've got several completed. I want to show you."

What can I do? Suddenly very hungry and unable to think about what's happening, mentally blocked as it were, but viscerally opened by the horror of an impending Henry scheme, I eat something. Eat and eat again. It's too late anyway. Henry knows me. He knows I'm already caught in his next scheme. He stands up, turns around twice, then leaves the kitchen, all the while speaking loudly and rapidly, almost as though I weren't even there. "Wait until you see these! You'll see. Christmas. Hah! Christmas! Wait until you see these cards. This will change things ...you'll see."

Waiting for Henry's return, I eat more pancakes and drink more coffee. The sausages are spicy and hot. The orange juice is fresh. The grits and gravy make me delirious.

♦♦♦♦

Henry has gone to his study and returned with a wooden box. It's an old wine gift box with a hinged top and a lock on it, probably a Christmas gift from his college days when wine and cheese were on a par with music and art posters. He forks a chunk of pancakes into his mouth, then shoves an assortment of dishes full of food to one side of the kitchen table with a sweep of his arm. He puts the box down, unlocks it with a tiny brass key and lifts the lid. Out come three drawings on three stiff pieces of Strathmore sketch paper folded in half to make cards.

The cover of the first card depicts a dimly-lit alley, apparently early in the morning. There are banged up overflowing garbage cans, old tires, boxes, cases of empty bottles and assorted rags and papers piled along the wall of one building. An outdoor light illuminates a doorway deep in the alley.

A series of thin, bedraggled men in shabby Santa outfits, all with the same morose expression on their faces, file out from the doorway and march forward. At the front of the line, you can clearly see the emaciated face, neck and hands of the first Santa, his eyes rimmed with yellow and his complexion sickly and sweaty. His worn-out, unclean Santa suit hangs on his bony body loosely, and the cloth is torn in places. One hand is held out in front of him. He has a forlorn, pathetic look on his face. Inside the card it says, "Can you spare a quarter for Santa?"

Henry. Oh Henry.

The second card has a man sitting at a table holding a gun to his head. The expression on his face is one of crazed bewilderment, fear and outrage. Henry has amazingly captured this combination of emotions in the drawing. Open the card and the man is face down on the table. His head, the gun and his arm lie in a pool of blood. On the wall to the side is a large splatter of blood roughly forming the words "Merry Christmas."

"I thought of including a couple of paper trays on the table in front of the guy initially. You know, a tray marked debit stacked high with bills and a tray marked credit next to it with just a few slips of paper in it. But then I thought, no, it's better leaving it ambiguous. Let the viewer think about why the guy is shooting himself in the head. Could be any number of Christmassy reasons. Right? What do you think?"

"Pretty sick stuff, Henry."

"Yeah, but people will love them, Harry. People want to have a way to protest Christmas. The whole idea isn't just the content of the cards. That's just part of the fun. The real idea is to begin using Christmas against itself. Start an anti-Christmas movement, which will make people feel free to choose, to think about what they really believe, what they really want instead of just buy, buy, buy and buy more stuff like mindless consumer robots. Let's cut Christmas in half, then in half again. Let's start living again."

"You've got a point, Henry. But, I don't know."

"What have we got to lose? It's worth a try, isn't it?"

"I suppose."

"Here." He hands me a third card.

A traditional picture of Santa, chubby and rosy-cheeked is on the front. Near the top, beside his head, it says, "Remember..." Inside the card, the message is, "Nothing is better than debt."

This one strikes me as pretty clever. I like it. It's definitely a card I would send. And it is an anti-Christmas card. I look at Henry. He's grinning and turning from side to side, eyeing me as he forks yet another sausage. He can see that I'm hooked. I'm sitting there like a dope, staring at the card, smiling at the thought of sending it out to my friends, acquaintances and colleagues. *Here you go again.* It's okay. I just wonder what part I'm playing in the scheme, how much it's going to cost.

"It won't be as much as you might think," says Henry, now a mind reader. "We'll get back what we invest in sales. I've talked to a guy about advertising through those weekly alternative newspapers. We've sent out a series of trial ads."

"What?"

"We've tried out a few ads. What's the big deal?"

"When?"

"The last two weeks of October. The response was terrific. I've already received orders for thirty boxes."

"Boxes of what?"

"Boxes of cards, idiot."

"What boxes of cards? I thought these were just an idea so far."

"The boxes of cards you've produced, Harry. That's your part."

"Whaaaat!!"

"Look, you were busy. You didn't have the time. I didn't have the money for both the ads and the production ...so you agreed to do the production."

"I don't think so."

"Yes. You did."

"When?"

"Just now. Shipping starts on Monday. You just need to pay Mannie down at the Mercury Press. Twelve hundred dollars."

Twelve hundred. Did I hear that right?

"Twelve hundred dollars!"

"That's all."

That's all, he says. This is my brother. I sit and stare at the table. The remaining pancake is cold, but I eat it. *Remember, this is your brother. Twelve hundred dollars. Everything will be all right. Mary doesn't have to know.*

We sit down together and work out a plan. It's going to cost, but if they sell in the trial run, next year, with a complete campaign, we could actually make a bundle. *Who knows?* Who knows? We swear a solemn oath to work in secret. Mary and Janette must never know. I look at Henry throughout this process, thinking, sometimes with great warmth, what a life we lead. *We're always up to something.* And then I look again and he's an alien, a complete stranger, very likely from another planet, who has devised this clever way to make it look like I decided to wreck my marriage and my life.

♦♦♦♦

The afternoon's poster madness exceeds my expectations. *But, why not one hour to madness?* Lives like our lives, except at Christmas time, always calm and contained, promulgate heart attacks and strokes. *Will insanity and its impulse save us from ourselves?* I don't know. *But, why not?* Henry has rented two Santa outfits for us to wear, his theory being that dressed as Santa we will not be seen as evil-doers up to no good. Police, security guards and the management will think we're just doing some necessary Christmas task. We might even be inconspicuous. However ridiculous this might sound, he's apparently correct in this surmise, for the first twenty posters go up without a hassle. We head for the mall, our final target, with the last ten posters.

Striking out on foot from the parking lot next to Sears, we turn toward the side entrance. I carry the glue pot in a large yellow and tan striped shopping bag with twine handles; Henry has the posters. We enter what Henry refers to as the throbbing heart of the Christmas machine, The Mall, a 750,000 square foot maze of shopping seduction, pumped daily with tons of oxygen-hyped air that induces a hypnotic shopping trance in the minds of the unwary masses.

The hardboard walls of stores under renovation, the smooth clean walls on the side concourses or any other prominent wall space will provide the best surface. Visual accessibility is the key to success. All goes well. We are next to the interior entrance to the

The Christmas Curmudgeon

Sears store. I slather up the back of a fresh 16 by 25 inch poster with glue and Henry presses it flat with a paint roller. This glue cures quickly and it won't be easy to remove our work. Henry has done his research. Good job! We move on down the hall into one of the main arteries.

While plastering a pair of posters side by side on the wallboard construction barrier surrounding the new GAP expansion going up, a shadow appears announcing an unwelcome presence.

"Hello there." A young security guard, a skinny fellow sporting a thin, black mustache, wearing a tan uniform and a shiny leather belt covered with leather-clad gizmos, stands behind us with his thumbs stuck in his pockets. Henry and I look at each other.

"Hello." Henry rolls the remaining posters into the shape of a cylindrical tube.

"Can't help but notice these posters aren't very Christmas ...do you have a permit?"

"Don't need a permit." Henry lies through his teeth. "We're with the downtown business association."

"Is that so?" The young guard nods, dubious.

"Right." A genial smile puts me into the spirit of things. "This is a public service announcement."

"Authorized by the city council," adds Henry.

"I see." The guard parts a space between us with his hands to examine the posters on the wall. The absurd, dangling poster Santa, a look of idiotic delight on his face, his legs and arms flying in random directions, seems almost to be in motion. "Amputate the puppeteer." The guard reads the message aloud. "I don't get it."

Henry is about to explain, but I interrupt. "That's the beauty of it."

"Uh huh." The guard frowns, clearly still puzzled.

In the past few minutes a small crowd has gathered behind us. The three of us look around. The crowd is small but intent: three women, a little girl

The Christmas Curmudgeon

and two young men. Other shoppers slow down as they pass, but move along. A tiny, wrinkled bird of a woman wearing a green knit cap and a purple and yellow sports jacket points a bony finger at the posters on the wall. "That's obscene." Her voice sounds like a cheese grater scraping cement. "Put them in jail, officer."

A younger woman comes up and grabs the arm of the little girl who is gawking wide-eyed at us.

"Look, mom," shouts the girl, pointing. "Two Santas!"

The mother is not amused. "C'mon peanut," she cautions, pulling her daughter away. "Those aren't Santas. They're fools. Don't look at them." Her face contorts, ugly with disgust.

The guard, apparently, has the good sense to see a potentially unruly situation developing as the young mother's red-faced, stocky six-foot husband approaches obviously concerned about his wife's distress and his daughter's innocence. The guard grabs my arm.

"Let's go, guys. I'll show you the way out..."

The guard speaks in a friendly, helpful way that tells us that he's on our side. He, at least, doesn't want to arbitrate between us and the big husband. He escorts us toward a narrow hallway that leads off to a metal door. As we enter the hallway Henry balks, but the guard thumbs backward to the crowd following. A couple of men have joined the husband and they stride toward us.

One of them shouts, "Hey, wait a minute."

Another mutters to his friend, "We're not putting up with no fake Santas."

"Take your hate posters with you," shouts a third man, scowling, leaning forward, fists at his side, disturbingly disgruntled.

Emotions seem to be escalating.

We go with the guard.

He unlocks the metal door and shoves us outside. We find ourselves behind a row of bushes next to a sizeable air-conditioning unit. We peer through the bushes. The sidewalk is about six feet away. It takes a few moments to gain our bearings; the car is visible, a pleasing short distance away, about two hundred yards to the left.

"Let's go. Did you see that guy?"

"Hard to believe." Henry clenches his teeth and turns down both sides of his mouth. "Let's put a couple of posters up here on the outside wall."

"Get out of here. Are you crazy?"

As if to confirm my worst fears, we hear a commotion coming from the right. The same fellows and a few more, along with a few growling angry women, turn out of the mall's glassed entrance 50 yards away. I don't even ask Henry what he thinks. Breaking for the parking lot, I heave my bag of glue to the side, assuming Henry has the sense to follow.

"Hey! Wait a minute! We want to talk to you!"

"Can't talk now ...in a hurry! So sorry!"

Whatever it is they have to say can be imagined as easily as it can be heard and with less discomfort than we presently experience. As the reality of our salvation comes closer, we discover a youthfulness in our ability to run that is unexpected and immensely pleasing. Once in the car, we lock up, happy and laughing between gasping breaths. I start the engine.

One of the men runs right up against the front fender and slams his hand on the hood. The slower, bigger, heavier red-faced men are coming. I edge the car forward to make the turn to head down the exit lane. Two men hit the trunk. They seem to be climbing hand over hand around to the sides.

"Check the door handles," shouts one. "These clowns need to own up."

We are owning up to the necessity of the moment.

I blast the horn repeatedly while accelerating down the lane.

Several of our pursuers give up. Henry turns to shake a fist at them. He cracks his window.

"Santa is coming!" His voice cracks; spittle flies from his lips. "And he's not happy!"

We're off, gaining speed.

The last of the pursuers drop off, arms swinging at their sides. Their mouths form words in the rear view mirror, crude but comprehensible.

Relief.

Hearts pounding.

Henry, showing teeth, lifts his right arm out the window, middle finger in the air.

We round the corner, laughing, and speed away.

Chapter Ten

The students come and go, most of them like zombies, half dead from sleepless nights and periodic bouts of drunkenness. I have gathered my resources to finish the semester: a pound of ground coffee imported from Sumatra, an eight cup Mr. Coffee coffee brewer, plenty of PaperMate red ink ballpoint pens and a jar of Advil.

I have secretly extracted the twelve hundred dollars from the cash value of my insurance policy. It's basically a loan using the policy as collateral. Boxes of anti-Christmas cards are going out at a slow but steady rate. I don't know what this means. Henry is in charge of the statistical predictions based on our small excursion into mass marketing. *If you make it they will buy.* I feel slightly nauseous. Maybe it's the coffee and the fatigue. Henry calls every afternoon with an official report.

"We mailed out thirty-three more boxes, Harry. These orders result from the ad in the alternative papers. A total of 110 orders so far, from just five advertisements. I've sent out ten more ads."

"Is that good?"

"Good! Are you kidding? The trial is a success. Next year we can sell a million."

"Will I get my money back?"

"Probably not this year. Start up expenses were high ...according to my calculations."

"I don't want to hear it." I interrupt. "I've got to go, Henry."

"It will come out all right, Harry. You'll see."

"Keep telling me that."

"I will ...talk to you later."

Sitting, staring at the phone doesn't soothe my nerves. For a while, I can't concentrate on my work.

Reviewing all the other financially wild machinations that are forming an evil vortex of doom in the center of my life doesn't help. Henry lacks complete awareness. Mary has decided that Tom is at a dangerous stage of development that requires special attention. According to Mary, fourteen is an important year, one in which you risk losing your child completely to peer influences, earphones and ugly teen song lyrics. He has been pressing for a Casio electronic synthesizer for months. This is a musical instrument that will record the sound of your burps and farts and turn that sound into a symphony. The only problem, of course, is that the Casio electronic synthesizer costs eight hundred dollars.

Mary brought forth her most recent contribution to the whirlwind at the breakfast table.

"Sure, it costs a lot, Harry. Everything costs plenty these days. But this is something he wants more than anything else in the world. Can you remember what that was like? And he loves music. It's a great opportunity for him to learn and grow."

Music? The last thing any fourteen year old should be allowed to be involved with is music. It's like selling him to a pimp in the Philippines. Lost forever. That was my thinking.

"I think this is an opportunity for Tom to learn about the amount of work it takes to pay for something like a Casio electronic synthesizer."

"Every child deserves one time in their life when something really special happens to them."

"Didn't he have that special moment a few years back with the bike he crashed?"

"Yes, but then his skateboard was stolen." This is an unfair tactic. No one could have retrieved the skateboard from that psycho woman from hell defending her kid like I was a madman planning to pull out his intestines.

"The lady was psychotic, Mary. She was screaming like I was pulling out her intestines."

"That's not the point. You made Tom work to

get a new one."

"So?"

"Every child gets a bike. This is special, Harry. Can't you see?"

The logic eludes me, but the attitude and tone are clear. Mary will not change her mind. *She rarely ever does.*

"Well, maybe. But, this doesn't have to be that time, does it? It could be another time." *One that doesn't involve financial ruin.*

"Oh, come off it. This is going to help keep Tom on the right track. He will know that he's respected, loved and appreciated, and he will want to honor these messages of parental confidence."

"He'll be spoiled rotten and think he can live a totally irresponsible life and still receive life's rewards."

"Trust me, Harry. I have done the right thing."

"What do you mean, I have done ...that sounds like you've already..."

"I have already..."

"What!?"

"Purchased the synthesizer."

"Where did you get the money?" Flabbergasted, I'm terrified to hear the truth.

"From my insurance policy."

"No!"

"Yes! I can pay it off quickly, Harry. Mr. Gregg wants me to work overtime and he's planning to expand the business. He'll probably promote me to a full time position some time next year and maybe assistant manager."

Fortunately, the cash value of either of our life insurance policies is only about a fifth of what our beneficiaries will receive in the event of our simultaneous deaths in, say, a house fire caused by an overheated Christmas bulb. *Or, possibly, a synthesizer explosion.* If we both die, the children will have enough money left over after paying off these cash value loans to cremate us and finish about one year of college.

Relax, if you die your kids will have to learn to be responsible. I don't even want to begin to think about the total cost of this Christmas. *You can say that again.* I don't want to think about it.

At the university the students' papers may pile up on my desk along with my own papers, journal reviews and correspondence that I'm trying to finish before the school break, but, at least, while I'm there, I have been able to control thinking about Christmas or money or anything else gruesome or scary. I don't have the time. This momentary violation, despite being only a few minutes of conversation with Henry and thoughts about Mary's money madness, gives me the willies. Is there no sanctuary? Can Christmas creep and seep into every corner and cranny of your life, like a poison gas, contaminating the clean air everywhere?

Yet, oddly it seems, I'm relaxed. *Losing time like water through a sieve.* Yes, this is true. *And what about this overtime with Mr. Gregg? Isn't that beginning to look a little suspicious? I'm not going to think anymore. I have quit thinking. Isn't it thinking that drives men mad? Isn't madness just thinking gone wild? The more I try to stop thinking, the more I think. There's something wrong.*

A black wave of dread forms in the space to the left of my brain. Turning my head, some dark creature flits across the periphery of my vision. Staring out the window, there's nothing. There's nothing there. Was there anything to begin with? I'm not sure. Mary's not here. Where did she go? What happened here? A section of time seems to have slipped away. I was talking with Henry not Mary. What happened to Henry? Did we finish talking? Did I hang up on him?

Sally makes an extra pot of coffee every afternoon before she leaves and Mary, good soul that she is most of the time, will have a hot dinner ready for me late at night along with a backrub at bedtime. Sometimes, I think about how much more she seems to accomplish than I do and I'm truly bewildered. I have asked her what her secret is and she tells me, "My children and husband help me every way they can." Perhaps, I'm being overly generous, but these kinds of statements make up for a lot of the day-to-day difficulties and even for the sarcasm and hurt. Mary can be an enchantress. Feeling strangely normal, I tilt back in my ergonomic reclining office chair wondering if one of these days, we'll have enough energy left over to romp in the Oval Office.

◆◆◆◆

Nearly finished, not much left to go, just the quantification, the scoring of the students' souls; a task that challenges even Brott, the most anal and critical of all the professors. No, it's not possible, but it's what we have to do, the reason we get paid – the numerical estimation of creativity. It helps them get ready for the real world.

The invisible fog seeps through the windows as I lay down my comments on the last student paper. She's a smart girl with a good idea and bad grammar. A good take on artificial intelligence, she used the issues involved in AI to comment on whether or not college courses actually enhance intelligence or just create a game called "Getting Good Grades," which you learn to play to advance to the world games. Freedom, which she defines as the ability to stop playing The Game is realized as the absence of thinking. The absence of thinking about The Game and the rules for getting good grades (passing courses, planning and scheduling, talking to the professor, neatness, being clever, asking the "right" questions and so on), is the basis for real intelligence. Without freedom there is no real intelligence. Every other kind of intelligence is programmed and unfree. Therefore AI, being a programmed intelligence, seems likely to never achieve a human level of intelligence. She gets an A.

Now, the fog is creeping toward me. I've got to get out of the office or succumb. As usual, the others have already gone. My footsteps echo as I walk the hallway toward the stairwell. Am I free, or have I just advanced to a higher level of The Game? Could I stop thinking about the rules, the grades, the course outline, the departmental politics, the striving, the pressure to achieve, to publish, to make a name? What would it be like to stop? *Your career will come to an end.* Does freedom have a price? *Financial disaster on a scale unimaginable.* It's time to go home.

The weather has changed. The cold front actually feels like a wall of cold wind advancing through the mountains, the coves and valleys, the flat places of my world, bringing with it the promise of punishment. Some people actually enjoy cold weather. They like to ski or build snowmen. Others like to sit by the fire at home and sip rum.

The walk home induces energy, but it's a nervous fearful energy, not necessarily invigorating, one based on the prospect of exhaustion, falling down from fighting the wind and cold and then being found a frozen carcass lying by the side of the road.

Willy greets me at the door.

"Dad, can I take Tiny for a walk?"

"How about letting me into the house first?"

Willy swings the door open.

"Is anyone home?"

"Mom and Tom went to the grocery store."

"You're here by yourself?"

"She said I could watch television, but then Tiny said she wanted to go out."

"Tiny spoke to you?"

"Well, you know, she acted like it."

"Right ...let me warm up and take a break and then we'll talk."

"Okay."

Tiny watches every move I make for signs of an impending walk. Taking off the coat, not good. Looking in the refrigerator, neutral. Sitting down at the kitchen table, ignoring her, reading the paper, all bad signs. She flops on the floor, her head between her paws, clearly disappointed.

Sock-footed Willy slides around the corner from the hall into the kitchen.

"Well, what about Tiny?"

"Tiny is resting."

"She's just waiting."

"Is that so?"

"But, she has to go."

"I'll tell you what. You go get your shoes on and a coat and get Tiny's leash and hook her up to it."

Willy ought to be a sprinter. He can go from zero to sixty in seconds. In minutes he and Tiny are dancing around the front door, ready to go. *You need the exercise. Spend some time with Willy. Go for the walk. It will be all right.* Once we're out there, it's tolerable. It's damn cold, but, hey we're going for a walk together. After a few blocks, Willy presses for the goal.

"Can I hold on to her?"

"Willy, Tiny outweighs you by at least thirty pounds and she's strong. She can pull me off my feet if I'm not careful. Does that tell you anything?"

"I can be careful."

Figuring the odds on catastrophe versus a mild, slightly bruising lesson on dog management and the limits of self-confidence, I hand him the leash. *There's a mistake, fella. Maybe the lesson on self-confidence will be for you.* It's against my better judgment, but how do you know what better judgment is if you don't disregard it once in a while? *Good thinking.*

Willy has two hands on the leash, and Tiny strolls along at a sniffing pace. Watching for squirrels, ready to grab the leash, I walk close to the other side of Tiny. No squirrels. All is well. Then, as my true underlying self knew all along, the little voice that unerringly knows the right way to do things at all times and sits smugly in the back of your mind watching you, whispering "I told you so, I told you so" even before anything happens, a cat head appears at the base of Mrs. Farrucci's hedge of ancient forsythia mixed with equally ancient hydrangea. Tiny has processed CAT in her specially designed dog brain long before I spot its slitted yellow eyes.

Flying Willy hits me waist high as Tiny lunges for the cat. Down on my butt, I can only turn to watch and hope for a safe outcome. Tiny's third or fourth leap takes her between the tops of two shrubs. Willy should let go.

"LET GO, WILLY!!"

It's too late.

He hits the base of the shrubs and both arms buckle inward as they crash against the sturdy stems – more like small tree trunks – of the shrubs. I'm up and over by the shrubs in moments. At first, it seems his head has taken the worst hit. There's a gouge over his left eye that will probably take stitches. It hasn't started bleeding yet, but it's going to be flowing any time. Folding my handkerchief into a square pad, I cover the wound. He's making a noble effort at not crying.

"Here ...hold this against the cut on your head."

"I can't."

"Why not?"

"My arms hurt."

While pulling him back away from the shrubbery so I can take a better look, he cries out in pain.

"Stop."

Damn. Life happens when you're not looking – when you're not thinking.

His arms are scraped up somewhat, but I see no damage.

"Move your arms, Willy."

He lifts both arms slowly.

"It hurts in my wrists."

"Move your fingers."

"No."

"Show me where it hurts."

He lifts his right arm, moves it across his waist and points to his left wrist.

"You're going to have to get up. We'll go to the hospital and have you checked out. Okay?"

"Okay ...what about Tiny?"

"Tiny will be all right. She'll go back home when she gets bored."

◆◆◆◆

Later on, at the emergency room, how many minutes I can't say, Mary swings in, shaking her head, coattail flying, dress askew, hair a mess, and finds us in one of the curtained-off spaces. I've just finished talking to the nurse and unconsciously eyeing her fit figure as she walks away. Two stitches have taken care of the gash by Willy's eyebrow, now nicely swollen and purpled. We're waiting for x-ray results.

"Is he alright?"

"He looks alright."

"I'm fine."

"They've given him something to reduce the pain and something else to relax him."

"I found Tiny sitting on Mrs. Farucci's front steps. Apparently, the cat went in through the cat door next to her front door."

"It looks like he's got a broken wrist."

"How did that happen?" I don't say anything, just stare patiently ahead thinking of comments about flying. She looks at me with squinted eyes, deep in thought. In a moment or two she figures it out. Amazingly she decides to let it go ...well almost.

"That's about as stupid as you can get, Harry."

"Well, at least we know now the boundaries of my stupidity."

Willy's left wrist gets the full cast and the right a plastic immobilizer and pressure wrap. Apparently the right wrist has a hairline fracture and a major sprain – nothing to worry about. He'll be using his right arm and hand in a few days, maybe a week, says the doc. Get him to bed. Get him some fluids. Keep him in bed a couple of days. *Right.* He hands us a follow-up appointment with a pediatric orthopedist, scheduled a week away. He's gone.

We head for home.

The Christmas Curmudgeon

Good-natured Willy, seated in the back, checks out his cast and laughs at the size and ungainliness of it. He sees humor in everything. We drive in silence through the streets of town, the storefronts sharp, the houses clean; each of us nurturing his or her own ideas. Then, Willy perks up; he's had a realization.

"Who's going to feed me?"

Mary laughs. "That's a good one."

"I'd be thinking about who's going to bathe me."

"Perhaps we could hire a sweet young nurse." Mary punches me in the ribs, but her look is smirky and hard.

"I don't want a nurse. I'll bathe myself."

It's not independence. I know it and so does Mary. He's become self-conscious. It's a revelation.

"I'll help with the bath and mom can do the feeding. Let's leave it at that."

Willy sits back. Peace and reason reside in a satisfactory outcome.

"Have some peanut brittle." Mary pulls a square plastic container with candy-cane stickers on it from her purse. "Mrs. Farucci and Laura made it."

I look it over, take a piece and hold it open for Willy.

"My ass she made it."

"Of course, she made it. She and Laura probably baked it yesterday."

"She got it from the grocery store. Mrs. Farucci sells real estate, and that's about all she does except complain about her ex-husband. She made this like you made a hand-crafted guitar to sing Christmas songs downtown on the street."

"That's not in the Christmas spirit."

"Neither is the peanut brittle. It's a passing nod."

"We should make something for her."

"Let's make her some chocolate covered cherries. You can get them cheap at CVS. We'll put them in a nice little paper box to make them look like we made them."

The Christmas Curmudgeon

    Mary groans and looks away. I look over at her, but she's lost in thought. Like the darkness that descended an hour or so ago, the hour when Mary came swiftly into the hospital emergency room treatment area, another darkness descends now, behind my eyes in the hollow universe of my mind. An image of Mary swiftly coming into the room, and now my wonder – why is she so disheveled?

Chapter Eleven

How does it happen? I look down and I look up and it's the second weekend in December. It's unbelievable. It's truly amazing. There are times when I just stand there, anywhere, wondering where the days went. If there is some time gremlin released during the Christmas season who gobbles up human time and saves it somewhere, in the bowels of some cave, perhaps, I want to know. *Demand the truth and you will get the truth.* I really wonder if I have blackouts or mental fugues. It makes me crazy to think about it. *There are cracks forming in my brain like dried mud after a desert rain. Something glows beneath the surface, revealed by these miniature canyons, orange, like lava, but cool, a glaze-hardened sheen, itself crackable, dangerous. It's better not to think. One should just live and not think at all.*

Mary is out again, shopping for the relatives, getting it done in time to deliver it into the mail so that when we receive what they send us we won't feel like what we bought them was simply a reaction to getting something from them. And doesn't that make sense. The kids have gone out to a movie, something about a woman who gives birth to an alien monster. What can I say? It's probably somebody's autobiography.

Christmas Day is a little more than two weeks away. The main highways in town are congested day and night. I'm glad to stay home by myself. The noon news actually has a report on highway congestion, the crowding at the malls, the congestion in the parking lots, and a comparison of this year's retail sales figures to last year's. After the news, there's a special economic report on Christmas sales figures and their relation to the overall health and well-being of the economy. Why is this considered news? There seems to be anxiety over the fact that "We the People" are not spending enough. Is this a sign of America's decline in world market share? Are we no longer the leader among nations? Is democracy failing? Consumption used to be what they call tuberculosis – a disease that ate you up, bit by bit.

Why is Christmas shopping an indicator of the well-being of America? And, more disturbing, God seems to have gotten involved. On the television images of people coming and going from churches are interspersed with those of people entering and leaving shopping centers. There's a sense in the news narrative, an intimation, that God smiles upon America when the gross national product gradually, yet continually, increases. In the commercials that follow, people are shown praying. Children, portrayed by child actors, are praying for the things they want, which are pictured in balloons above their heads. These commercials blend with the news almost indistinguishably. Have commercialism and news become intertwined so inextricably that we can't tell the difference? The surrealism of it makes me feel disconnected from the world.

Then, in a bizarre corrective reaction, I feel totally enmeshed, absorbed into the stream of news as though it was intentionally designed to enter my particular mind. Is it a personal message about my stinginess, my desire to control the family, to keep them from spending money, my lack of generosity, my lack of willingness to go along with the Big Party, to flow along tossing presents to the peasants, my unkingliness, my lowness, my lack of loving? Gahh, what a withered, self-enclosed, spiteful, nasty grouch I am. If shopping isn't going well, then God is disappointed. God isn't directly mentioned, but He is, mysteriously, invoked. God wants us to shop. Can this be right?

I find these thoughts disturbing enough to turn off the television and fix myself a glass of rum. Why not an eggnog rum? Mary and the children are out at the mall. I pour a double shot of rum into a six ounce glass of eggnog. Later on, I've got to go to the office to add up and average all the scores for the semester – as though a writing course was so many innings of baseball, some hard hits, a few fouls, a lot of running around, fielding, double plays and pitching – all with words, of course. A somber task, but nothing that can't be enhanced by rum.

Tomorrow morning will be a true test of my Christmas spirit. Tomorrow, Henry and I will purchase Christmas trees. Mary and Janette feel that we're already a week late. Like everything else Christmas, the good ones will be gone. This viewpoint of theirs resembles a forty-year-old spinster's picture of life. I call this view of diminishing possibilities facsimile need. When I first told Henry about facsimile need, he thought it was an important Christmas insight. He took me out to dinner to celebrate my heightened awareness.

Facsimile need isn't simply a function of massive advertising. Advertising, of course, plays a role in creating a need for products that you don't really need. But ad campaigns are aimed at boosting sales of a particular product for special markets – a market being a certain group or type of person. Acme acne medicine for teenagers who feel rejected. Suave shampoo for middle aged housewives with dry hair who think they look frumpy. Black & Decker power tools for power-hungry men. And so forth and so on. *On and on ad infinitum.*

The eggnog rum is good, so smooth and creamy that it's like drinking a cold glass of liquefied custard. The rum doesn't burn at all and before I know it I've finished the whole glass. The afternoon is about as mellow and fine as any will ever be during the Christmas season. I mix another eggnog rum and stare mindlessly into the gas logs flaming in the fireplace.

Facsimile need is more refined, more insidious than advertising. It has to do with the perceived scarcity of consumer products. The products need not really be scarce. They must only be perceived as such. The act of shopping itself, by reducing shelf congestion, actually creates the sense of scarcity and the perceived need. News reports feature updates on popular items that are being "sold out." This fake scarcity then creates a form of panic, a nervous awareness of the possibility of thwarted satisfactions, an awful tension of anticipated frustration and fears of being left out or left behind. Shoppers flock to the stores and pick the shelves clean, thereby increasing the "need." More important, once the scarce products are gone, it doesn't matter anymore. Facsimile need becomes so intense under these conditions that the need takes over, and the actual objects desired become less important. When they go to the store, most people will then buy anything. They are frenzied by facsimile need.

Manufacturers and merchants, of course, encourage this shopping frenzy. The mindless purchasing of massive quantities of cheap substitutes and inadequate alternatives make for huge profits. Remember – facsimile need is not a real need, so it doesn't matter what you buy. If you can't get what you want, get something you don't want ...as long as you get something.

◆◆◆◆

The wind whips through the trees in gusts and lashes, tearing leaves from branches, lifting layers of the fallen leaves from the ground and sending them into swirls. A thousand golden thoughts; the leaves know nothing of each other yet are all connected. A few moments peace inside this storm, always with walking. I sit in seats so much it's a wonder to be outside in the air, brisk, chilled, with a warm spot of rum in my belly. It's better to feel this way, walking across the empty campus, than to sink into the chaos of worry, chased by ghosts of guilt into depression. Then, I can't work. Empty of ideas, I sit in my office imagining phone calls, doodling, reading other writers' great works. Even my students' works seem more creative, brighter, and more inventive than anything I might do.

Money, it's always money, or the lack of it, it seems, that rends my mind, cleaving it so that interpretations come from every direction, self-referential fantasies in which the fools around me, strangers – even friends are strangers in this condition – all speak to me in code, in sly references and innuendo, intimating their knowledge of my academic weakness, my lack of even one good idea, my marital issues, my doubts and fears, my desire for escape – things which I think only I think about. How do they know my thoughts, my life secrets?

In my office, halfway through the numerification of artistic effort, the rum wears down, leaving in its place a raw uneasiness. Putting the work aside, head in my hands, a gray cloud of doom sweeps through my consciousness clearing the way for an upheaval of thought. Thoughts I don't want. But, there is rum. I know there is, somewhere in the office. While searching the shelves and cabinets, the hideyguy reminds me of his efforts. *You're a clever one you are. Found me out have you? Have I hid it here? Have I hid it there? Or, did I change my mind, put it down in the boot of the car or somewhere safe in the files out in secretary Sally's realm? Plenty of room out there. No, no, I know it's in here. You're not going to dupe me this time.* Then it comes to me. *Yes! I've beaten you. Ha!*

Lifting up the corner of the desk, I reach under the lower drawer and there it is, concealed by the false panels that make the desk look as though it's built into the floor. Whoever designed it knew my intentions. It's a fine half full pint of Bacardi Black ...ready for sipping. There's a glass, too, in the back of the top drawer. Now, there's a fine solution to apply to anyone's problem.

Kicked back in the ergonomic reclining chair, glass of Bacardi in hand, I'm once again master of the universe. I'm thinking about Hedler. Maybe, I should invite him over for a drop of dew. Nix that. It has always been my unspoken pact of safety to never share this bottle-in-the-bottom-drawer secret ...trust and friendship aside. There are things better kept quiet if you want them; if you want peace and the things you want kept quiet, keep quiet. That's the answer. Still, Hedler is a good man. I toast him. *The loyalty of a true friend is a priceless treasure; it cannot be squandered nor can it be measured.*

As I recall it, coming down the hall, on the way in, Hedler, as usual, stepped out of his office. How he manages to appear at the exact moment I arrive is incomprehensible. Does he wait secretly behind the crack of his door peering down the hall? With his private office he could do this. Is it out of the question? Would anyone spend his hours in such a way?

Perhaps, he has a gift for encounter, psychic antennae tuned to the approach of colleagues. Clearly, he doesn't appear when students amble by. They wait by his door for opportunities like supplicants at the gates of a Buddhist temple, willing to cut off an arm just to hear one word from the mouth of the master. They sit around in two's and three's, chatting amiably as if they had nothing better to do. Maybe I should write a play: "Waiting for Hedler."

Anyway, he jumps from the doorway like he does, like a kid really, as though to surprise you, and he does surprise you. It's so incongruous – department chair slash adolescent clown. He starts talking right away, before I can go through any absurd amenities, no greetings, no observations about the weather. He has no patience.

"I've got the shakes, Harry. Sale of the book diminishes hourly, maybe even minute-by-minute, right now as we speak. The invitations for lectures are dwindling. My penis is worried."

"You had a great ride."

"That's so, but now what? I've been resting for over a year. Nothing is coming to me. Nothing. Nada. Zip. Zilch. I'm dried up."

The Christmas Curmudgeon

"Don't worry."

What else can I say? He speaks my thoughts. He describes my condition as if it were his own.

"My students have some good ideas." He smiles pathetically, mixing wistful thoughts of youth and energy with a questioning eye that investigates whether or not I understand his questionable intentions.

"So do mine."

"I've thought of stealing from them."

"It's only natural."

"It's not natural!"

"No you're right. What was I thinking? It's not."

"It's like eating a baby."

"Oh, that's awful."

"It's awful all right. You can't do it!"

Switching to the second person there in that last statement catches me off guard. Does he mean I can't do it? What does he suspect? It sets in motion another of my personalities – a suspicious untrustworthy fellow who thinks the people out there in the world know what I'm thinking (all of them out there who for unknown reasons are watching and gossiping, as though they had nothing better to do with their lives except to monitor mine). This personality, unnamed as yet, therefore searches through all the words they say, today, yesterday, even last month (it has a great memory). For example, during that conversation at the restaurant when the guy raised his eyebrow as he raised his head, then looked around at me and said, "Fish are slippery." What did he mean? Why did he look at me from that table across the way at just that time? Fish slip away through your hands? Is it a sly reference to women? Am I losing my grip? Is my life getting away from me? Is my wife ...?"

While standing at the bathroom stall pissing at the movies, after the movie, the guy next to me says, "I'm here at this action flick staining the ceramic stall while my part-time wife is out parting her hair with her part-time boss at her part-time job." He looks aside toward me and slowly, ever so slowly, as though he were indicating an acknowledgment that he knows, he's certain, that what he's saying is about me. I can't stand this kind of thing.

Caught up by these thoughts, I miss most of Hedler's next idea. Gathering my attention, I pick up his last line and interpolate the obvious gist of his inclination.

" ...It's incredible. She suspects me of screwing around while I'm off at these lectures, making the bucks, by the way, not just for me but for her, and the fact is I'm too tired to tool around like a teenager – not that I haven't had the chance – but the fact is I haven't. I'm beginning to think it's her way of telling me that she's screwing around."

That's it. I've heard enough. Does he know this is what I've been thinking about Mary? Or, is this just something all professors' wives do? And we the dour dons talk about it in hallways, crying and whining like newly-castrated slaves, holding our detached organs in our hands for a last pathetic look, disbelieving yet knowing the truth, saying goodbye before our parts are taken and thrown to the baying dogs out the window as offal. The growling and snapping in the distance offers a vicious presentiment of what's to come as age and failure take us. Eunuchs.

Enough. Enough is enough. I'm tired of thinking this way. This can go on for hours. Rum is the only proper solution. Two thick swigs go right to the head, knocking a blur into the brain. Rum soothes like nothing else. It should be shared. It really should. Two more swigs, twice again, and then I'm out. Unh.

The woman of my dreams comes into the room and stands behind my chair. I can hear the slight rustling of her silken gown as she moves her hands across my shoulders and down my back digging the deep tension out of my muscles. I can see her reflection in the mirrors on the walls. She's younger than I am and beautiful like a woman is beautiful in a painting. Flames dance in the background behind her in the mirrors. The room glows and seems to change size and shape as the light from a fireplace changes.

"Commander," she whispers.

"Yes," I say. "Harry ...call me Harry."

"Harry."

"Yes."

"How would you like to put me on the Lay-Away plan?"

She slides around the side of my chair and stands beside me. Her waist tilts as she sits on the arm of my chair. I clearly observe the curve of her thighs, the concavity between them that sucks at the silk of her dress intimating ideas of nakedness. She smells like eucalyptus. Her movements are soft like a breeze. Her face is next to mine. The power of her body pulls at mine with its magnetism.

She whispers in my ear.

"How about making your first installment, commander ...Harry?"

She's like a drug. She sits on my lap and kisses me. It's wonderful. It's the eggnog rum of kisses. My groin stirs. As the magnetic momentum builds, invisible energies pass between us. Cracking sounds like popping vertebrae travel through my neck, exploding spasms of light in my brain.

She leans back, pushing against me, smiles and waves a finger.

"There's only one thing you should know."

"What?"

"Buy now, pay later."

"What?" An electric storm emits waves of energy through the sky, a thousand strings of lightning in each wave.

"You know what buy now means." She nuzzles my neck and kisses me.

A tiny black glider emerges from a thunderhead, sailing incredibly fast, drifting downward, headed for clear air.

"Yes."

"You should have some idea of what pay later

means, too."

"Yes ...I should."

The glider crashes into a cliff and explodes into pieces. One of them propels toward me like the blade of a guillotine set free, flying sideways, hurtling, rotating, making a whoosh-whoosh sound as it heads yet, yes, for my neck.

"AAAACCKK!"

The chair has an automatic pneumatic device that adjusts the height of the seat if you tug at a lever placed handily to the side of the seat bottom. On the forward lurch precipitated by the dream, I've hit the lever with my hand. The seat descends rapidly taking me to its lowest level, a convenience of the apparatus apparently designed to aid midgets. I'm fully awake now, bobbing slightly from the ride, with a nearly eye-level view of the top of the desk. The sheen of the desktop like a thin layer of perfectly smooth ice reflects the random objects there. A paper clip, magnified by the residue of dream consciousness along with the change in perspective, looks like a section of twisted conduit.

Three small knocks at my office door seem a mile away, yet clear and clean, precise, as though offered by a drummer.

"Professor?"

The door cracks, swings open and Sally's bright face edges through the opening. Her cheeks and nose shine red from being outdoors. A sporty blue headband with white snowflakes holds her hair back in a bunch so it looks like a thick stand of reddish grass growing from her head. The tips of her hair curl over and bend every which way creating a carefree appearance; they lend a frisson of unruliness.

"Are you all right?"

"Come on in, Sally."

"I heard a sound like choking."

She steps into the office uncertainly. Come to my senses, I quickly sweep the rum glass into my hand and deftly let it drop into the top right hand drawer, which I have swiftly opened with my other hand. This kind of coordination and timing, admirable under any circumstances, makes me feel almost youthful. Sally stands in the room now, wearing an ice skating outfit. The bodice covers her torso and breasts snugly, it's a shiny blue synthetic material sprinkled with silver sparkles. The short, pleated skirt, also blue, flows like a flower from her waist, her legs, the stem, are clad in that tan nylon made for stockings, neither transparent nor opaque, that suggests tightness and suppleness and every other erotic thing you can imagine. My breathing becomes taut and turgid. Our eyes meet and we smile.

"I've been ice skating at the campus rink. A bunch of us go every year ...a kind of secretaries' party."

"It's been quite a year."

What an inane comment. By pushing the lever on the side of the chair, I make my body elevate. Sally, meanwhile, digs in a small handbag for something. As she retrieves whatever it is, a tangled gob of keys, baubles and beaded strings comes out over the edge and falls on the floor. Something breaks and beads begin rolling in every direction.

"Oh, damn it." She throws her purse down.

Meanwhile, I've taken the opportunity to place my hand over the flat side of the rum pint, which is still on the desk, sliding it slowly, all along watching Sally carefully to see if she notices what I'm doing, which she doesn't. As she stoops to pick up her keys, I grab the bottle, deftly again placing it in the desk drawer with the glass. A small clinking sound. Now, Sally being the young, cheerful, unselfconscious person that she is, characteristics which gave her the appeal to be hired for the receptionist chair, along with her other professional qualifications, bends over this way and that picking up beads from the floor, in the process tilting her back down at a low angle, lifting her hips high and spreading her thighs slightly to aid her stability. Each turn and bend reveals her derriere, the nylon stretched to heighten the roundness, the firmness and the shades of her skin beneath, and then, too, her crotch, the underwear underneath, pink satin, slightly bulbed by her position and the natural attributes of contour, thickness, fullness, shape, responsivity to torque and twist and tension of the flesh in that so lovely focus of her body ...what. I've lost track of myself. Who wouldn't stare? I admit that I tilted back, angled the chair to a pitch as far back as possible in order to see as well as could be seen all that the view had to offer.

Sally remains absorbed in her task, muttering to herself, finding and capturing each bead, then standing, places the bead in a zippered pocket in her bodice, a feature someone figured would create a marketing edge. Sally bends down again. This slowly repeated liquid movement reminds you of those plastic birds with round balls for bottoms filled with a strange red fluid that makes the bird's head at the end of a long plastic neck bob up and down regularly once set in motion. From my angle, Sally's bottom is so much more appealing, so beautiful, so enjoyable that I can't really describe the depth of my professorial pleasure.

As stated, who would not stare? Life is made for these moments.

"Harry Jenkins!"

I look up, shot through electrically with a jolt of recognition, truth, fear and awfulness that jams my brain suddenly with the entire contents of my childhood reserve of theft guilt, sneakiness guilt, pornographic sexual shame, what have you. I'm caught. Mary stands in the office door, staring at me fiercely.

Aaahhhcckk!

The jolt from her appearance and words is physical enough to throw me backward, which at my already precarious angle creates an unsupportable distribution of weight, as well as kaleidoscopic emotions, and the chair goes over backwards and sideways as I try, arms flailing, to rectify the fall. Crash. Down. My head hits the bookcase behind the desk, hard enough to hurt, seriously hurt; a crack of sharp intense pain, then dizziness and confusion. I sprawl out on the floor and lie there for several moments looking at the wood in the flooring; a dark knot next to my right eye particularly captures my interest. *Quickly, quickly, quickly. Thinking.* I'm better off prolonging the appearance of head injury, confusion, dizziness than by doing anything else. I pretend to try to lift my head, but let it back down slowly.

"Ooof."

"Hi Mrs. Jenkins."

"Hello, Sally. Get up, Harry. There's nothing wrong with you."

"I think he banged his head."

"Better than banging something else."

Light enters Sally's mind. You can see it.

"Oh, no. Mrs. Jenkins. I just came in from ice skating."

"I was taking a nap and she knocked on the door." I'm sitting up now, exploring the back of my head with one hand, the other hand on the floor as a prop.

"I was out shopping and came by to see if you wanted to go to dinner, but I see now that you're far too busy, too ...deeply absorbed in what you're doing."

"Oh, geez. I really did bang my head."

"Good. I hope it hurts."

"C'mon."

"Mrs. Jenkins. You don't think ...I'm not that kind of person."

"Oh. I think you're not, Sally. ...Harry and I ...Harry?"

"What."

"I'll meet you at the Sushi House."

"What?"

"The Sushi House at 5:30."

"All right, all right. Now, will you help me up and look at my head. I think it's actually bleeding."

Mary helps me up. Sally takes this opportunity

to leave. A few beads remain on the floor. *Make sure to save them, these wonderful beads.* They're reminders, treasures really. I'll save them. I hold my hand out in front of my face. Blood covers my fingers, plenty enough blood to be concerned. Blood oozes down my neck. Mary takes stock of the wound. She puts a hand on each side of my head and turns my head slowly this way and that, finding that it works well enough, mechanically speaking.

"Go to the campus clinic and get patched up. Then we can meet for dinner."

She steps back, turns and walks away.

♦♦♦♦

At the restaurant, it's as though nothing happened. Mary doesn't ask about my head or say anything about Sally. A couple of Advil, a bandage and I'm walking upright, though a headache looms and it would be nice of her to ask. There's something wrong here, no question. *She feels relieved about her affair with Mr. Gregg. She thinks she's off the hook because of Sally. But nothing is going on with Sally.* Who wouldn't have stared.

Somebody has to talk. It might as well be me.

"You know, I would probably like Christmas if I didn't think about it."

"So don't think about it."

Is attempted conversation anything like attempted murder?

"Right," I say. "And don't breathe, either. Besides, Henry has got a new scheme ...a Christmas scheme." *Don't tell her about the money.*

"What is it this time?"

"Anti-Christmas cards."

"No!"

"Yes. You should see them." *You better change the topic.* "Henry's so crazy. Sometimes, I wonder about him."

"Ohh, I don't know. Janette thinks he's just being a curmudgeon. She's more worried about his cholesterol than his rebellious nature."

"Well, maybe." But something in me isn't totally convinced. I wonder if Henry's getting a little loose above the noose. Maybe he needs to go to a doctor ...a head doctor.

"Guess what?" says Mary.

"I can't guess."

"Oh, come on, Harry ...guess."

You're having an affair with your boss. You're sucking your way up to assistant manager. You do it in the shoe storage area, like animals, like dogs on the floor. "Oh, let's see, our troubles are over. You won one of those big lottery scratch offs ...no ...no ...you're pregnant."

Mary shrieks. She loves the thought of having another baby.

"No," She pinches my cheek. "Bad boy ...I got something for Willy."

"Oh yeah? What did Willy get?"

"A new Pro-tech mountain bike." She looks down as though she has done something bad. "It was six hundred and fifty dollars."

Oh God. I reel. Then I feel good because the cost of the anti-Christmas cards will match her crime. Thoughts of the debt we are accumulating assail me, but I shove them aside. Who cares? What difference does it make? My mood becomes calm, peaceful, almost spiritual. I'm at that stage in the season when you become disconnected from it all, from everything and everybody. In this state, you drift along, almost as though you were floating in the sky watching the hordes swoosh and clash, rending each other with elbows and cars, boxes and carts and brittle hard glares of greedy me-first consumption.

"It's okay. Willy should get something better than usual this year, given Tom's monster gift." *Can it really matter when doom and disaster are clearly inevitable?* "I approve."

"It takes some assembly."

"Oh no."

"Sorry."

"Fine. But, you know the agreement. You stay away until it's all done. No matter how much swearing you hear coming from the garage. No interference, no matter what."

"I promise."

It occurs to me now, with Mary's good mood, that I can solve a problem that has been bothering me. It may be risky, given the events of the day, but what the heck, nothing matters, everything is just fine. *Bangs on the head. Bangs on the floor. Who cares? It's Christmas. Be happy. Don't worry. Smile.*

"How about doing me a favor?"

"I can do favors."

There's no point in hesitating. I know she'll resist but hopefully not too severely. The problem needs to be solved before time runs out. I figure that such a transparent fact along with Mary's hidden shopping guilt will carry me through to the goal.

"I don't know what to get Sally."

"Oh no," Mary, shakes her head, frowning. "It's your responsibility to buy a present for your secretary. You should show her that you think of her."

"I do think of her. I appreciate her. I just don't know what to get her. She's a twenty-five year old single woman."

"How about getting her a tutu for the office?"

"Yes, I'm sure that would go over well."

"She might like it. She could do ballet while she picks up beads amidst your daydreams of dancing bears and lollipops."

"Get serious, will you? All I want is a little help here."

"You knew what to get me at that age."

"That's not fair. That's completely different. I was after getting in your pants."

"Oh, I see. You can only think of a twenty-five year old as an opportunity, a physical possibility? You can't think of her practically."

"You're twisting things into something they

aren't. Sally's a nice young woman. The trouble is that I don't think of her in any way clearly enough to guide me."

"And you're a dirty old man." Mary certainly enjoys herself. She laughs at me.

"So, that's it ...You think I'm after Sally. You're jealous and you won't buy her a present!"

"I didn't say that." Her eyebrows rise speculatively.

"You might as well have." It's my turn for a laugh.

"I'll buy her a present for you, Harry." She nods, a hint of sly purpose in her eye. Her voice is as hard as her nails but misses the shine of the lacquer. "But I think it's wrong."

"I'll tell her that I bought it."

"Oh, how couth."

"Asking you to help is thinking of her. I know you'll get her the perfect thing where I would get her something awful, an elephant end table, a set of plastic containers for leftovers or worse, something my old granny would cherish, a horrible ceramic figurine of a ballet girl, Empire State building salt and pepper shakers. God! I hate to think of what could happen."

"How sad. You can't even understand the ordinary needs of a young woman."

"Yes." A little hurt by that remark, I sneer back at her. "I'm such a pathetic fool. It's a wonder I can understand or do anything at all."

"I hope you remember that I didn't say that ...you did."

"Hmmm." Of course, saying something doesn't make it true. I know that it's better to let it go at this point. She will get the present, and it will be better than what I'd have thought up. After all, maybe I really don't understand the needs of a modern young woman. *Is that so bad?*

"There's one condition."

Now what? I had it sacked.

"I'll do it if you agree to go to a psychiatrist."

"Are you kidding?"

"No. At least go and see Dr. Temple at the university and see if he can't give you something. You're irritable. You're depressed. You think too much."

"They have drugs now to prevent thinking?"

She looks at me like I'm an idiot. "You worry too much. And you drink too much."

Considering her points and the deal rationally for a moment, it becomes clear that there isn't much choice. It's the path of least resistance, not always the right path, but certainly the path of the moment. *Bring the curtains down. Let's get on with life.* I agree to check in with a psychiatrist.

Chapter Twelve

Christmas tree morning.

As soon as we're out of bed, Mary starts pressing me to go to a psychiatrist to discuss my "problems." She thinks I'm a depressive neurotic with secondary personality disorders, probably multiple personality disorders with sleep disorder and alcohol disorder thrown into the mix. She has developed these ideas with her female co-workers at her place of work. They're all the time discussing their husbands as if we're a bunch of lunatics who somehow got lucky enough to marry reasonably normal, wholesome women. She's done this before and it usually passes, but this time she's being exceptionally persistent. I wonder if she's trying to set me up so she can hit me with the Big Truth about herself and Mr. Gregg. *Push that thought aside.* Rather than argue with her, I remind her that I agreed to make an appointment. I bite my tongue literally in an effort to stay calm, and it hurts, but I don't react. She might see it as a symptom of some sort of self-loathing disorder.

I'll tell you what though; I'm ready to escape the cause of all my problems. I'm really in the mood to get going and get this Christmas tree task out of the way so that Christmas can materialize and disappear as quickly as possible. Mary barks at me all the way to the front door despite the fact that Tom stands in the hallway, waiting, and is privy to what she says. Once there, she takes a turn at Tom.

"Remember what we talked about, Tom, Okay?"

"Yes, Mom. You only told me five times."

"I told you twice and it's just to make sure you understand."

"I understand. I'm not an idiot."

"Okay." She smiles at Tom then turns back to

me. "Do you want me to call and set up an appointment with Dr. Temple?"

"I'll make my own appointment. And, I'll choose my own doctor."

"No need to be snappy."

"It comes with the personality disorder."

She backs off, apparently satisfied, but probably doubtful, yet unwilling to drive me over the edge of sanity into regrettable acts of defiance, self-abuse, drinking, brooding on violent thoughts, whatever. These are the things sick people do. *Hmmm. She must be plotting to keep me sane. Why would she do that?* We'd better get out the door and get going.

Young Tom and I set out eagerly in the good ol' 1995 GMC Jimmy. The back seat folds down so we can put one tree inside with the back gate open and one tree on the roof. Tom will have to sit in the back with the tree. A cold front has settled in like a boulder in mud. Overnight the temperature has dropped to eighteen degrees and it's starting to snow. The car warms up slowly, then starts running smoothly. What can I say; with 182 thousand miles on it and no car payments for two straight years I can't complain.

On the way to Henry's, Tom turns on the radio and I turn it off. Asserting my authority is a necessary correction to Tom's hidden agenda. Tom knows his role this morning. He has been sent by Mary to insure that the two dads do not slight the rules for proper tree selection. Over six feet. Perfect symmetry. By all means, a straight trunk. Scotch Pine or Fraser Fir only. Tom perceives correctly via the radio struggle that his role as top-notch tree consultant, a.k.a. spy and informer for the moms, is unappreciated and under siege. He will be put to the all-for-one-and-one-for-all-brotherhood-of-males-like-father-like-son loyalty test.

"Too bad," I say.

The silence surrounding his disgruntled look feels as deep and cold as the weather. The look on his face, the grotesque twist of his lips and the side-to-

The Christmas Curmudgeon

side shake of his head, tells me that he thinks he knows what's up and thinks he's ready, too. He's not brave enough to mock me outright, but cocky enough to make ugly faces. He has no doubt been instructed thoroughly by his mother regarding the nature of Dad's and Henry's stingy self-serving attitude regarding the annual Christmas tree and, probably, through extensive explanation and bribery, she has fortified his resistance to the ploys we will use to alter his commitment to a proper, time-consuming and ultimately expensive tree purchase. He has a tape measure and a picture to go by. The poor lad is in a terrible fix.

Henry's standing on the front steps shuffling his feet and clapping his hands when we pull into his driveway. He has chosen the original classic leather WWI leather flight helmet with the grim reaper insignia we gave him eight years ago. The flaps are down and the strap secured beneath his chin. His bright red nylon football jacket balloons around him; a black and orange striped scarf flies from his neck, to the East as the wind blows. Goggles with round lenses would complete the zaniness. Gusts of blue vapor stream from his mouth as he trots to the car. He climbs into the front seat after Tom slides into the back.

"Brrrr," goes Henry. "It's colder than a bald man's bottom taking a dump in the woods during a blizzard."

Tom laughs.

"I'll say." I back out of the driveway. Even on this residential street there are so many cars out that I have to wait. Christmas car congestion annoyance tightens my back.

Henry unsnaps his straps and lifts his flaps, then turns sideways to take a look at Tom in the back. "Hey, hey, me boy. I guess they've sent you to keep an eye on your old dad and me, huh?"

"Mom and Aunt Janette are paying me to pick out good trees," says Tom.

"Ahhh, I see," Henry is clearly surprised that Janette has been included in the scheme. "So it's come to that. They're paying you. Is that right?"

"Right," says Tom.

"He won't say how much either, Henry."

"Ohh, reaaally. Well. How much is it, Tom? Now that it's just us guys, you can tell."

"No way," Tom leans back folding his arms across his chest.

Henry looks at me. "Looks like it's going to be a tough day, Harry. Let's talk this up over breakfast. What do you say to the IHOP? I'm buying."

"Sounds good."

"Me too," Tom leans forward. "I'm hungry."

Poor lad.

"Oh I don't know about breakfast for you," says Henry. "You may have to stay in the car. Conflict of interest you know."

"Divided loyalties," I add, chuckling along with Henry.

"Man, I love those pancakes at the IHOP," chortles Henry, "especially those Swedish ones with the Loganberry butter." He knows this is Tom's favorite.

"It's lingonberry," says Tom.

"I think I'll have a double order."

An advertising sign for IHOP appears on the right. I see no escape from the long line of cars we've joined. We inch forward. There's a meaningful silence. Henry turns the dial on the radio, picks a classical station and hums along.

"Say, Tom. You could go across the street to McDonalds if you like ...you know, just while Uncle Henry and I work out our tree strategy."

"C'mon, Dad. That's not fair."

"Sure it's fair. It's as fair as your mom and Aunt Janette paying you to make the tree selection. You know your Uncle Henry and I can't just say no to Mom and Aunt Janette about their sending you along. It would make us look like Christmas ogres."

"You can't be on two teams at once," adds Henry, with sage indifference.

Tom sits back in the back seat, brooding.

"Say Tom," Henry turns toward the back to speak directly, sympathetically. "How much was it the moms paid you for this bit of U.N. style watchdog activity?"

Tom hesitates but finally relents. "Ten dollars."

"Ten dollars!!" Henry and I shout simultaneously.

"Hah!" Henry's exclamation reflects my own certainty about the situation.

"You've been duped, son. Is this discomfort you're experiencing and the loss of a really fun IHOP breakfast with your dad and your favorite Uncle Henry worth a paltry ten dollars?"

"Give us your ten dollars," Henry puts his open hand in the air, "as a token of your loyalty to the secret brotherhood of men and no one will be the wiser."

What boy can resist membership in a secret brotherhood? There is not one, not even for a hundred dollars. "C'mon, Tom. This is your chance. We men must stick together."

Henry extends his hand over the back seat. "The ten dollars please."

"Why can't I just keep the money? Mom won't know, right?" Tom looks to me for an endorsement of this idea.

"Fair is fair, Tom. It's a matter of principle. The ten dollars reveals the sincerity of your commitment."

"And your courage," adds Henry. "It's a token of your trust and true intentions."

"All right," says Tom. "Here's the ten dollars ...but I'm getting a double order of Swedish pancakes." He digs the ten out of his pocket and passes it to Henry.

"You're on, my boy. You made the right choice. Silence is the password." I reach back and pat his shoulder.

"And Janette's ten, too." Henry eye's Tom steadily.

"Awww, C'mon."

"Give it."

Tom fishes out the ten and hands it to Henry. He folds his arms as he leans back in the back seat, scowling.

We've reached the West end of Main Street. The road divides into a boulevard lined with shopping plazas and restaurants. The IHOP is the last restaurant before the interstate. The parking lot is jammed. We pull into a space at the far end and walk through a blast of ice-cold wind. We add our bodies to a line that has formed outside the front door.

"Geez." Henry shuffles his feet. "It's colder than an ice fisherman's toes sloshed with slush on a bad day in Wisconsin."

"I'll say," says Tom.

I put my arms around their shoulders to form a huddle against the wind. The line moves forward a few steps. "Men must be brave during the dark hours of the Christmas season."

"As we stand together in our pursuit of the cheapest tree that meets the basic requirements," Henry smiles with glee, "knowing that we will endure the harshest scrutiny and peer into the very face of judgment, weathering guilt, disappointment, scorn and accusations of betrayal, let's remember the immortal words of President Bill Clinton ...I would not and did not do what you think I did!"

◆◆◆◆

Once we're seated and have hot coffee, we relax and let the cold slip off us like water off walruses. The IHOP packs people in on a regular basis but this is incredible. A huge crowd jams the entranceway and another huddles outside. Amazingly, breakfast arrives in a timely manner. We all chow down eagerly once the plates of food are served and the coffee is refilled. Tom's double order of Swedish pancakes with lingonberry butter looks awesome, Henry's steak and egg plate mouthwatering and my pancake, sausage and egg combo stupendous.

While we're sipping coffee after the feast, except for Tom who at fourteen can eat continuously, Henry asserts the inevitable.

"You know, we cut down thousands upon thousands of trees every year for this madness. Why don't we just go and buy one of those green plastic-coated aluminum jobs. They look nice and they stand up straight. And, they last for years."

I hesitate, "Can't do it. It's a wrong idea."

"There's nothing wrong. What's wrong?"

"Mom and Aunt Janette will kill me – that's what's wrong." Tom peers up from his third stack of pancakes to see if we object.

Henry fills Tom's coffee cup. "Well, besides that there's nothing wrong. It's a good idea. Plastic is the answer. Why don't you face it?" He looks at me.

If we go plastic we're lost. We'll become plastic ourselves, like human Barbie dolls, meaningless simulations of real people adrift in the cultural sea. A real tree preserves some sense of continuity with nature and the past. Sure, it's not environmentally sound to cut down so many trees, but they do get replaced. Plastic just accumulates into piles of unrecyclable junk.

"Why don't you get some plastic hair?"

Henry leans back and drinks his coffee. His face changes. A sober, serious look transforms him from Jolly Henry Flying Ace to Darth Vader Henry. The entire restaurant seems to become quiet.

"Okay. If we're going to get serious, why don't we just completely forego cutting down one of nature's wonders. We can do without any kind of tree. Let's stick to our convictions. Let's bring the battle to the field."

Tom, noticeably uncomfortable with Henry's passion, speaks up.

"Have you forgotten about me being killed by mom and Aunt Janette?"

Henry smiles at him. "Every battle has its casualties, Tom. You're a good fellow and we'll miss you."

"So, let me get this straight." I jump in, nodding

The Christmas Curmudgeon

at Henry, noting his duplicitous intent. "You want me to sacrifice my first born, either that or go plastic?"

"Get some balls, Harry."

"Get some brains, Henry."

"Can't we just get a tree?" Tom asks. "You know you won't go back without one. Mom and Aunt Janette will kill you, too."

"He's got a point."

"A definite point there," concedes Henry.

"We should go."

"Let's do it! Let's destroy nature and become true Americans!"

We put on our coats and turn toward the aisle, committed, brave, fools for Christmas, fools for our wives, just plain fools. Henry drops Tom's ten on the table as we leave. Tom's pathos at the loss strikes our funny bones. We're feeling spirited again by the time we reach the car. The cold wind slams into us like an invisible door.

Back in the car, waiting for the engine to heat up, we're ready to head out to find Raymond Nixon's cut-your-own tree farm. Janette heard about it through one of the secretaries where she works. The secretary is apparently a relative of this Raymond Nixon fellow. He's got an enormous farm, half of which is planted in Christmas trees. "They're the best," said Janette. Mary concurred though she has never been to Nixon's tree farm and has never met Janette's secretary's friend.

This is how things work with women. When one says she's sure of something, they all are certain of the validity. This is how support leads to the actual creation of a "truth." It's an unscientific yet powerful approach.

"I don't know if I can trust a guy named Nixon, Henry." We both recall those Watergate years.

"That's what I said to Janette."

"What'd she say?"

"You can cut your own tree for ten to fifteen dollars. Downtown the price starts at thirty bucks and goes up from there."

"Can't everybody named Nixon be a crook."

"The man's probably a saint."

I back out and turn the car toward the highway. We have to wait for a line of twenty cars to pass before we can go. At last, we're on the way. Main Street turns into Hastings County Road on the other side of the interstate where it then winds through New Hope Valley. Once we're in the valley, the road clears. The houses thin out until we are riding through farmland backed by mountains.

Any one of these farmhouses, if surrounded by snow, with its roof thickly iced and white like a cake, could adorn the cover of a traditional Christmas card. It's pretty damn scenic. Unfortunately, I mention this to Henry as we pass by a particularly quaint stone-sided home with an old gray barn set off to the side. The place seems to have been deliberately enhanced by woods and a still pond reflecting the house and the barn perfectly on its surface.

"Damn, Harry! You've hit upon another winner."

Tom, now one of the guys, sits forward, his head between the backs of the two front seats. Tom smells a scheme and wants to know.

"What's another winner?"

"Should I tell him?"

"I don't know what you're talking about, Henry," I say dryly, shifting the responsibility back to him.

"Anti-Christmas cards! For God's sake, Harry, have you gone dim?"

"Anti-Christmas cards?" asks Tom.

"Your dad just gave me an inspiration."

"Go ahead and tell him, Henry. Fair is fair. He's part of the secret brotherhood now."

Henry doesn't need a green light to get started. His enthusiasm is a marvel. He serves Tom the whole scoop on the anti-Christmas movement spearheaded by the anti-Christmas cards. Tom listens rapt, smiling broadly at his Uncle Henry's antipathetic attitude.

"So here we are driving through the very heart of quaint." Henry's tone has the right sardonic edge it needs to impart the wicked joy he takes in the project. "You just know there has got to be a run-down old shack surrounded by broken pots, hubcaps and litter of all sorts down one of these side roads. We've got to find it and put a scraggly geezer in suspenders and long johns in the doorway; maybe he has got a dead gopher or raccoon in one hand hanging down by its tail. He's got a broken-toothed grin and flies flying around his head. Inside the card it'll say, 'Christmas dinner ain't always got to be turkey do it?' We'll take a few photos just to go by. It'll be card number five."

"Number five? What happened to number four?" I say, at the same time tapping his shoulder and pointing to a roadside sign.

Raymond Nixon's
Cut Your Own Christmas
Just 5 miles ahead

"We're almost there," I say.

"Good," says Tom.

"Number four is a Santa on a crucifix. The hills behind him are covered with the stumps of cut down trees. A golf ball has just bounced off his head. Inside the card it says, 'Fore!' It's a sort of ecology-religion-sports combination," claims Henry, a little defensively, embarrassed by his own depravity. "It's a protest card."

"Geeez, Henry. Nobody's going to buy this stuff. Where do you come up with it, anyway? Are you sick? What's next?!" I'm trying to let Tom know that while I'm involved on an investment basis, I don't necessarily approve of all of Henry's ideas. *It's an American approach to responsibility.* I can tell by the look on his face that his Uncle Henry amazes Tom. He doesn't know what to think.

"Next year we'll have two boxes ...the standard and the deluxe with two extra Christmas scenes. Six more cards. Twice the price for the deluxe collection."

"Can we afford it?"

"If we reinvest all our profits."

"Have we broken even yet?"

"We're doing well enough," says Henry, mysterious with promise.

It seems that we aren't the only ones late to get their Christmas tree. There's a line of cars backed up ten deep on the road. We make number eleven. An old coot with a grimy face driving a beat-up Ford pick up chugs by passing us from the rear on the left. The old guy slows, looks over at us, beeps his horn and waves. One of his eyes is shut, and his mouth is open with a leer bordering on idiocy. He repeats this gesture as he passes each car ahead in the line.

The dirt drive into Nixon's is rutted, the ruts frozen solid. A small cardboard sign with an arrow and the word "trees" is stuck in the ground. We cut across Nixon's front yard, bounce and lurch along another frozen, rutted trail over a hill and end up at the front of a huge field where the Christmas trees fan out in spiraled rows with mathematical precision. About thirty cars are parked to the left in a lumpy field. There's a small shed with another Raymond Nixon sign nailed to the wall.

You cut, you carry - $2.00 a tree foot

I cut and carry - half again as much

"Looks like a bargain," says Henry. "You bring a saw?"

"Sure did," I point back to Tom, "and a sawer, too."

Tom grins and jumps out of the back. Henry and I get out. A blast of wind cuts the air and stabs at any place we've got bare skin.

"Whooh! That's cold. Make your hair curl or

what?" The rough country voice comes from behind us.

We all turn to look at a creased-faced man in a tan Carhart jacket. He's about six feet tall, lean and ruddy. He looks to be in his mid-forties, a man primed with vital energy.

"Raymond Nixon here. How about you?"

"Harry Jenkins," I say and point to Tom. "My son Tom."

Henry nods and says his own name.

Nixon nods at Tom with approval, obviously pleased that Tom has a saw.

"Most of these women want me to cut and haul for 'em." He waves his hand at the people walking through the field looking at trees. Nearly all of them are men. "Bunch of ass wipes," he says, spitting a line of tobacco juice from the left side of his mouth. "C'mon."

We follow him out to the field, and he directs us up a hill to a nice group of trees.

"You'll find what you want up there. Just haul them down to the shed. Johnny can measure and price them for you if I ain't there."

He coughs and spits, then runs his finger inside his lower lip to the side and cleans out a wad of tobacco. He throws it to the ground. It looks like a piece of chewed liver. He scans the field, looking for something. We all look with him, wondering what we'll see. Wild Indians maybe or lost sheep. A man about two hundred yards away starts waving his hand over his head.

"Well, that's the sign," says Nixon. "Got to go. One of them fairies has found what he wants. Better get to it before he starts crying or wets his pants." Nixon starts walking away. He waves his hand behind him as he goes. "Nice meeting you folks."

"Nice to meet you," Henry stands with his hands on his hips, a smile on his face. He has clearly enjoyed Nixon's colorful way of speaking.

"Well," I shake my head after making sure that

Nixon is far enough away. "He's no saint."

"Probably not," growls Henry, clearing his throat and spitting as he speaks. "But he ain't no whining crybaby pants wetter neither."

♦♦♦♦

We start climbing the hill. Tree selection should proceed without undue deliberation. It's damn cold and I know that Henry is ready to cut down a tree and haul it away as fast as he can. In this regard Henry and I are the same. There's a line you cross, and after that, cold is nothing but cold. There's no way around it. Get through and get home.

"Now the thing about Christmas trees, Tom, is that they only need to look good on one side. All that crap about symmetry is just that – crap. When you put it up, nearly half the tree is back against the wall where no one can see it."

Tom looks at me to see whether Uncle Henry is joking or not. His mother has impressed upon Tom that symmetry is a necessity. She has even used a football to demonstrate her point. Imagine throwing a football shaped like a saddle.

"What you want is a straight trunk," I look directly at Tom. "From a guy point of view a straight trunk makes up for all other deficiencies."

"If you can't get the tree to stand up straight when you get it home," adds Henry, "what good is it?"

"That's a fact."

With these thoughts in mind we begin our search. The trees on the uphill slope do look nice. None of them is perfect though. No one in his right mind expects a tree to be perfect. I let Tom select ours. It's nice looking, a little flat on one side, but fully branched and tall enough. He cuts it down with some pride.

Henry has culled an eight foot monster that is pyramidal in shape. It has a gaping hole near the bottom of one of its elongated triangular faces, but the green of the tree has a hint of turquoise that's admirable. Tom cuts the trunk. Then, sliding the trees behind us, we struggle down to the shed to get measured and pay up. We're all chilled to the bone.

When we get there, Johnny comes out, and we're all surprised to see that he is a she. She's a comely woman, around thirty-five or so, with a full head of auburn hair and an energetic, outdoor complexion. She looks at our gawking faces and laughs.

"Ray didn't tell you I was a woman, did he? He likes to do that. People expect me to be some thick-headed boy. Ha Ha!"

She has a robust laugh. None of us knows what to say. The more you look at her the clearer it is that she's truly beautiful. Her collar is open at the neck, and for a second I watch the pulse of her heart beat. Finally, Henry gathers the courage to speak.

"You must be Mrs. Nixon then."

"Oh, nooo, noo. Hah! I'm Ray's daughter."

"Nahhh," says Henry with disbelief. "That guy who took us up the hill?"

"Yes, the same one. He doesn't look a day over forty, does he?"

"No, he doesn't," I say, really amazed. "What's his secret?"

She looks us both up and down, deciding something – whether we're honest men, perhaps, and worthy.

"If I tell you will you keep it to yourself?"

We're all eager. To the last, including Tom, we give our word. She holds her arms out and waves us forward into a small group. She smells like pine trees and fresh fruit. She whispers.

"He doesn't celebrate Christmas." She emits another robust laugh.

"Is that right?" Henry openly displays an attitude conspicuous with conviction, as though he had known it all along.

"That's right," she says. "Every year he cashes in on the trees, closes up the house and from December twenty-third to February first he basks in the sun on a beach in Aruba. It's downright healing to his body and soul. He feels that there's too much pressure up here in the land of hungry souls."

"You see." Henry nearly chokes with admiration. "You see..." He has gone into a fit of recognition. All that he can say, over and over, is "you see, you see." He can't articulate the truth of his awareness. It's too powerful to him, too astonishing.

We pack up the trees without difficulty and pay Johnny. She waves as we bounce out across the frozen ruts. The underside of the Jimmy orchestrates crunching metallic noises that make me wince. Lining the car up to follow a pair of ruts that lead out of there improves our progress slightly. The car rocks sideways and up and down, sliding on ice and catching on gravel patches. Before we attain the top of the hill on the way back toward Nixon's house, the car slides and loses momentum. The tires slip and whirr on an icy patch. I race the motor and spin the wheels, trying to rock it back and forth, but it's no use. Finally, Tom and Henry get out and push, and, slithering sideways, the car veers upwards and over the top of the hill.

We arrive at the highway feeling safe and free, unaware that the afternoon will open to a strangeness that will be transforming in its power.

Chapter Thirteen

Henry insists on taking a side trip. He's convinced that the perfect Christmas tree cabin for the anti-Christmas card photograph is back here in the wilderness. We take a right on Bear Creek Road. No doubt a plenitude of bears roamed this area at one time. Beyond the cleared land along the roadsides the woods are thick with hemlock and pine, poplar, oak and sourwood. We pass a grove of holly trees that fills a depression to the left, the orange berries on the male trees glistening. From the near distance where the steep mountainsides rise abruptly, a whistling wind carries the call of the wild to our car windows, but we don't answer. We only look. This is not our place, but a place of no time where spirits come and go. Magic from an older age rests in the depths waiting for a proper shaman to incorporate the image and the word.

The road, in some disrepair, turns to gravel and the washed out holes and hollows on the surface slow our progress. Here and there, junk of various sorts along with uprooted tree trunks off the shoulder on each side give a ravaged appearance to the wound this road makes in the wilderness.

"This looks good." Henry slaps his hand on the dash. "Keep an eye peeled."

We keep going several miles, climbing steadily. I figure we're no more than ten miles from the Tennessee border. We pass a couple of shacks with wrecked cars sinking into yards like dinosaurs trapped in tar pits. The road rises steadily and angles more steeply as we proceed. I don't notice the engine overheating. Everyone, including me, is looking for Henry's perfect anti-Christmas scene. We climb over the crest of a long uphill curve and he starts yelling.

"There it is, there it is! Look at that place."

The Christmas Curmudgeon

We pull over. Thirty feet back from the road, an unpainted wood plank house, with a porch that is broken and caved in on the far end, occupies a low knoll. A rusty stovepipe extends at an angle from the roof. One of the two windows on the near side of the house is covered with cardboard. The other has three windowpanes intact; the fourth pane is broken and stuffed with rags.

Various containers fan out across the yard, some stand at slight angles, others lie on their sides: oil drums, tin cans, washtubs and the like along with a great number of plastic buckets and jugs. Empty beer cans and soda cans form piles as if they had been raked like fall leaves. There's a rusting Dodge Caravan half sunk in the ground and several engines torn down into parts, the parts sitting atop cinder blocks as though placed on display. An irregular footpath winds its way through the dry, brown stalks of bushes and clumps of weeds and grass that provide a surreal countryside for this junk-strewn shambles and its shack. Henry beams with delight.

Suddenly, the car seems very cold. No heat flows from the vents. I check the gauges and see that the needle inside the temperature gauge has tilted to the red. Before I can think or say anything, the engine compartment begins smoking. I turn the key and the engine dies, making a strange clattering sound. The smoke is thick, acrid and poisonous.

"This doesn't look good at all."

Tom and Henry agree.

While we're huddled under the hood, presenting theories to each other based primarily on other people's car stories we've heard, ones probably constructed from ignorance and superstition, a man appears on the porch of the shack.

"Car broke down?" he shouts.

"Looks like it," I shout back.

He reenters the shack then reappears in a short time wearing a dark blue coat. He stands on the porch and watches. We alternate looking nervously at him and ignorantly into the engine compartment.

"Why don't you go and talk to him, Henry. It looks like we're going to need a tow truck."

"Why don't you go and talk to him." Henry eyes me defiantly.

"It's you that wants to photograph his quaint back-woods shack. We wouldn't be here if it weren't for you."

"It's your car."

"I'm cold." Tom crosses his arms, annoyed at us. "I'll go."

"No, no, Tom. We'll all go."

So we turn and wend our way along the nearest part of the path toward the house. Tom takes the lead, but then as he comes within range of the man he slows down. I almost bump into him because I've been looking at the stuff in the yard. Henry chuckles.

"C'mon in." The man on the porch motions toward the steps with his hand.

At first glance he looks normal enough. The open front of his coat reveals a gray cotton shirt that clings to his chest, which looks hard and flat. He's wearing blue suspenders that hold up a pair of baggy oil-stained blue pants. A few days' growth shadows his sunken cheeks. His hair is thick and sticks out sideways from the top of his head over his ears, which protrude some, too. A wide smile, lacking some teeth, contributes to his likeability. Along with a deeply-relaxed bearing, the crinkly tanned skin around his eyes and neck give the impression that he's in his late fifties, a working man who has probably quit working.

When we reach the porch, he appraises our appearance, giving Henry's fashion ensemble extra attention. Then he leans down extending his hand. "I'm Morgan Critzer. Who are you?"

We introduce ourselves.

"Sorry to bother you on a cold day like this, Mr. Critzer," I say, "but it looks like we need a tow truck."

"That'd be Cyrus Budd down the road a piece."

"Does he have a truck?"

"That's what I said."

"Oh, uh..."

"Come on in." He turns and walks into his house, leaving the door open.

Henry steps up on the porch first then Tom. Something in me doesn't want to go into the house, but, clearly, there's not much else to do. I follow Tom in and we are all stunned silent.

The place is dimly-lit, and wisps of smoke leak from a wood stove over by the far wall, making the room hazy. Something steaming on top of the wood stove smells rank. The front wall is covered with shirts, pants and jackets hung on nails. Part of the odor in the place must come from these clothes. An array of boots and shoes is piled against the wall on the floor.

We stand on bare sub-flooring. The sheets of plywood are stained from spills, and rusty circles surround the nails in the wood. Some wood shavings, dust and litter swept into a pile near the kitchen door move slightly, probably the burrowing of a bug. Around the wood stove many cigarettes have been squashed out on the floor. But, the rest of the place appears to have been recently cleaned. There's no dust on the shelves or the furniture; and everything is orderly, even thoughtfully arranged.

Henry turns his head from side to side and up and down, taking it all in. Tom stares open-mouthed at a doorway to our left. In the doorway, a man in a wheelchair slowly, calmly edges forward. His skin is pale and his eyes gleam with a strange intensity. His entire being seems focused on a destination not of an earthly nature. His mouth is stretched to each side and his teeth are showing.

"That there is Virgil," says Morgan. "He's the oldest of us three brothers. Got his legs blowed off in Vietnam. Say hello to these folks, Virgil ...stopped by with a broke down vehicle."

"Hello." Virgil, stretches out the vowels as he speaks.

"Go ahead," Morgan Critzer invites us with a hand extended toward his brother, "shake his hand. He loves it. He's proud to meet you."

"Proud to meet you." Virgil speaks with enthusiasm as each of us shakes his hand. "Can't say how much I appreciate your visit." His green work pants are cut off and pinned back just above the knees. He's wearing a soiled red and white plaid flannel shirt, which is unbuttoned over his belly. His wrists are thick, and the grip of his handshake strong.

Henry looks at me with shifting eyes and a determined face that says he's ready to leave right away. I ignore Henry's discomfort.

"It's nice to meet you folks. And, I don't want to seem unfriendly, but I'm worried about, uh, what to do about our car. I wonder if we might use your phone?"

Morgan tilts his head and looks at me like I might be sprouting broccoli from my ears.

"Phone?" He breaks into a series of short snorts of nasal laughter. "Did you hear that, Virge? He wants to use our phone."

Virgil slaps the arm of his wheelchair a couple of times, laughing with Morgan. Henry, Tom and I look at each other.

"Have no worry," says Morgan. "Everything is going to be fine. We don't have a phone. Don't need one. Come and sit with us. Have a cup of coffee. Cyrus will be by before you know it."

What does he mean - everything is going to be fine? How does he know Cyrus is on his way?

"Don't worry." He repeats the words with great calm and self-assurance.

Improbable as it may seem, I'm captured by the man's confidence and reassured by the warmth and sincerity of his tone. In my hurry to solve the car problem and with Henry's nervous looks, I'm also concerned that we may have been rude.

"Well, I guess we could visit for a bit."

Looking around for a chair, I see an old woman

sitting in a rocking chair over in a dark corner. I guess it's because of looking for a chair that I notice her at all. She's so quiet. She's wearing a dark brown dress that matches the color of the walls and, sitting in the shadows as she is, so totally immobile, none of us has noticed her. Henry and Tom are looking at her, too.

"That's ma over there. Don't think nothing of her being so quiet over there. She ain't dead. She just don't move much. Tired, I guess. She gets up to cook and then she sits. That's it for ma. Tired is all. Nearly ninety-one years old."

Henry moves to my side and leans close to my ear. "Harry? What the hell are you doing? Look at these people. Look around. We need to leave here, Harry."

Morgan looks at me expectantly. Virgil has stopped laughing. I feel strangely at ease, despite Henry's ill feeling. I understand that we're not really in this place, that the whole scene, these two brothers, Virgil and Morgan, the entire shack of Henry's imagination, the disorder and the poverty and the isolation of the place have all been brought together in something like a time warp. It's real, yes, and it's also a dream. The Critzers carry an aspect of otherworldliness, a peacefulness that transcends the ordinary. It's only a moment in our lives, but it's a special moment, one that we should follow and attend to as one might listen closely for the first time to the lyrics of a song or to the words of a psalm. Morgan smiles. He sees that I understand.

I put my hand on Henry's shoulder and nudge him forward to the chairs in the kitchen. "Come on, Henry. Let's sit down with these nice folks and have a cup of coffee."

Henry looks at me like I've gone wacko.

◆◆◆◆

We sit down at the kitchen table and Morgan pours coffee in five metal mugs coated with speckled blue enamel. Virgil pulls up to the table and reaches for his coffee. His hands are heavily veined, thick-fingered and look strong. He notices my observing them.

"I'm a carver," he says to me. "A wood carver."

"Ohhh."

"What do you carve?" asks Henry.

"Wood," says Virgil, looking back and forth among me, Tom and Morgan. He has a restrained look of wild joy on his face.

"Ha haaahh!" Morgan slaps the table and laughs. We all laugh along, even Henry. "Virgil, you joker. Show the man."

Virgil shakes his head no.

"Aww c'mon, Virge."

Virgil picks up his coffee and drinks, smiling at us, but neither says nor does anything.

"I'd like to..." I begin to express my interest in Virgil's carvings, but Morgan holds his hand up.

"Ol' Virge really likes you all. I can tell. He'll show you his carvings in good time, I'm sure, but first he wants me to tell you the story."

Henry rolls his eyes. Tom hunkers down over his coffee, blowing across the mug to cool it down. He seems more alert and attentive to the people here than I've seen him be toward anything for a long time. He's like a child at a circus, totally involved, watching everything he can. I wave a hand and nod at Morgan, indicating my desire to hear his story.

"There was three of us boys, born one after another ever two years. Virgil there is the oldest, then there was Wyatt and then me. Our life was good as boys. We grew up right on this land, fishing and hunting when we was old enough.

"Our daddy was a great fan of the Wyatt Earp story and, in fact, had met the man once. He wanted us boys to feel like the Earp brothers ...good strong old boys who would stick up for each other. That's why we got the names we got." He looks over at Virgil just at this point and smiles softly at him. Virgil has a tear in his eye, which he wipes away. The kitchen is

The Christmas Curmudgeon

silent and deeply peaceful.

"Anyway, things went rough for daddy. His heart went bad and he couldn't work none. Well, Virgil, being the oldest, took on most of the work. He done good too. Me and Wyatt helped out, but not like ol' Virge here. He was a working fool. A real dog. Ha Haaa!"

Virgil grins at this.

"So, one day, Virge was just nineteen, me fifteen and Wyatt seventeen years old – that old Vietnam was hot about that time, gooks and Congs and commies and what all crawling around causing a commotion – we none of us could figure who was what and what side we were supposed to be on. That didn't matter much. We was just boys and didn't expect ourselves to understand the work of the government. God bless America we thought, God bless her, the best country in the world. Whatever it was going on over there, we figured it was our job to fix it.

"But that's getting ahead, ain't it Virge?" Virgil nods his head, but doesn't speak to Morgan's question. He doesn't want to slow the story down. All of us are mesmerized, wondering what he will say next. The way that Morgan speaks, with a kind of reverence for the story and love for his brothers, makes me feel that I'm in a small theater listening to one of the great American storytellers, Mark Twain maybe, or Ring Lardner.

"So, Virgil was out pulling stumps, clearing some land right over yonder." Morgan points through the back window of the kitchen. "Wyatt had got the idea that he could grow flowers out there and sell them down to the city folk and make some money. He had got the idea from one of our visits with daddy to the hospital where they checked on his heart. There was a lady there with a cart selling flowers. It was a good idea, too. We all thought so. Wyatt was always the smart one, coming up with an idea. He was just naturally smart. God, we loved that boy. His heart was bigger and gooder than the rest of us put together.

And his brain was just bigger, too, following after his heart."

"Now, one of them stumps out back was just not cooperating. Ever time Virgil put the chain hook to it and pulled with the tractor, something would go wrong. The stump was not going ...and it was a big one, too, a big old beech tree stump. Been there about a hundred years the tree was, I guess, until Virgil cut it down. Anyway, ol' Virge, being small of brain, taking after his pecker I guess, was in a confusion. He couldn't figure nothing."

Virgil shakes his head indicating that he has heard this joke about his pecker and his brain a few too many times. Morgan looks up at us, looks at Virgil, runs both hands through his hair and takes a deep swallow of coffee, then resumes the story.

"He calls out Wyatt to do some thinking. Wyatt is going to watch what happens when Virge hooks up the chain and gives the stump to the tractor. So it goes. Virgil wraps the chain, buries the hook and gets on the tractor and pulls. Rrrrunn, vrrunn, rrun, vrun. The tractor is whining and the wheels digging and churning in the dirt. Next thing ...Whang!! The chain flips loose and slams into Wyatt's head killing him dead on the spot. Oh God, God almighty. How could it happen? No one had planned or even thought of such a thing. Wyatt was such a fine boy. He looked like a broken angel lying there on the ground. It was the most terrible thing we could ever know. Daddy couldn't bear it at all. He died a month later of heart attack."

"My God." I sit back in my seat. My eyes have teared up and I don't know what to say.

Virgil is crying and Henry is shaking his head in wonder, partly in amazement at the strangeness of the Critzers, but also, I'm sure, over life's cruelty. Even Tom, who at fourteen isn't going to cry for anything, struggles to keep himself under control.

"That's a sad tale," says Henry.

"Oh, that ain't the end of it ...as you can plainly

see. It's because Virgil felt to blame, like he was a dumb fool who had killed his own brother instead of just a regular fellow whose brother had died in terrible misfortune, that he run off and joined the army and thereafter through no fault of his own got his legs blowed to pieces in that God-awful war ...trying to help one of his fellow soldiers, he was, risking his own life to help another man."

"Oh, oh!" Morgan shouts so we should all restrain ourselves from any comment. "Don't say nothing, don't say a word, for it's all come out all right. If it don't beat all. I do not understand the hand of God and I won't claim to, but look for yourself fellows, look at him." He points to his brother Virgil.

Virgil has finished his coffee and is resting in his wheelchair. His face is soft and kindly, a look of pure beatitude, his eyes sparkling and gleaming like two charms set in glass. A feeling of wonder passes through us all. I'm as sure of that as anything in my life. I'm sure we all felt the same way at the same time ...and that was a feeling of pure peace and wonder at the beauty and mystery of life.

"Virgil saw the face of God in Vietnam," Morgan continues. "As he lay there bleeding and broken at the door of death amidst the jungle weeds and the heat and the insects, he looked into the sky above and there above him, gigantic and in Technicolor, was the face of our brother Wyatt floating in the sky. 'Have no fear' was what Wyatt said. 'Have no fear, Virgil. You are forgiven. Everything is going to be all right.' And the knowledge of God was in it. Pure peacefulness, safety and protection. Complete comfort and a sacred trust; a belief in the goodness of life. Virgil came home a changed man, as you see him now. A man of peace. A simple good fellow without guilt or shame, a man who never did and never would hurt a living soul. Now ain't that something?"

Virgil's face radiates a strange combination of sorrow and joy. "I'm glad you come to visit," he says. "I can't tell you how glad I am."

I have never felt more moved or more well received in my life.

Perhaps another fifteen or twenty minutes pass before Cyrus arrives with the tow truck. We never called him, yet there he was. No messenger had left the house, no signal had been sent. Yet, there he was.

During this brief period before Cyrus's arrival, Virgil shows us his carvings. He wheels out to the living room and pulls a wood crate from under a shelf, then takes about thirty carved figures from the crate. Each of them is a richly-detailed sculpture of a person doing some ordinary activity – reading a book, smoking a pipe, a young fellow fishing, a man carrying a briefcase, a woman brushing her hair and so on. The pieces are superb, absolutely beautiful, full of wonder. No doubt each figure has occupied many hours of his time. Before we leave with Cyrus to haul the car to the city and ourselves to our city lives, Virgil gives each of us one of these small wooden figurines.

As he hands me my carving, Virgil holds it up in the air so I will look at it. He speaks softly, almost whispering, his voice scratchy, yet soothing. "The world gets turned upside down sometimes, that's all. You'll be back on your feet before you know it and so will I." He laughs then, at the impossibility of his statement, looking back and forth between Morgan and me. "Back on my feet. Ha, Haahhh! Ha ha Haah!!"

Henry and Tom study their carvings, slightly puzzled looks on their faces. I'm not to know it at the time, but this is the beginning of troubles between Henry and me. *How would I know?* But I do remember wondering for a moment if something had gone wrong. Then Cyrus arrives, walks in through the front door, slaps hands with Morgan and tosses a pack of Marlboros to Virgil who catches them with a clap of his hands. Cyrus steps back out the front door and returns with two boxes loaded with groceries, one stacked atop the other.

"This oughter do you, Maw." He grins at the old lady. Then, he stands there looking at us, sizing us up. He pulls his head back at the sight of Henry's outfit.

"You got a burnt out vehicle?"

"That's right." I nod.

"Well, all right. Let's go. Anybody Morgan sees fit to guest has got to be qualified."

Cyrus is a whole lot more like the kind of person we all expected to see at the Critzer's house than the Critzers are themselves. He smells like tobacco plug and animal skins. His teeth are brackish and brown along the gum lines. There's a tattoo of a flaming snake on the left side of his neck. He lifts a window and spits a stream of brown fluid outside. We all stare, but it makes no difference to him.

After shaking hands all around and sincere thanks expressed by us to the Critzers, we trail Cyrus out to the car. We then stand by uselessly while he arranges a couple of heavy rubber-strapped contraptions under the front wheels of the Jimmy. He pulls a lever by the side of the truck near the back and the half-inch cable he has attached under the front somewhere starts slowly moving, lifting the Jimmy's front end as the crank motor grinds and whines.

After he's finished, he waves us around to the side of his tow truck and tells us all, "C'mon, boys, let's go. Get in. It ain't getting any warmer."

Morgan Critzer waves at us from his porch. We each wave back as we climb into Cyrus's truck. I hope Virgil will appear in the doorway, but he doesn't. Staring out the front window of the truck, I have the sense that I'll never see him again. Closing my eyes for a moment, I picture him in my mind. Henry would scoff if he knew what I was doing, but I want to store the memory, and I'm not going to tell him what I'm doing, anyway. Something has moved deep within and I can feel myself changing. I believe I have picked up some of Virgil's peace.

"That's the place. It's perfect. We've got to go back and take some pictures. Old Morgan will pose for us don't you think? He's got to."

By the tone of his voice, which is softer and friendlier, even Henry's recalcitrant attitude seems to have changed. Oddly enough, I feel hope for him. But, neither Tom nor I answer.

On the way home, crammed into the secondary seats in Cyrus Budd's truck along with Tom, Henry up front with Cyrus, who's driving, I hold the small carved figure in my hand to look at it carefully. Henry and Tom are looking at their own carvings. Every once in a while, Henry will say something like, "Isn't it interesting how country folks keep an eye out and come to each other's aid?" Or, "That certainly was an unusual bunch." Now, there's a tone of sarcasm to his words, but, except for the mysterious appearance of Cyrus Budd at the Critzers, I'm not sure what it's about. It feels like he's baiting me.

"Look at this," he says, holding up his carving for all of us to see. "It's two men ...one chasing the other. Now why do you suppose he would carve something like that?"

"More to the point," I say, "why do you suppose he gave that particular carving to you?"

"I knew it!" says Henry, striking the dashboard. "I knew it. You're going to make this one of those meaningful cosmic things, aren't you, Harry?"

"Don't you think there might be some meaning in the choice of this carving for you? Didn't you see the way the man looked, Henry?"

"Oh, ga, grrr, gggit." Henry splutters with annoyance and frustration, slapping his head as he turns it from side to side. "Gaaa, gnnn. Grrr. No, no, no ...no!" he says. "Don't do it, Harry. No! You'll make me sick or crazy with that crap."

I ignore Henry and decide to avoid further conversation about the topic. I roll my eyes at Tom to suggest that Uncle Henry is already crazy and Tom grins. I feel better. At least Tom has some sense. But I can't help studying my own carving again.

The figurine is no more than four inches tall, the figure of a man in trousers and a tight shirt. He's in a kneeling position with one leg extended back behind him. His arms bend out in front with the palms of his hands facing upward and backward. The hands are about level with the top of his head. You could imagine him balancing a large tray on top of his hands and head. The face has a look of great concentration.

It's a most curious work. I'm quite moved by it and feel in some strange way as though the figure is myself. Virgil, I'm sure, when he chose it for me intended it to deliver a message. I'm puzzled but not upset or disturbed. I can look at the figure and laugh or look at it and feel sad about the absurdity of my life. It's all right to feel either way. There exists a renewed and deeper acceptance in myself for myself because of Virgil. The rest of the ride back to town is quiet and peaceful. Cyrus says nothing. Henry stares out the front window, a stern look of inward concentration on his face. I wonder if Tom experiences the same peaceful sense of wonder as I but don't ask him. He seems perfectly satisfied with his own gift, which is the least mysterious of the three. It's a figure of a boy seated, legs crossed, on top of the world. He is gazing contentedly out at the universe. I don't say a word about it. I don't want to change the way things are.

Chapter Fourteen

Cyrus tows us to a gas station he knows in town and heads back out, charging us thirty dollars for the tow, which is more than reasonable. The car sits in the garage at a place called Joe's Exxon. Jerry at Joe's Exxon is suggesting a pressure test to see if we've blown a head gasket. Nothing against Jerry, but he looks twenty years old and seems as though he has undergone a number of pressure tests on his own head.

"Look, Jerry," I'm looking around for someone with some managerial experience. "Is Joe around?"

"Joe?" Jerry looks puzzled.

"Yes, Joe. The Joe of Joe's Exxon."

"Ohh!" He laughs in a way that suggests he believes I must gladly share in his enjoyment of my ignorance. Not in the mood, I leer back at him. "You must mean Gene. There is no Joe."

"Is Gene the owner, then?"

"Gene's the manager."

"Where's Gene?"

"He's not here."

"Well," I try to retain a spirit of good will and patience, "is there a way you could reach him, or that I could reach him?"

"Sure. He'll be back in about ten minutes. Gone to get a wheel bearing for that old Ford over there." He points to the stall in the garage past the one where my car sits.

Okay. About an hour later, Gene shows up. Gene appears to be about forty. By the look of his jacket, he could be the head mechanic for Dale Earnhardt Jr. He's a walking advertisement for numerous car parts companies.

"Never heard of Filco." I'm looking at a particularly colorful patch.

"Filco?" He furrows his forehead. I point to the patch sewn on his jacket. He nods knowledgeably. "They do spark plug wires."

"Oh." I'd appreciate this more if it weren't about fifteen degrees inside the garage.

Gene wants to know if Jerry did a pressure test. I tell him I want his own professional opinion on what should be done. After we get the pressure test done, he tells me I've got a blown head gasket and for his money, with that many miles on the car it doesn't make sense to replace the head gasket. I'd be better off installing a remanufactured engine. They can do the work right there ...they do it all the time. Only cost about twenty four hundred, total. *Twenty four hundred!?* I'm not suspicious. *Why should I be suspicious?* After all, I'm talking to Gene of Joe's Exxon. Joe doesn't exist. It makes sense. What do I know, anyway?

Meanwhile, it has turned extremely cold outside. A hard wind blows in from the North carrying the breath of polar bears and walruses. Henry and Tom sit in numb silence inside the small office at Joe's Exxon. I tell Gene that I'll have to get back to him about the job.

"No hurry." He snorts and swallows. "That car ain't going anywhere."

"Right." I smile and ask to use the phone.

Mary and Janette come in separate cars. We transfer the Christmas trees to their separate trunks. There are looks of dismay and disappointment. Tom hides his traitorous self. His mother sees through his behavior and accuses me with stoniness in her posture and squintiness in her eyes. I transport myself to a higher plane of awareness.

By the time we get home, I'm ready for dinner. Of course, this could be seen as a euphemistic thought. In fact, there is no actual dinner, no meatloaf and green beans, no steaming plate of spaghetti. Mary has been too busy decorating the house in preparation for the tree reception and installation of the tree. There is no aroma of roasted beef lingering in the halls, no sweet scent of fried chicken. Instead, the house is redolent of quarter pounders with cheese and large orders of fries – virtual food, food I despise, but eat with bestial hunger. Few words are spoken. Minutes drag by like a series of captured traitors being towed across the tundra by prisoners in chains.

My theory is that to return to Mary's good graces I must install the tree without delay. It's a working hypothesis. Things aren't going too badly. I've got the tree inside and have put the cunningly designed metal stand together. Without the downward thrust of a tree to force the parts together thereby achieving cohesive stability, the parts rattle and slide threatening discombobulation at any moment. The tricky part then is getting the tree into the stand, standing. It turns out the trunk has a nasty bend right at the base. It's going to be a monster.

I find Tom, pull his earphones off and, putting my arm around his shoulder as we return to the living room, explain to him the horror of the situation. It's going to take careful blocking of the trunk inside the tree stand ring and probably a wire pull tacked to the wall to keep the tree right. It's definitely a two-man job. Is he up to it; as one of the loyal and true brothers of the secret brotherhood? He is.

Tom holds the tree steady. The damn butt of the trunk won't sit square on the circle of dagger-shaped prongs that are supposed to root the tree into place. I shove a triad of two-inch wide pieces of wood between the ring of the stand and the trunk and then screw the L-shaped bolts inward. That done, I step back to take a look. The tree wobbles if Tom loosens his grip.

"Okay, Tom, keep holding. We're going to wire it to the wall."

"Word."

I have the wire and a pair of eyebolt screws on hand. We try a few angles, find the sturdiest position, then attach the guy wire to both tree and wall. Good. The tree is up and standing as stable and true as possible, not perfect, but from the front the view is terrific. The guy wire holds steady three quarters of the way up to the top of the tree, screwed at the other end into a wall stud. The job has taken about an hour, but it's a manly job.

Mary comes in to inspect. She's immediately displeased.

"This won't do, Harry. What we're you thinking?"

"It's pretty straight, Mary, and good and solid ...it won't tip over."

"It's not straight at all, Harry." Mary, stands back, circling, eyeing up and down. "This is not how I want it."

"The tree has got a crooked end, Mary. It can't be helped."

"Can't you saw the end off?"

Tom and I look at each other. I can almost read his mind. *Don't do it, Dad.* Fool that I am, I consider my argument. *Fool ...fool.* Just be silent and say, yes, of course, Mary, why didn't I think of that.

"You know what I'd have to do." My tone belies the day's frustrations. "It's a problem ...I'd have to untack the guy wire from the damn wall and drag the tree back out to the garage to work on it. The damn stand is hardly worth keeping, it's about ready to fall apart, anyway ...the damn bastard is standing up as straight as it's going to, Mary ...probably, I'd bring it back and it would be crookeder than it is right now." I'm a little red in the face. It has been a long day.

Mary's eyes are welling with tears. She looks at the tree. She looks around the room that she has spent the day cleaning and decorating. Suddenly, she bursts into tears, speaking through them like a sailor facing an ocean squall, gasping for breath and wiping away the wetness in order to see. Anger and hurt rise and fall as she rides the waves of her emotions.

"I work my fingers raw scrubbing and cleaning

and have got ...have got the house ...decorated ...just for Christmas ...for the whole family. Why do I do it? I would like to know! I just want everything to be beautiful ...I try to make the house beautiful for us ...what's the reason, Harry? Do you even care? Why have Christmas at all? Why don't we just go out for hamburgers on Christmas? Oh! Oh, forget it ...just forget it ...I don't care!"

She retreats off to the kitchen.

There's a part of me that would like to second the hamburger idea. Go out for hamburgers? A great idea. Let's take off the whole week and go to a distant shore where they don't celebrate Christmas. Some place where they haven't even heard of Christmas, where Santa Claus is dead and the elves are fat and retired, where nothing artificial twinkles or blinks on and off, where they serve good food and leave you alone.

I stand by the tree, look at Tom, look at the tree, shake my head and stop myself from further thought. I look at Tom again. He's standing still, in teen zombie land, hypnotized by the radio in his mind that plays who knows what. Whatever it is, it's as effective as a drug. I suspect that he's not really even there. It's just his body, running on automatic. Tom knows that I could never have succeeded in this argument. I can see the awareness of impossibility there in the patient blankness on his face. I know there's no reason but selfishness and laziness for my unwillingness. I know it and I feel it.

Though the words have never actually been spoken, Tom knows that women are in charge of Christmas. Women, mothers, wives make all the important Christmas decisions. They conjure the Christmas spirit with unalterable will, ritual-power and hidden design. It's an event with a yearly predetermination, as ancient and foreseen as the journey of the Magi. Our job is to be silent and do.

Then, for another few moments there is silence, the silence of defeat. It's the silence of acceptance. It's the silence of the acceptance of defeat. It's the silence of knowing what must be done and the gathering of the resolve to do it. It's the silence of forgiveness. It's the silence from which the Christmas spirit emerges, rising like an insane elf that has been kept forever in a dark dungeon, scheming and stewing, waiting for that moment of freedom to enter the world and destroy the last vestiges of reason and self control that exist in the worldly world of men.

Tom and I laugh maniacally as we take down the tree, drag it to the garage and then realize – how terrible and real is the knowledge as it shoots to the center of the soul – that the saw, our one and only outdoor saw, is safely stowed in the rear of the broken down '95 GMC Jimmy now sitting in the frozen lot of non-existent Joe's Exxon at the far end of town.

In a frenzy of concentrated intent, we cast about, find the old rusty camping hatchet and hack away the lower ring of limbs and then the gnarled and twisted bent bastard butt end of the tree trunk. Tom holds and I hack. But holding the branches back in the midst of the fierce blasts of my blade proves difficult for Tom; understandably, in hindsight you might say a man-sized wrestler would run for his life. One of the lower branches springs free just as I lunge in for another whack with the hatchet. A spray of green needles swipes my face, cutting across my open right eye like a switch of razors.

"Gaaahhh!!" My scream sends Tom back a foot.

"Sorry, dad. It just happened."

Raising my head slowly, hand over my eye, I turn to Tom.

"Maybe you better just leave."

"I can hold the tree, dad, but slow down a little."

"No, Tom. That's not what I mean. Go on back into the house. Your job is finished."

The clarity and the calm determination of my voice can't be refused. Tom throws out his hands and leaves without looking back. I hunt around to find the emergency garage rum pint behind a pile of lumber stacked against the far wall. It has about two inches of the cure left. *Time to restock.* After finishing the rum and letting it settle into my brain, I turn back to the tree.

"Now, you bastard, we'll have at it. You're going to be missing a few limbs when I'm done."

And then, I can't stop myself. I hack farther and farther up the trunk, wielding the rusty hand axe like a man possessed by demons, frothing at the mouth, spittle flying as I shout.

"Damn this tree as no tree has ever been damned before! I'll cut you to the core. I'll butcher you, you beast, and make you what I want! A perfect tree! Hah, Hah! PERFECT!!" A perfect tree, eh Tom?" I look for Tom but he's not there. "A little bereft maybe, but Perfect! Straight, symmetrical, and by God, missing a few limbs!"

A few more whacks and I'm finished. The trunk of the tree shows a series of yellow scars where the lower limbs were once attached. I stand it up on the garage floor. About three and a half feet of the trunk have been exposed, the upper portion where the 'tree' remains, a perfect cone of greenery, about three feet additional altitude, with a matching circumference at the bottom row of limbs, creates the overall appearance of an oversized conical spearhead at the end of a gnarly, yet straight, shaft.

I drag it back to the house, stumbling through the garage door, falling, hitting my forearm hard against the edge of the step, banging my head then settling in a heap on the floor, the tree in my face. Gritting my teeth and using all my strength, I lurch to my feet and in one smooth run speed through the doorway into the kitchen, heading full bore toward the door to the living room. Flashes of light burst in my eyes. I crash into the door jam with my left shoulder sending a hot jolt of pain into my forearm. *Did I just have a stroke? Has something exploded? No. It's Willy in the kitchen taking pictures. He has learned how to*

The Christmas Curmudgeon

use the flash.

At last, the tree is restored to its rightful place as king of the living room space, awaiting its coronation Sunday, tomorrow afternoon. Mary can't believe what has been done. She stands before the tree dumbstruck. For now, she's silent. Tom and Willy appear, intruders in the dust. Willy holds his plaster and plastic covered arms in front of him like pincers, his camera dangling at his waist. Tom pulls out his earplugs. The four of us stand there stricken by the incomprehensible. No one can speak. The silence and stillness continue unabated, minute after minute, what seems like an hour, a day, a lifetime, while everyone stares at the tree comparing it in their minds to trees of yore, to an ideal set forth in ancient times perhaps by Plato.

"Think of it as conceptual art."

Mary turns her head slowly toward me, saying nothing.

Willy begins laughing and keeps on laughing. Tom catches it and starts in laughing, too. Mary and I smile at our children's willingness to accept life as it is. They haven't developed the adult propensity for judgment. Looking inward, I see that the tree doesn't matter, but who I am and how I live does matter. I've been too dark, too resentful and should change my way.

My black intent, my heartless tension, an answer to the truth, slaughters the devilled saint, who, with his bag and charcoal streaks, ravages the lives of men. My enemy is known, is near and ready to appear. I am ready, too, at last prepared and strong enough to make freedom home. At last, I can be happy. Money doesn't make the man.

My fierce intensity prevents remarks from Mary. She sees that I'm still slightly crazed. There will be time later she thinks. I know this is what she thinks so I can say it here with no doubt. She's thinking, with her grim set jaw, that she will speak with me later. My left shoulder feels bruised, but my right forearm throbs. Whenever I lift it, shooting pains travel up to my shoulder. Swelling has started at the site of impact. Not a good sign, but I'm not in the mood to deal with it. *Ignore it. Maybe it will settle down.*

All is calm and quiet. I turn the lights down low. Tom retreats to his earphones and the meaningful lyrics of R.E.M. I can hear the lyrics of the song, he's got it turned up so loud. "That's me in the corner ...that's me in the spotlight ...losing my religion."

I sit on the couch, exhausted, and, amazingly, in a clear offer of concession, Mary, at first tentative, doubtful of my reception, then increasingly at ease as she finds that I don't repel her, snuggles next to me. Fatigue overwhelms me, but before I fall into a deep restful sleep, for a few wonderful moments I'm conscious only of the sweetest feeling of peace and pleasure. Not a creature is stirring. The cold winds blow outside and rattle the windows. But, for now, we are warm and I don't care. Let tomorrow bring what it will, let tomorrow be tomorrow. No doubt, Mary will recover from this act of forgiveness and I will have to suffer. The season being what it is, it will probably be a cold and prolonged period of endurance.

♦♦♦♦

Sunday afternoon I get a call from a guy who assumes I recognize his voice.

"We got to talk," says the voice, distinctly familiar with its rough New England accent. "You don't want to do the job at that Exxon station. I've heard about that place." I'm listening. The voice is coming to me. "I know a guy who says he can do the job for around fifteen hundred."

Ah hah! I've got it. Mary's sister, Ellen, has a boyfriend, Lee, from upstate Massachusetts. We have met him two or three times before. A good fellow. For a second, I'm doubtful, but then I'm sure, sure as the sting in the tail of a wasp that my mind has it right and has fired the right connections. Lee works with a guy who knows a mechanic named Ray who has a

The Christmas Curmudgeon

shop down by the river who does all of Lee's work. He apprises me of some useful facts about engine replacement.

"Lee, fifteen hundred sounds a lot better to me. Are you sure that's for the same job? A completely remanufactured engine?"

Lee convinces me I'm having a torque wrench ream job on my backside by the people at Joe's Exxon. "Hell," announces Lee. "Nobody even knows who owns that place. How can you deal with that?"

"Who can you trust?"

"That's right," says Lee.

After resuming our acquaintance for a few minutes – Lee and Ellen are still dating; he has a new job at the Sears loading dock – we hang up with assurances that we will get together over the holidays.

Cyrus Budd's tow truck isn't in the phone book. I'm just as glad because, to tell the truth, I'm not too interested in another ride with Cyrus. The smell of him was enough to ruin your appetite. I remember seeing a weird looking triangular shaped thing on the passenger side floor of his truck and then realizing it was a piece of very old, dried-out pizza. Cyrus was a good old boy and he did a good job. That's about all I would like to remember of him.

It turns out that Ray at Rick's Automotive will arrange to have the car towed to their shop on Monday. He explains, with enough clarity that even I understand, what will happen with the engine replacement deal, and I'm impressed. I go ahead and sign the contract, so to speak, over the phone.

"Before I hang up here, Ray, I wonder if you could tell me something?"

"Shoot."

"This is your own shop isn't it, your own business, right?"

"That's right," he says.

"So how come you don't call it Ray's automotive instead of Rick's?"

"That's an easy one. When my son grows up,

The Christmas Curmudgeon

he'll see that the business will belong to him one day."

"I see. So your son's name is Rick?"

"Well, no ...I don't have a son yet, but when I do, I'll name him Rick, after the business."

"Uh huh." It's worth a laugh – some time later. Henry will enjoy this addition to the story, a thought which makes me realize I haven't heard from Henry for a while. Of course it's Christmas and the pressure builds relentlessly these last days before the implosion. Henry may be having his own breakdown, maybe a rampage involving the loss of the heads of the heads of corporations. Ray responds to the lengthy pause on the phone with a smoker's cough and a "howdy, are you there?" His voice startles me. "Yes sir. It makes perfect sense. I appreciate your talking to me on a Sunday, Ray."

"No problem. Give me a call around Thursday or Friday. I'll be able to tell you more then."

Good. Just what I need. More. Just fix the car is what I'm thinking. I don't want to know more. It's like hearing about your wife's mother's fibroid tumor operation. Maybe she could bring that baby over in a jar so we could really talk it up. This, to me, is an engine transplant, too specialized to be accessible, too fundamental to be denigrated by common talk. I don't want to see or know about the innards or the procedure. I'm afraid of what I might experience if I were present during the operation.

Meanwhile, it's nearly tree decoration time. Traditionally, it's my job to make homemade eggnog. I do it with pleasure. Since the tree installation, Mary and I have been civil if not altogether pleasant, but she hasn't insisted on a replacement though her murderous looks suggest I may need to be replaced. This reminds me of Mr. Gregg and, as a result, I rummage in the kitchen gathering the ingredients for egg nog scowling with resentment and suspicion. There's a pint of rum in the pantry I'd forgotten. The atmosphere of our home is now one of tense preoccupied anger and gloom; the kids hide in their rooms. I

The Christmas Curmudgeon

feel I'm to blame for ruining the pre-Christmas tone, but I'm not going to say that. No way. Blame is for eight year old kids. *No one is to blame. If anything, it's Christmas that's to blame, the symbol, the corporate monster that stands in for the corporate culture, the culture of mass-marketing, massive consumption, and the mastery and control of the masses.* I take another draw on the rum. *What did you think, I just looked at it?* There, now, I'm feeling a little better. My arm seems better, too. *Maybe a little more rum will help.*

Mary calls the children out of hiding, and a quiet ceasefire begins as I present glasses of eggnog on a tray and open a box of holiday cookies. The rum stands boldly on the tray on the coffee table. My look is nonchalant. Mary acts as if it's fine with her. She unloads old cardboard boxes marked "Christmas" from the top shelf of the hall closet.

The kids wrestle the boxes into separate stacks and we gather around and start unpacking the decorations. A spirit of good will gradually develops among us. I put on my homemade tape of Christmas music favorites. "Grandma Got Run Over by a Reindeer." "The Twelve Pains of Christmas." A few selections from Alvin and the Chipmunks. Everyone is happy. Healing occurs. Home regains the appearance of being home.

Tom and Willy, get along well. This is, in part, due to Tom's understanding that I'll kill him if he humiliates or tortures Willy. I was a younger brother once myself and know the truth about spirit killing. Tom gets a pretty good dose of rum in his nog to celebrate his entrance into the secret brotherhood. *All right dad!*

As we approach the end of the tree decoration, Mary stands aside and surveys the work. She carefully directs the movement of Christmas bulbs from one location to another until the tree approximates the new picture she has in mind. The majority of the decorations hang down from the lowest branches like a circular fringe, a cascade raining down and around the space below. It could be a green rocket shuttle, the ornaments representing the firing of the jets around its base. Despite the truncated branches, the tree looks fantastic, kind of amazing and futuristic. With a pile of presents underneath, the gap between branches and floor won't be so awful. It's good.

Here's Willy's chance to practice formal portrait photography. He directs us into different positions for each shot, leaving room for himself either standing to one side or kneeling up front. He's full of enthusiasm for the task and its responsibilities and we cooperate by making faces and pretending we don't understand what he wants.

Mary has conceded this one thing that I won't allow. For the eighteen years of our marriage including the fourteen years of children, not a single photograph has been taken Christmas morning or Christmas day. I have never given her my real reason, not the story from my own childhood. I don't know why. She asked only once – our first Christmas together. What I told her was that it was the only family tradition from my parents that I wanted to preserve. It was a lie, but she could see that I really meant it. I explained it to her in this way.

The joy of Christmas is a spirit. It cannot be captured. It should not be put on display. It should be experienced as it is, inside yourself, and between our selves, in the silent acknowledgment of our smiles and the bright lights in our eyes. These mental images we have of each other and the feelings and thoughts that go along with them comprise the secret memory of love given and received that we each hold inside. That's what keeps us alive and gives us strength. An artificial record must not weaken our memories of these things. Photographs weaken the mind. We must make our memories strong by the practice of attention we give to each other and our life together.

That was all I ever wanted her to understand. She never asked again.

સ

Chapter Fifteen

Late Tuesday morning.
Three days before Christmas.
Mary has spent the last day and a half cleaning the house in preparation for the day of the red-suited devil. I can't say that I've been much help. I've slept more than three people deserve. Since the tree decoration, Mary has been the very soul of Christmas peace. She hasn't complained a bit about my lethargy. How long will it last? I'm a little suspicious.

My remaining university responsibilities are complete. I've put the graded papers in the outbox where the students can pick them up, and the grades are recorded and undergoing bureaucratic processing. For the next two weeks I'm free. The Jimmy remains in the shop and I couldn't care less. I can walk anywhere I want to go. I have but one errand: deliver Sally's gift. If I'm ever going to do it, I'd better do it today.

Tiny comes over to where I'm sitting at the kitchen table, nudges my arm and wags her tail. Mary concentrates on a cryptogram in the newspaper between sips of Earl Grey tea. She contorts the features of her face with the effort. This is how ordinary and peaceful things have been since Sunday. Except for some aggravating phone calls from Henry during which he fulminates about Christmas, the erratic sale of anti-Christmas cards and Janette's indifference to his frustrations, I feel completely relaxed. It's so pleasant that I'm almost able to forget that Christmas is only three days away.

Mary looks up from her puzzle and smiles.
"Are you going to take Tiny for a walk?"
"I guess so. Maybe it will give me some energy."
"Good. I mean good that it will give you some

energy." She stares at me for a second with a puzzled look. "How was your visit to the psychiatrist?"

"Well, it was more of an appointment to make an appointment. They're busy this time of year."

"Hmmm, I suppose. What did he say?"

"She didn't say much. She listened to what I had to say and then told me to take two aspirin in the mornings and come back after Christmas."

"Are you going to go?"

"I said I would and I will, so let's leave it at that."

"Alright, Mr. Touchy." She pushes her puzzle aside and sips some hot tea. "Oh, you know what?"

"What?"

"I figured out what that little carved man is doing, you know, the one you got from those people."

"The Critzers." My tone is a bit harsh.

The experience with the Critzers has been a source of teasing and mockery for the past two days. It isn't Mary's fault and I shouldn't take it out on her. Besides calling with his worries about anti-Christmas cards, Henry has badgered me three and four times a day to ask if I've seen an angel or possibly even Jesus. He wonders if Virgil Critzer speaks to me in my dreams. He calls me Mr. Christmas and snorts with derision. He cackles like a madman. He's gone over the edge, in his own way, far more than I have. The more he thinks about the Critzer's the angrier he becomes. Every time he calls he has some added vexation to register, after he's done teasing me about my mystical awakening or my transcendental titillation. The whole thing is a thorn, but so far, I've managed to put it aside.

No one seems to understand what I feel about the experience. I've been changed. I see life, people and even ordinary events with greater clarity. I have a broader perspective. People are more interesting, even my students, even the less scintillating students. Mary nods her head and does listen when I try to tell her about it, but I can tell she's just appeasing me. She thinks it's just an oddity and it will pass.

"So, what do you think he's doing?"

"He's trying to stand on his head."

This is some cause for thought. I had never considered the possibility. Then I remember what Virgil Critzer said when he gave me the figure. "The world is turned upside down sometimes. You'll get back on your feet. Don't worry." I thought he was just making a bad joke at the time.

"Go get the figure, Harry. I'll show you. I'll bet he's as steady as a rock when you put him upside down."

I retrieve the little wooden man from the living room and bring him back to the kitchen. Mary takes it from my hand and turns him over on the table. It's astounding. The legs almost look as though they are in motion, the way Virgil has carved them. One sticks out back, pulled in from the push off the ground, and the other is bent, ready to be straightened into the air. It's as though he's caught a man in the act of standing on his head. Even the look of concentrated effort on the face of the little man makes sense now.

Mary is transfixed.

"Now do you see what I mean?" For a moment I'm transported by the memory of Virgil's peaceful presence.

"There is some spirit in this, Harry. That's true." Mary pulls her chin in to her neck and tilts her head. She's moved. She appears to be struck with wonder. "It's quite a piece of art."

"The man touched me, Mary, in some way I've never been touched before. It's like he set something in motion in my life and I'm just there along for the ride, but also I'm really there, in my life, waiting to see what comes next."

"I always thought you were that way, Harry." She smiles at me lovingly.

This strikes me as a strange revelation, something Mary has never mentioned before. I look at her. Her eyes twinkle. Her hair seems to glow.

The phone rings.

I pick it off the wall and put the receiver to my ear. It's Henry.

"How are you boy? You still talkin' 'bout dem critters?"

"Critters?"

"Dat Virgil critter still on your mind?"

"Oh, c'mon, Henry. Critzer, their name was Critzer."

"Boy, you sure do like to joke around."

"I don't believe you, Henry. You were there just as well as I was. Didn't they affect you in any way? Didn't they make you feel anything?"

"You know, they did," he admits. "I have been pissed off ever since. C'mon yourself, Harry. You want me to feel like the Christmas spirit has descended upon me and made me over. Now, I'm supposed to go out and shop 'til I drop because I've been magically awakened to the Christmas spirit?"

"Didn't you feel it, Henry? The spirit of the man, the peace of him, his caring?"

"Harry, Damn it. You're not going to do this. I saw two men and an old lady living in desperate poverty, eating beans and dried-out cornbread, totally unable to cope with the world. That's what I saw. Do you think they're going to have Christmas, Harry? Do you think ten thousand other people worse off than them are going to have Christmas? That's what I saw, Harry. And, I look around downtown and see the frenzy and the shopping and I think, Jesus, I don't know what to think. I see all the people with money gobbling up everything, piles and piles of stuff, mountains of it, and I think this is going on all over America while a world full of Critters sit on their haunches, clothed in rags, gnawing at bones, and watch us. Gaahd! It just makes me sick."

Henry will make a point from time to time. I don't know what to say. For a moment, there's a vast gulf of silence between us. I don't know whether Henry experiences the silence in the same way I do. I'm

The Christmas Curmudgeon

aware that his experience of the Critzer's has been different than mine, that his experience of the world is different than mine, that his experience of himself is different than my experience of myself.

The space between us suddenly seems immeasurable. I think that we're now experiencing ourselves as strangers to each other and because of that, since our brotherhood has always been a relationship in which we have validated each other, confirmed our sense of ourselves, I'm suddenly nervous, wondering how far this estrangement will go. Are Henry and I going separate ways? That would change me more than I can imagine. I need a little time to think.

"Henry, I'm going to have to call you back. Something has come up. Henry? ...Henry?"

"All right, Harry. Whatever you say." His anger is surprisingly strong. "I won't call you anymore. How's that? I see you've gone nuts. In fact, I don't ever want to talk to you again. How's that!"

"It sounds a little extreme, Henry."

"Good," he yells into the phone. "Now you know how you sound to me."

He hangs up.

Henry will settle down and call back later. But then, I'm suddenly convinced that Henry won't call back later, that he has gone around some bend of self-discovery into a place where I'm not going. Maybe, I'm wrong about the Critzers; maybe, Henry is right. I don't know. I look around the kitchen, which, at the moment, seems unusually large and hollow. Mary is back at her cryptogram. Tiny awaits her walk. It seems as good a time as any to let the dog lead the way. It seems the dog has more of a mind of her own than I do.

◆◆◆◆

Settle down, I tell myself, while Tiny squats to water one of the neighbor's plants. Henry is your brother. Relax and wait awhile. Everything will be all right. Henry and I have too much shared history to give up speaking to one another. We've been through more than forty Christmas celebrations together. Forget the argument. Remember the fun we've had together.

Tiny doesn't seem to mind taking a little break under a tree. I sit down cross-legged and lean back against the tree trunk, and she sniffs around before settling down. The afternoon air is cool but not uncomfortable. Altostratus clouds stretch across the sky, a thick blanket promising snow. In places, the undersides take on a nacreous iridescence that makes me think of ancient cities and journeys to the east. Tiny sits up by my side and we watch the movements of a number of small birds inside the bushes nearby. It's a wonderful, relaxing interlude. Sometimes, I think it's a good thing to have a dog. Tiny puts her head down between her paws while I close my eyes and reminisce.

The first Christmas I remember enjoying was the one Henry and I pulled the chair out from under Aunt Dorothy. How could such a thing happen, totally unplanned? I don't know. We were only nine and eleven years old. We didn't plan anything.

Aunt Dorothy was humongous, a puffy overstuffed chair of a woman, well over two hundred pounds, one of those women who wore vast black dresses with tiny white dots all over the fabric. Organza. Gorgonzilla. Something like that. She had round red cheeks and a complete set of false teeth. Her thick arms seemed stuffed with rolls of recently kneaded dough. Her hair was a ball of fluff. She could have been a giant puppet of herself.

Aunt Dorothy was coming to sit at the dining room table. Mom shouted from the kitchen, "Help Aunt Dorothy with her chair." Henry wanted to help her with her chair. I wanted to help her with her chair. Somehow, when he pulled the chair from one side and I pulled the chair from the other, it ended up about a foot and a half back from where it started. All this happened within a matter of the few seconds it took

Aunt Dorothy to decide to arrange herself into position and sit down. The timing couldn't have been better if it had been planned. She descended swiftly once the barrier of the chair had been removed, and she seemed to swing backwards a short distance as though in search of some purchase by which she could alter the course of events. Alas.

She bumped the chair with her rump causing it to teeter and spring out of our hands; then she hit the floor with a resounding thump. Henry and I were stunned as much as Aunt Dorothy. Our mother rushed from the kitchen. Aunt Dorothy sat, flustered and dismayed. Her fake, flesh-colored knee-length rubbery stockings were exposed. Her false teeth clacked as she put them back in place. Henry and I grinned at each other, despite the knowledge that grinning was wrong under the circumstances and might even be fatal.

"What have you done?!" Mother shouted. "Did you pull the chair out from under Aunt Dorothy?!"

We shook our heads. We protested.

"We were trying to help her sit down."

Well, even though it was a truthful statement, it didn't sound right.

"I was trying to pull the chair out," Henry shouted.

That sounded even worse.

"It was an accident," I said, too late.

"How could you boys do such a thing?"

It wasn't a question. It was an indictment. Mom, convinced that we had done it on purpose, sent us to our rooms. After the grown-ups had finished eating dinner, Dad brought us cold meat sandwiches and glasses of water. He looked at us and shook his head.

"You boys are in for it, now. You might as well stay up here for the rest of your lives."

Cold winds blew at the windows and clouds filled the darkness outside. It rained and thundered. Life was gray and ugly, but we made the best of it.

Henry snuck into my room and we played cards – War and Crazy Eights. There were no computers in those days. Kids had to look to each other for entertainment. It was hell. But, it was one of the few times as youngsters that my brother and I got along without any trouble. We actually had a great time together, playing cards, then building forts in our rooms and taking turns attacking each other with missiles made from Lincoln Logs and Tinkertoys.

Our mother came to inform us that we had to come downstairs before bedtime to apologize to Aunt Dorothy. Her dignity had been rumpled. We had to kiss her. Sure, it was a disgusting thing to have to do. Aunt Dorothy was huge and spongy and her teeth clacked. She smelled like medicine. At that age, we were not great kissers anyway. Hugs were enough. When you hugged Aunt Dorothy you had the vague sense that you could be absorbed and disappear.

We went downstairs in our pajamas. Everything was quiet. Our father was reading a book and the television was off. He would have ignored the whole incident from the beginning anyway, but this part was certainly of no interest to him. He was a businessman. If it didn't have to do with dollars and cents, it was either foolishness or nonsense. We went into the kitchen. Aunt Dorothy retained a slight look of indignation and mother, still awash in the wake of the singular odiousness of our behavior of the afternoon, was as stern as the back of a boat.

We knew it was going to be tough, but we knew we had to do it. At least, Henry and I had the satisfaction that each of us would have to go through the same ordeal. I looked on as Henry spoke his few words of apology. Then the entire front and both sides of his head disappeared in the folds of Aunt Dorothy's bosom as she hugged him. Henry's arms went out to her sides but his reach was insufficient. It was more like he was trying to grab hold of a dirigible. Then, at the end, Aunt Dorothy leaned over and Henry kissed her on the cheek. He turned away. I looked and saw an indescribable countenance, a fractured, demonized picture of his former self. As for my own experience, I cannot speak of it.

The most important thing about that day, what made it so enjoyable, was the genuine vitality of everything that happened. All the varied feelings that we had were a truth about ourselves and about our life together. Nothing was contrived. We had not been manipulated into laughter, shock or fear by someone else's media-fashioned pretend existence as seen on television. These experiences were real and our own. I felt like I belonged to my family then in a way that is continually under threat and being eroded now. Television, computers and the information age undermine this sense of empathy and community. I've come to recognize that sharing and belonging are missing in my post-modern electronic, commodified existence. And Christmas with all its gifts and trimmings has come to symbolize something from the past that we all need but don't realize that we have diminished to the point of being lost.

Tiny and I return to find the house empty again. Mary doesn't need to leave a note. I know where she has gone. She has taken Willy to the mall to see Santa Claus. She does this despite the fact that Willy knows that Santa is as bogus as a plastic wreath. Tom has probably gone along for the ice cream sundaes they will have to end the outing. The fact is that for Mary and the kids going to the mall is like going to heaven. That's what it is. I don't pretend to understand and I keep my opinions to myself. Most of the time.

It's as good a time as any to take Sally her present. Another walk, about a mile and a half, to the department office won't do me any harm, though Tiny is clearly put out about being left behind. The package is neatly wrapped in gold foil with green satin ribbons and waits for me, as it has for several days, on the hall table. Attached to the top, there's a note card to Sally that says, "Merry Christmas to a wonderful secretary.

I don't know what I'd do without you!" Succinct but sincere. *Mary has a better way with words than the English professor.* Grateful to have the task finished and the responsibility nearly off my back, the shame of my inadequacy disappears.

The uphill trek to the department building takes my breath away, and the stairs up to the second floor seem daunting. *Get back in shape or end up in a wheelchair.* I make the effort and arrive at the top bent over for a few breaths. Strangely, Hedler doesn't pop out of his doorway like a curious, erudite Jack-in-the-Box. Sally has decorated the outer door to the reception area with a huge snowman with a large-print quote in a balloon above his head, "We all come home, or ought to come home, for a short holiday ...the longer the better." The empty office hums with the life of machines. Surely, a human hand is near. In a moment, Sally comes out of my office, startled by my presence.

"I was just returning some finished papers to your desk."

"No need to explain, Sally." Holding the gift in my hands, I recall Mary's admonition. "I want you to know I think about you and that you are appreciated." She grins and laughs as I hand her the gift.

"Thank you, professor. That's sweet."

"Go ahead, open it," I'm eager to find out what it is. *Mary, the stinker, wouldn't tell me.* She just told me to say, "It's something nice for the kitchen."

Sally carefully removes the ribbons and the wrapping, opens the paper box and looks inside. Her eyes widen.

"Excuse me," she blushes as she reaches into the box, retrieving another hidden card. She looks at me, then looks away, blushes again deeply, then turns around, turns back and throws her head around. "Oh, wait, wait, I've got to go to the bathroom." She runs from the office. There's something suspicious here, but I don't have time to think about it. *Damage control. Warning. Something is wrong.*

The Christmas Curmudgeon

There's an awakening in the consciousness of man that comes at times either of great success or disaster. I already know this is a disaster, even before looking in the box to discover the frilly French maid outfit, the little black apron trimmed in white lace, the tiny panties and the sheer see-through fabric. Oh my God. Mary, what have you done? Horrid images flash through my mind, scandal, departmental hearings, harassment lawsuits and disgrace.

Find Sally and explain.

Out in the hall, looking this way and that, a frantic madman, perhaps a murderer trots down the corridor to the bathrooms. Professor Hedler, fully present now when not needed, nods his head from his office, eyes the madman quizzically, but says nothing. I know where to go. *Swiftly, swiftly.* Hedler nods again, grins and slips backward out of sight into his office like a turtle back into its shell. I plunge toward the women's room and push inside shading my eyes to prevent the sight of anyone who might be in there whom I shouldn't see. No one screams. There's no one there.

"Sally ...Sally! ...There's been a mistake!"

"Professor Jenkins! You ...are ...in ...the ladies room." Her voice comes from a stall at the end of the room.

"Well, so I am." I muster calmness and professorial dignity. "I apologize. There's been a terrible mistake. That's not your present."

"Surely not," she assents with certainty. "Please leave, will you? I am actually in the bathroom here."

"Oh, I'm sorry. I mean, well, I'll be out in the hall. Actually, it would be better if I went back to the office, I guess. Standing around in the hall by the ladies' room door doesn't seem too auspicious either, you know, it wouldn't look..."

"Professor Jenkins!! Get out before someone else comes in!"

I stand in the hall for a minute anyway, preferring a little thought to more action. When Sally emerges, she holds a note card in one hand in front of her face. She walks past me slowly, straight-backed and deliberate.

Calmly, with dignity, she states, "Your wife left a note in the box explaining the gift. So, you don't have to pretend. I like it very much and thank you." With that, she walks back to the office, leaving me mortified. Hedler pops his head out again as I approach his door. I grab his nose quickly and give it a turn.

"There's for you, old boy!"

The best plan will be to call Sally later. We can talk safely at a distance over the phone. A little more time to think won't hurt either of us. I pass on down the hall, down the stairs, outside and downhill toward home. It's all beginning to look pretty funny, in a twisted sort of way, and, suddenly realizing anew Mary's hand in this fiasco, I figure my best strategy will be to pretend nothing has happened. Let her wonder. Yes, indeed! Let Mary wonder.

Home at last, I putter in the kitchen, doing the dishes and cleaning up the counters. Eventually, I drift into the den and into my chair and back into the tiredness again. I've come to recognize it as a kind of bone-deep weariness that is as much mental as it is physical. Henry doesn't seem to feel this way. Maybe his is the right way. Maybe people should express themselves outright as he does, without restraint. *Then again, maybe not.* What seems good to me is sleep. Yes, sleep is very good. *Stretch out on the couch and relax. Soothe your sore muscles.*

I'm drifting, looking at the stars. There is the sense of an opportunity that could arrive at any moment. The star cruiser Jules Verne is moving successfully under the power of the magnetic field engines. We're literally surfing, drawing energy from magnetic waves in the fabric of space-time. Ours is a dream speed, faster than any reality would allow.

The woman from the fourth dimension sits next to me in the officer's lounge and we're viewing surreal vistas, the changing horizons of deep space. When I look to the side, her face seems to shift and change in composition as though it's made of fluid, moveable parts that create facial expressions quite unlike the normal third-dimensional ones to which I'm accustomed. Still, her company sends thrills through my body. There's something so wonderfully commanding in her way that it's clear that she's a special person with unique powers, perhaps a spiritual being, or a visitor from a highly advanced culture. I stare at her, trying to understand a peculiar sensation of recognition combined with amazement and curiosity. It's an oddly dizzying experience.

"At this speed you could easily cross into the fourth dimension, Commander. Would you like to go?" she asks.

""What's it like?"

"It's joyous."

"Joyous?"

"Touch my hand, Commander, and I will take you there. Don't think about what to do. You will know automatically. If you feel you have to do something, you will not be able. If you feel you are able, then you will have to. These are two very different ways."

She extends her arm towards me. Her eyes kaleidoscopic with light, she urges me on telepathically. Feeling her thoughts guide me, I reach out and place my hands in hers. And then we're gone. The fourth dimension opens. It's a grand universe of spirits. Everything is made of energy, composed like music into infinite varieties of harmony and understanding.

"You can't deny the beauty of life, Commander. You can't deny what you experience as true."

"Yes."

Floating in a sea of peaceful joy, waves of heavenly energy surround us. Then suddenly she's gone. And, I'm in the star cruiser again, walking toward the helm of the ship. Crew members pass and look at me strangely. I feel a rush of urgency and begin running to the helm. The ship is slowing down. The magnetic field engine has shut down. I'm running as fast as I can, running with increasing fear and urgency. Everything on the ship stops. The lights go out. A voice speaks in the air, directly in my mind. "Oh, that's not the end of it. Oh, no. It will all come out right, you'll see."

I wake up in the dark in the living room. The house is quiet. I feel so deeply moved by the dream, by the sense of joy and reassurance, and so relieved of some pressure, that I'm crying with gratitude. My emotions settle. A great calm pervades me and the space around my body.

After awhile, I'm thinking about things that need to be done, my list, my responsibilities. There are only two days remaining before Christmas. I realize I haven't bought Mary a present, haven't even thought about what to give her. Christmas shopping is something I have to do. It can't be avoided any longer. Accept it. *What's the point in ignoring Mary?* Will it do any good? It's doubtful. And then, without any reason and surprisingly, I actually feel like going shopping. It almost makes me laugh.

What would Mary like for Christmas? The idea of spending a day looking for something unique and wonderful for Mary surprisingly seems quite appealing. I could go out for lunch along the way. I could even buy myself a little something that I want. What would be wrong with that? Christmas doesn't have to be all about the presents. It can be about having an enjoyable afternoon to yourself. But then I think it would be more fun if Henry went along. Henry. I wonder if he's still not talking to me. Well, I feel defiant and insistent; it's up to him to make the call. Henry will have to get over his problem. I'm his brother, after all.

Chapter Sixteen

Wednesday, I sleep till ten. Even Tiny doesn't rouse me. I sit up on the edge of the bed and stare dully at the gray light out the window. Slowly I rise; slowly I walk. The house is empty, the hallway empty, the kitchen empty and my brain empty. A note on the kitchen table tells me that Tom and Willy are at friends' houses and Mary has gone shopping. She says she will be home for lunch. Will I make soup? I look in the utility room and Tiny perks up and wags at me. Closing the door, I leave her there. My brain won't start up. My hard drive has crashed. I'm operating on a pre-electronic level, feeling organic and slow, like a mud turtle or maybe a troglodyte. A hot shower and coffee should help.

Out of the shower, wrapped in a towel, I head for the kitchen. The coffeemaker's light indicates readiness, and the coffee is good, hot and hearty. *"The best part of waking up is —— in your cup."* Where did that come from? What's the brand name of that coffee? One of those flesh-colored rolls of elastic athletic wrapping was in the bathroom cabinet and rolling it snugly around my arm helps. The swelling has reduced and three Advil ease the pain. But, maybe a bone is cracked. I'll check with the doctor after Christmas. In fact, now that I'm thinking about it, this visit to the doctor will be a good time to pretend that I went to a psychiatrist.

Now, it's time to make a list, my one and only Christmas list. The time passes slowly because this is Christmas thinking, which is a tedious, more agonizing type of thought. Tiny whines at the utility room door, pleading to be inside. That's all the excuse I need. Tiny's good company has been a source of solace over the past few weeks. She deserves a break.

The only item on the list so far is three pints of rum.

A quick check reveals nothing but a puddle on the floor. I'll clean up the puddle, pat her on the head and we'll start out, man and dog, into the wilderness hunting something rotten, something smelly and not okay. We'll put things in our mouths we shouldn't. We'll pee on trees and bushes. We'll growl at people or jump at them seeking affection. Me and Tiny, two old dogs on the prowl. We'll go back and forth on the scrubby grass on the border between the sidewalk and the road.

It's a good plan and nearly plays out as such until Tiny breaks free, almost yanking my arm out of its socket going after a squirrel. I don't need two bad arms, so off she goes, set free. She'll come back when she's ready.

Back at the house I chop up some mushrooms, carrots and onions and sauté them. Add two cups of chicken stock and noodles. After the noodles are soft, add a can of Progresso soup. Let it simmer. This is how it's done. Plenty of time before Mary's arrival. Time enough to consider the observations I've made; the thoughts that repeat; the evidence for the possibility of her infidelity.

There exists an opinion in the world that many occurrences that seem intentional are, in fact, coincidental. You're thinking about an old friend and in the next moment as you walk around a corner you meet that old friend. You're puzzling over a question in your life, some personal difficulty perhaps, and then you pick up a book or magazine to distract yourself and begin reading. Within minutes helpful thoughts regarding your problem appear in print before your eyes. Any one of us could probably provide ten examples of such incidences. And, often, there is an unmistakable feeling that this appearance of someone, these words, this particular event occurred with you specifically in mind. How could it be otherwise? It was intended for you and, if so intended, then a will, a consciousness beyond your own must have caused it to happen. People dismiss this notion outright as either superstition or self-centeredness and label it coincidence. But, I think there's no such thing as coincidence. All these events, the special ones we notice and many others we never suspect, are part of a vast matrix of events that, indeed, are intended to move our lives toward a higher level of awareness, a profoundly better way of being and living.

It's with these thoughts in mind that I wait for Mary. These thoughts give me courage. They tell me that Mary and I alone are not entirely responsible for our dissension, that we are being impelled toward a better life, perhaps toward greater honesty and trust. There are forces in the spiritual world that make arrangements in the worldly world. They hint and indicate, and even startle us at times. But, they must be here for us; even if what they reveal is difficult to see, they're for us. I don't know why I believe this; it's a new idea that feels like the truth. And, I'm beginning to trust my intuitions.

Mary breezes in, bringing Tiny along, just as I finish setting the kitchen table. My serving the soup allows her time to deposit her bags and take off her coat then settle down from the exhilaration of shopping.

"What are we having?"

"Progresso Fat Free Chicken Noodle ...want some bread with it?"

"Sure."

We sit at the table, sip spoonfuls of soup and munch thick slices of flax seed bread with Smart Balance Buttery Spread. Mary regales me with shopping successes. There remains little left to do. We have each other to consider. We agreed years ago never to ask what the other wanted. Otherwise, you might as well go out and buy it for yourself. Hints are allowed but not encouraged.

"That was a pretty nasty little present you put up for Sally, Mary. Why'd you do that?"

She holds her head steady as a stone and

glares at me. "To teach you a lesson."

"I don't need a lesson."

"Then quit ogling Sally."

"So that's your excuse?"

"I don't need an excuse."

"What did you write in the note to her? Did you tell her to ignore me? I'm just an old lecher? If she makes an issue out of this present, she could raise a big stink in the department. I could lose my job."

"She won't. I explained to her ahead of time, and she agreed to go along with it."

"She knew she was getting that present?"

Mary sits back and stares at her soup.

"I'm sorry. It was mean, but I was so mad at you – you can't imagine."

Nodding away agreeably, I decide to drop the subject and go after my paramount concern.

"I've been spending a lot of time with the dog lately."

"That's nice. I'm sure she appreciates it."

"Yeah ...I go for walks with the dog, I talk to the dog, I eat with the dog, I even take naps with the dog. I spend more time with the dog than I do with you."

"I haven't had time to take care of the dog, Harry. I'm sorry, but I've been busy."

"I'm not talking about the dog!"

She pushes her empty bowl of soup to the side and wipes her mouth.

"Alright, I've been working extra hours at the store to help with the bills. What do you care? You're busy or you're drinking rum."

"I don't drink that much."

"Yes, you do."

"Look, that's not what I'm talking about. Don't change the subject."

"Well, then get to the point."

"Does your paycheck reflect all these extra hours?"

"Since when have I ever had to account for my paycheck? What are you getting at?"

The Christmas Curmudgeon

Why are you beating around the bush? Get into the bush. Get it out. Get it over with.

"You've been spending a lot of time with Mr. Gregg, haven't you?"

"What?"

"Are you sleeping with him?"

"Harry!" She puts her hand over her mouth, then lowers her head in a challenging manner. "Are you sleeping with Sally?"

"Unh uh. You aren't going to turn it back on me. You know I'm not sleeping with Sally. We already did Sally. So, spill it."

"Spill it?" Mary tries to hide her amusement at these words, then begins to laugh lightly. This, of course, is infuriating, but I sit back calmly and wait, staring at her with cold appraisal. "Harry, Harry. Mr. Gregg is as gay as a maypole. Besides, I'm your wife. Haven't we always been faithful and true? Don't we have children together? What's wrong with you? Did you go to the psychiatrist like you said you would?"

"Yes. *You liar.* She said there was nothing wrong with me."

"Really?"

"He's as gay as a maypole? Where'd you get that?"

"From a movie, I think. But, he is. I'm pretty sure, anyway. Nobody at the store knows for certain, but you never see him with anyone and there's just something, you know, gay about him."

To create a break, a moment to reflect, I clear the dishes from the table then stand at the sink running the tap until it's hot. Looking back at Mary's back, it's clear that she's tired. She's rubbing her neck and her shoulders. *What a mess. What a colossal pile of speculation and precarious dubiety.* I'm overwhelmed by my own stupidity. *You've not been stupid. There's nothing stupid about this. How would you know? You haven't been spending any time together. You haven't talked.* Pulling a chair around to her side, I sit with her and speak calmly, earnestly.

179

"We haven't been talking to each other. That's the problem. If we talked more, I would worry less."

"Is that what the psychiatrist said?"

"Yes." *Liar.*

"Did she give you medicine?"

"She suggested a natural alternative ...St. John's Wort."

"What? Is she some hippie New Age type, Harry?"

"She's an authentic psychiatrist."

"What's her name?"

"Dr. Maypole."

Mary stops and stares. Then she starts laughing. It's good to see her laugh like this. Our lives have been so busy and controlled, so pressured and demanding. It's an enormous relief. Now, I'm laughing with her.

"Why don't we go to a movie tonight and let the kids stay home and eat pizza? Melanie and Vivian can come over and we'll let them have the house. They can ask some friends over."

"A party?"

"Why not? They're big enough. Melanie can take charge. She acts older than her mother sometimes."

"I wish I could, but Janette and I are going to finish up tonight. Why don't you call Henry and go out, the two of you?"

"Because Henry decided he's not talking to me. So, Henry can call me when he gets over himself."

Mary ponders the point. "Janette said he's been acting as weird as an Eskimo in England."

"Maybe that's so, but I'm not calling him. He has to call. Where does she get her similes?"

"From living with Henry, I think."

◆◆◆◆

Maybe a walk will help clear my mind, help deal with the stress of the Christmas season. Christmas stress. Yes, I see it clearly; that's why I'm so tired. But, the talk with Mary has done me good. My fatigue can be countered. Certain wisdom has entered my awareness. I need to change the way I do things. I'm going to change the way I work. The dull exercise of the routines at college wears me down, as dull routine would anyone.

The fact is, I'm out of shape to an extreme. Flabby, soft, sagging wads of flesh hang from my bones, and, though I'm not terribly overweight, it's enough to make walking unpleasant, despite the fact that it's the discipline of walking every day that I need. I can actually feel the need, a truth that even the devils of doubt and denial can't hide. *I'm not going to wait; start now, start making changes now. Just do it and let the rest of your roles and responsibilities adjust.* And, going for a walk right away is as good a way as any to escape the inevitable return home chatter about Christmas presents, who gets to turn on the lights on the Christmas tree, the depressing niggling over Christmas wrap and ribbons and the awful music, the endlessly terrible Christmas music on the radio that the children and Mary turn on to accompany their activity and complement their conversation. I can dwell on these realities while strolling down to the park. Perhaps by focusing on the dreadfulness of the unbearable one makes it bearable.

So, here I am, out in the cool air, taking an evening constitutional. A number of the houses I pass are lit up so garishly that you can inspect the pores of your skin under their light. One has a Santa that waves his arms in a sleigh on the roof. Santa and the reindeer are backed by strings of "stars" that swoop from the roof to the trees around the house in every direction. Several of the houses have all their corners and edges lined with white bulbs. *Strange.* These houses seem to lose their sense of sturdiness and strength. They look as though they're made of cardboard. Perhaps the people inside are equally bendable and flat.

I pass on to a stretch of darker houses with only lamplight in their windows. The nighttime sky is crystal clear, sparkling with real stars, and the air is crisp and truly refreshing. This is what I need. The chill of the air invigorates. Viewing the sky is something that Mary and I enjoyed in the past. We should do it again. In the distance, there's the sound of a man and woman arguing. It seems to project from a house behind the house in front of me. They're really going at it. Their words aren't clear, but their tone is fierce and combative. In the midst of the calm peaceful wonder of sky-viewing, these harsh noises seem like madness; truly, the ugly meanness of people must be a kind of madness.

What is it that makes a man go mad? It can't be some sudden thing, the realization of a dark truth, the failure of one attempt, the first overwhelming manifestation of loneliness, fear or rejection. It has to be the result of an accumulation of insults. As in those stories of Chinese water torture, it isn't the awareness of being tortured, nor is it the fact of the torture itself. It's the accumulated experience of one drop following another, the anticipation of the next drop, the acknowledgment that you are alone, abandoned by your fellows and far from hope or rescue. Then your suffering is exquisite, the distortion of your pain extreme, the accompanying descent into dread too much to bear and it is then that your mind turns to madness. It's the failure of your murderous rage to defend you, the failure of your God to save you, the failure of belief to reassure you, the failure of your mind to maintain a reasonable perspective. By this account, we should all go mad, for the accumulated stresses of society and modern life are a kind of torture. And we do accumulate that stress, year after year, and we do so most clearly during the months surrounding Christmas, during the pre-season pressure and during the post-season melancholy and sudden drop into debt and the iron chains of winter.

It's a wonder more of us aren't mad.

◆◆◆◆

About ten blocks from the house, near the edge of the downtown district, there's a wonderful park. One side of the park is across from the city library. The marble plaza in front of the library as well as the stone steps down to the street are lit up and give the place a grand elegance, creating a feeling of nobility that spreads out across the street into the park. The park is landscaped with small, rolling hillocks clustered with flowerbeds and shrubbery. Well-placed trees lend dignity, and interesting sculptures honor the grounds. An asphalt path curves around with no apparent direction. There are benches and street lamps scattered throughout that create a special aura of friendliness and familiarity.

Approaching the north end of the park, I notice a small crowd of people lining the sidewalk. Some are in the street and some are leaning against parked cars. They're standing quietly it seems, facing into the park. At first, I think they're listening to carolers or a Christmas choir and head over that way to listen.

An outdoor choir or a group of carolers singing Christmas songs, actual live music, not music pumped at you from the radio, is one of the few things I like about the Christmas season. It seems a truly noble thing to do, and I actually wonder why we don't, as a people, go around in small groups singing all through the year. It would be a lot of fun. It would improve community relations.

But walking nearer the congregation, I see that the people aren't listening to a choir at all but to a man giving a speech. I can tell also that there's a lot of energy in the crowd. They're stirred up.

Coming into their midst, I'm startled to hear the man next to me raise his voice in a shout. "Right on, brother. Tell it like it is! Say it man ...you're right!" Didn't this sort of enthusiasm die out in the sixties? Apparently, the person speaking to the crowd has touched some common chord, and the people here are willing to respond. I'm amazed.

Edging my way toward the center of the group, I can now hear and see the man speaking. He's stand-

The Christmas Curmudgeon

ing on a slatted wooden crate waving his hands in an animated fashion. He's quite impressive with his balding head shining under the street lamp, his huge belly hanging out and a wild kind of cheeriness to the blush of his cheeks. A red Santa jacket, with white-edged cuffs and hems and big black buttons, fits snugly on the man's large frame. I stand and watch in awe. I'm tickled by the finger of fear. Of course, it's Henry.

"Listen people, I know as well as you that Christmas started many, many years ago, and that it's considered a cultural tradition, a necessity, to celebrate Christmas. But, even if Christmas is a tradition, we might still ask what does it represent in our culture now? What does it celebrate ...the spending of money?

"Did it start ages ago with the giving of a small gift to a loved one? Maybe. Now it's a multi-billion dollar gift-giving enterprise. Think of the sales and the tax revenues. Don't you think the government and all the corporations would be interested in perpetuating Christmas, perhaps even in emphasizing its commercial aspect over its religious aspect?

Several women on the edge of the crowd boo Henry.

"Are you drunk?" shouts one.

"I am not." Henry shouts back at them.

"Why don't you go home?"

"You go home if you want. I have a right to speak out about what I believe. I know I'm not alone."

A couple of the women do leave, throwing a hand behind them in an expression of disgust. Still, many of the people stay. They seem interested in what Henry has to say.

"Every year they try to add something to the Christmas extravaganza. Christmas cards sold and sent by the millions, a postal service bonanza. Christmas foods and Christmas shows, movies, parades and ice capades, and Christmas decorations, expensive Christmas celebrations and Christmas sale specials on nearly everything that can be sold and

Christmas books and Christmas music and incredible, incredible as it may seem, Christmas clothing, ties and sweaters, shirts and jewelry to give you that special Christmas look. Is there no end to it? The answer is no, not unless we stop buying into it."

There are some who shout, "You got it, buddy!" or, "That's the truth!" and others who form a single, purposeful chorus of "Go home, go home." Some of Henry's supporters turn and glare at his detractors. They're angered by what they see as an attempt to suppress him.

"You go home!" one man shouts angrily.

"Let the man speak," another says.

"Yeah, let the man have his say."

I think for a minute that the crowd will erupt into a shouting match, but it's Henry who shouts them down.

"Listen to me! Listen people! Let me finish."

The crowd settles, but the restlessness and tension level remain high. Those that take offense whisper to each other, making fists in the cold and shaking their heads. In a daze, I look at the people, wondering at the strangeness of this event. There's a man taking pictures. Two other men talk calmly as they watch. They aren't really listening. Something about their attitude bothers me. Then I realize they are waiting for something to happen; for an encounter; for the police.

"What's it about? What is Christmas all about these days, right now? I'll tell you what. It's the most massive extortion scheme in the history of the world. Who benefits? I'll tell you who. Corporate America ...Big Business, that's who. AND WHO PAYS FOR IT?!!"

"We do!!" shouts one man in the crowd. There are many who grumble or shout their assent.

"That's right," shouts Henry. "You do and I do and every other regular working person does, many of them people who can barely afford to pay their bills and put food on the table."

More of those who disagree with Henry walk away, aware that they're being ignored. The people

The Christmas Curmudgeon

remaining applaud the last remark.

"Look, look over there!" Henry points across the street. A Santa Claus walks along the sidewalk, ambling toward the downtown shopping district. A red metal bucket hangs from one of his hands. I turn to look along with the rest of the crowd as Henry shouts behind us.

"There's your symbol of the true meaning of Christmas. A businessman disguised as Santa with his bucket ready to take your money! Do you see it? Do you understand? He doesn't even pretend that you'll get anything in return. Just fork over the dough, friends, just pour it by the bucket load into the Christmas coffers. Where does your donation go?! Does anyone know? Doesn't it seem like there are more homeless, poor, and needy than ever before?

"Where does your donation really go?" Henry shouts louder now to regain their attention. The crowd turns back to face him. "I'll tell you. It pays for the perpetuation of the bureaucracy, the business and government of it and for the advertisements that keep you notified of what it is you need and when you need to buy it. You pay for the advertising and the marketing strategies that control you! How about that?! You're all SUCKERS lined up at the Christmas carnival, the biggest in the world. Drop your dollar in the bucket, friend!"

Several patrol cars have pulled up and a number of police officers approach the crowd. Several more patrolmen arrive on foot from different directions. Henry seems oblivious to their movements. But, surely, he will step down and leave. The police move in among the people and tell them to disperse and go home.

"Don't let them tell you to leave!" Henry shouts. "You have every right to be here!" A number of them turn back to listen. I edge toward the side of the crowd, hoping to spot an escape route that will allow me to grab Henry's arm and pull him away. We can run to safety. This has gone far enough. Some of the people are arguing with the police. Most are leaving.

The Christmas Curmudgeon

Henry continues speaking, apparently inspired. "The mass of Americans – that's you and me, people, you and me! – we support the mass culture, we keep it going, we pay for it, but we don't design it! We're like a huge family of children, and the corporate parents keep us dumb and silent in our living rooms with television, Xbox, Internet ...an endless supply of toys and games from childhood to adulthood to the grave! Wake up! People! Wake up!! You're dupes. You're Christmas slaves!"

The police split the crowd and turn them back, instructing them to move on or go home. Two hefty policemen move toward Henry from the front, and another stands by to intercept anyone who might try to interfere. Several more official looking cars arrive and newspaper reporters and photographers scramble out.

"Henry! Henry!" I shout and wave at him. "Come this way!" I point to a relatively open space where we might make a run for it.

Henry looks at me as I call his name again, but it's too late. The policemen are upon him. They grab his arms and start pulling him toward the street and their waiting cars. Henry deliberately lets his feet slip out from under him. He's being dragged away. He lifts his head to shout. The photographers rush forward.

"See! See people! They don't want you to hear what I'm saying. But, I have the right to speak, don't I? Is Christmas more powerful than freedom? Do you see? Is Christmas more powerful than the Constitution? The Bill of Rights?"

The crowd is well dispersed by now. Most of the people have left, but a few stand at a distance and watch as Henry is pushed against a patrol car. I walk toward Henry and the police, feeling, as his brother, I should try to intercede. Amazingly, he struggles to say a few more words.

"Look at the Christmas thugs! Look at the Christmas thugs! The Christmas police! This is the meaning of Christmas!"

Something happens now that I would never

plan or prepare. It's a spontaneous act, beyond my own self-reckoning. I stride forward intentionally, holding a hand in the air.

"Officer, officer. Please. This is my brother. Let me take him home."

Then, without thinking, I reach forward and grab Henry's arm and pull. He grins at me like a madman and we begin laughing. Stumbling backward, as the officers push me aside, both Henry and I realize our plight, our foolhardy adolescent idiocy. But, it's too late, we're clearly on the wrong side of the law, and some of the officers are riled. Electronic flashes sear the air repeatedly as the photographers capture our faces, the police and the action of the arrest. Six policemen surround Henry and me, pull us apart and push us both to the ground. We take a few shoves that seem unnecessary, but nothing terrible happens. I guess it's routine for the police; they do their job with certainty, strength and self-control. We are actually being handcuffed.

Henry and I are yanked to our feet, and pushed and pulled toward the back of two police cars. Thoughts of hardened criminals in jail teaching us more about sin and crime skitter through my mind. A couple of reporters stand near the police cars. The police want to hurry out of there, but the news people are persistent. One reporter asks for a statement, and Henry responds clearly and with dignity.

"We aren't criminals. I was only exercising my right to free speech, my right to protest in this public park."

The reporter turns to one of the cops. "So, what are they charged with, officer?"

"Public disturbance. No permit. Resisting arrest."

Flashes continue as we're turned by hand and pressed into the waiting cars. Tomorrow morning's paper will carry some strange news.

Chapter Seventeen

Getting out of jail isn't a complex problem. The officer at the front desk actually laughs when we arrive. When he laughs, his forehead turns red. His collar is too tight for his neck. The officers on the night shift are sympathetic and don't see either of us as a threat. We're allowed the requisite phone call and we contact Mary and Janette. Mary is incredulous but cooperative. Janette laughs in the background and then Mary starts laughing.

"Professor Jenkins goes to jail. Ha! The kids will love this. Disturbing the peace was it?"

"Just come and get us, Mary."

Henry and I are taken to separate rooms for processing. Who knows why? Apparently they are doing him first. I sit for quite a while in a metal chair in front of a plain table with a female guard standing by. About a half an hour passes, and then a cop in street clothes enters the room. He's tall and lean with a square jaw and a wide smile that reveals oversized teeth.

"So, you're the brother." I nod. "He's been telling us how you got stuck out on a side road and met some of them mountain critters."

Be tolerant. This is a law officer "Yes, we did. It was quite an experience."

"Basically," the cop clearly enjoys his position, "your brother thinks you ought to be locked up and not him."

"Is that so?" *What in the world is this? What is Henry up to?*

"Yep. He says he wouldn't be out on the streets sounding off about Christmas if you hadn't gone soft on him." *Soft?* "Harry the Good, turned against his own brother." He chortles, enjoying the tease.

"What? I'll tell you what. He's the one making the public speeches, inciting the crowd and causing the disturbance."

Startled by my outburst, he stiffens and scowls, then recovers quickly. He winks at me as though we share some secret, a view of Henry that allows us both to truly understand Henry's view. But I don't understand. And I don't have any interest in making anything clearer. Let the police think what they will.

"Let's get on with this. Are we ready to be released?"

"He's already released." He waves me up from my seat toward the door. He points down a hall to the left. "Just go down there to room three on the right. He's in there."

Room three has "Interrogation" stenciled on the front of the door at eye level. I knock on the door and a voice shouts, "Come on in." Then another voice I recognize quite well says, "Is that you, Harry?" He sounds okay, in a good mood. Henry and three officers are playing cards on a card table in the center of the room. There's a pile of loose change on the table. Poker. Henry's favorite.

"Come on in, Harry. Join the game."

"Sure. Pull up a chair," says one of the officers, indicating a stack of chairs by the far wall.

It turns out Henry hasn't actually been sent to jail and neither have I. They've been holding us in custody. Henry is merely waiting for someone to give him a ride. He knew I would be right along. He's annoyed at having to leave the game, but arranges for another. In a matter of moments, after a few friendly words, we walk past the front desk and leave. Standing outside in the cold evening, Henry informs me on how things proceed from here.

"The captain is one of my clients. He talked to a lawyer friend of mine, who'll represent both of us. We'll have to go to court, but they'll drop the resisting arrest charges. We'll pay a fine and that will be that."

"But I didn't do anything."

"You intruded. Police don't like that."

"I should have let them drag you away."

"That's what I would have done."

Mary pulls up in her Honda and toots the horn – just in time – before I punch Henry in the nose. Janette's not with her because Janette was undressed in a changing room when we called. Mary just told her to take her time. She said it's probably nothing. A gigantic pile of packages cover the front passenger seat.

"Get in the back." Mary accompanies her command with a look of bewildered amusement.

We get into the car and head for home.

"I'll drop you off, then go back for Janette." Mary pretends to tend to the road. She mastered the art of eavesdropping, as most girls do, in grade school.

I say nothing and keep my eyes on the road, avoiding Henry. *Harry the Good.* How annoying. *How can you let him get away with that?* Looking to the side, I shake my head and stare at him like he's an idiot.

"C'mon, Harry. Don't look at me like that. Didn't you ever want to do something, to just quit being so damn mild and pleasant and well behaved. Didn't you ever want to just shoot your mouth off, tell them all to go to hell?"

Now he's staring at me. It's not clear where Henry's anti-Christmas energy is headed. Otherwise, I understand his feeling, even think he has been courageous. But, here's the worry. He has no remorse and seems far from finished. He could have another crazy scheme ready, something madder yet. *And what about Harry the Good.* That's going to bother me all night.

"Harry the Good?" I point at him, angry. "Isn't that going a little overboard?"

He aims a sly chuckle at my anger. "Would Saint Harry be better?" He laughs. "Would you rather be Good King Harry? Or, Harry the Fairy? Or possibly, Harry, my brother, the Enlightened One? Oh Harry, Great King Harry, have you come to save me in this my hour of mad misgivings?"

"Alright already." *This kind of talk goes nowhere.* "What in the world were you doing?"

He looks at me, considering for a moment what must be the truth in his heart.

"I'm tired of sitting around gnawing my knuckles in fear, Harry. Like a damn prisoner here in the land of the free and the home of the brave."

"What fear? What are you talking about?"

"Not doing something, Harry. I'm afraid of becoming comfortable and letting my life slip by and finding out at seventy that I'm unsatisfied with myself, that I didn't do what I wanted to, what I need to do to live with myself."

"I see."

But I don't see, not really. I don't understand the pressure that Henry feels about these ideas. I don't know, for example, that Henry believes that Christmas has become so entirely corrupted, so enmeshed in the socio-political-economic structure of America that defying Christmas tradition is tantamount, in his mind, to revolt. He has become more and more radical in his thinking about Christmas, but he's still a middle class man and his radical thoughts don't jibe well with his middle class existence. Inside, he's tearing himself in two, and – I don't know this either – he's suffering physically from the stress and has been for some time.

"Let's go to your house, Harry. I want to sleep on your couch in the den."

"How come?" I look over at Mary. She seems surprised, too.

"I don't want to go home. I don't want to deal with Janette tonight. After all this shopping, she'll be fired up for a rodeo and I'm not in the mood. Besides, she will have heard something. She'll want to know what happened. And she'll be worried and upset."

"She probably doesn't have any idea about what happened yet, Henry."

Mary knows Janette well enough to be reasonably certain in her claim. Plus she left Janette trying on clothes at the mall. All Janette heard from the call was that we were being taken in by the police and we needed a ride.

"Are you kidding? Janette? She knows who I'm having lunch with before I do. If she hasn't already heard, she'll take one look at me and she will know."

"I suppose you're right," concedes Mary. "Apparently you made a pretty big scene at the park. By now somebody who knows somebody who knows Janette will have reached her and told her the whole thing."

"And probably made it sound like I've gone nuts and got taken to the loony bin, too."

"You probably should call and let her know the truth, Henry."

I'm staying out of this conversation.
"You call her."
"You want me to call her?"
"That's right. Do me a favor."
"Are you and Janette having problems?"
"No."
"Really?"
"For God's sake, Mary. No. Really! I'm just not feeling well. I want to lie down and be quiet. I want to be away from everyone."

"Ohh." It's my chance to make a point. "It's probably just all the excitement making you feel a little sick. How many times do you get dragged off screaming by the police?"

"Heh, heh, heh." Henry chuckles with satisfaction. "That was pretty good, wasn't it? I wonder how it will look in the newspaper."

"Sure, Henry. Maybe they'll want to interview you again. I can see the headline now. Christmas Lunatic Speaks Out. It'll be a follow-up story to tomorrow's tabloid piece featuring pictures of the local professor and stockbroker who went bonkers. Pictures of them being handcuffed and dragged away."

"You didn't have to jump in."

"I'm not sure why I did, in fact."

Henry swivels his head, offended.

Mary frowns at me in the rearview mirror.

"Okay, okay, I'll say it again." *I'll say it and you better acknowledge it.* "I couldn't just let them drag you off, could I?"

Henry can't contain himself. His laughter barely permits him to utter a word. "Sure you could. I would have let them drag you off."

I'm strangling him. I'm biting his ear. I'm punching him in his bald face. Mary bursts out laughing. "You two are like two boys!" She keeps on laughing, which settles us a bit. But as all fools do, we have to get in a last word.

"Maybe I'll call them in the morning and see if they want an interview."

"Right. You do that. You can wear your Santa suit."

We arrive home and no one is there. Henry crashes on the couch in the den and falls asleep immediately. I get his shoes off and cover him with a couple of blankets. He looks okay. I haven't taken his statement about not feeling well too seriously. It's clear that he's gotten himself overly worked up, but beyond that there doesn't seem to be a problem. His face is flush and rosy. He looks solid and strong like a fat Viking. I turn the lights down and leave the room.

Mary calls Janette. Janette has found a ride home from the mall with a friend. She listens to the story and laughs.

"By God, Mary," she says. "I knew he was going to do something crazy some day. I actually feel kind of relieved. Now that he's done it, maybe he'll settle down and enjoy the rest of Christmas."

This is what she says, and I believe that she feels relieved. Maybe she's right. Henry's outbursts could have led to anything. But even Mary won't try to disillusion her with regard to the idea that Henry will settle down after this one mad moment. It's enough that she accepts Henry for who he is and that she's good humored about it. By the time they finish talking, the kids are coming up the front walk. They sound cheerful and we're both looking forward to seeing them. Have we got a story to tell.

"All right, Janette," Mary says. "The kids are coming. Harry will bring the old grouch home in the morning. Good night."

I go to the front door with my finger to my lips. Here's my family, happy and bright. I feel a deep sense of gratitude. They're such good people. They're immediately considerate of the situation. We close Henry off in the den and sit around in the kitchen telling tales of the day. The kids gape with amazement. They can't wait to see tomorrow's newspaper. Then Willy takes photos of us sitting at the table. He has learned how to set the camera on time delay so he can be included. Cool. Eventually, midnight clocks in and we put it to rest. We all go eagerly to sleep and dreams.

◆◆◆◆

Henry is up rummaging around in the kitchen when I come out to make coffee. The rest of my family sleeps, no doubt worn out by the previous day's expenditures. Outside, the morning light casts a gray glow through the mist. Apparently, warm air moved in overnight and we're seeing the earth respond. There's a primitive jungle quality to the back yard due to the partial emergence of tree trunks and shrubbery in the mist. Man-made objects aren't visible. All is well, despite our new identities as criminally insane insurrectionists. *An odd thought, but not bothersome.* I'm happy. I could sing.

"Say, Henry. Have you got Janette a present yet?"

"No, I haven't."

"What say we have some coffee, head out early and get it done?"

"I guess we have to," he admits.

"There's no escaping it, Henry. Tomorrow is Christmas."

"Where's the coffee?" He's digging in the freezer part of the refrigerator.

"Mary keeps it in a jar now, instead of in the fridge. It's on the shelf there." I point to the green ceramic Bee House jar with an airtight lid. Henry retrieves it from the shelf and together we brew a pot of six cups in the Mr. Coffee machine. Henry digs out some Cheerios and fixes himself a bowl. Skipping the cereal, I nuke up an old bagel in the Sharp microwave.

"What are you going to get Janette?"

"No idea," says Henry as he munches.

"Me neither. I'm trying to think of something different. You know, something special."

"It's all overpriced crap, Harry. That's the problem."

Maybe we need to try a different approach, look in new and unusual places. *Let's do it right for once, make it look, at least, like some thought went into the decision.*

"I don't want to go to the mall."

"Now you're talking," says Henry. "I never want to see another mall in my life."

"But where?"

We both sit and think. Henry munches his cereal while I chew bagel and gulp down more coffee. It feels like were building a little momentum. There's a marketplace on the south side of town, which has hundreds of booths filled with unique, hand-made items. The possibilities seem promising. I'm even considering ignoring any thoughts about money. *Get something really neat.* What the hell. We're already thousands and thousands in debt, what with the new engine transplant for the Jimmy and the synthesizer gizmo and the anti-Christmas cards and the bike. *What madness.* The crazy idea comes to mind to spend another thousand on Mary. Why not? But, what can I get her? Absorbed by my thoughts, I don't really notice Henry right away. He's sitting back from his cereal with a strange look on his face.

"Boy, that milk is cold. My throat is cold."

"Like eating ice cream too fast."

"Yeah," Henry's voice is weak. "Just like that, but the freezing feeling is in my chest and not my head. Jesus, Harry, I think I'm having a heart attack."

"Are you kidding?" It's difficult to believe. He looks fine. His face is a normal color. He acts like he finds it difficult to believe, too.

"Well maybe it's just the milk ...it's gone away."

"Good. Are you sure?"

"No," Now he sounds scared. "No ...I'm having a heart attack ...it's back."

He sits back farther and puts his hand on his chest. His face looks puzzled and strange. We're both sitting there – like idiots – trying to come to grips with the idea. Maybe he's having a heart attack. Maybe he's not. He's sitting there talking to me. It makes me think he's okay. Maybe it's just indigestion. He stands up.

"Let's go to the hospital, Harry."

Suddenly, we mobilize.

"Okay, let's go. Get your shoes on. I'll start the car."

"To hell with my shoes, Harry. Let's go."

"It'll take less time if you put on your shoes. Don't tie them. Let's just get going."

He does what I say.

Luckily, the hospital is only ten minutes away and it's early morning. There's no traffic and we make good time. Halfway there, Henry angrily says that I'm not going fast enough. He's scared. It's like a shot of adrenaline. It is a shot of adrenaline. I push down the pedal and move into race car mode.

By the time we get to the emergency room door, Henry looks pale and sickly, but he's still moving under his own power. We pass through the double doors and stand before a window where a nurse sits looking out at the waiting area.

"He's having chest pains." A strange urgency has altered my voice.

The nurse takes one look and starts moving.

The Christmas Curmudgeon

Within a minute, he's on a gurney and plastered with a dozen wires and stuck with tubes. They give him the nitroglycerine. I'm a few feet away looking on. I can't hear all the words. It's like watching a silent movie. Two doctors enter. They get his permission for the TPA clot dissolver. Henry knows what it is and what the risks are. He tells them okay. After all, he's got stock in Genentech.

Everyone moves competently; they seem so knowledgeable about what they're doing. Then suddenly, there's a spike in the activity. He's having a heart attack for real. Even I can tell that. The clot buster goes in. A few tense, motionless minutes pass. Then all the nurses and doctors relax. Henry's going to be alright. It's not just being hopeful. He really is.

A nurse approaches and tells me to go to the waiting area. "He's had a heart attack," she says. "We'll need some information from you."

"Is he okay?"

She ignores my question. "How much time was it from when it started to your getting here?"

"I don't know, all told, about eighteen minutes, I guess." *Why eighteen? Why not fifteen or twenty?*

"That's good," she answers and points me to the waiting room. "He's doing fine."

Another nurse takes the information about Henry's health insurance, address, occupation, so on and so forth. By the time we're finished, she feels confident that Henry will be able to pay for his treatment. She's noticeably more relaxed. I can't help but wonder what would happen if this weren't the case. Is there a poor person's treatment option? One for which they just give you a shot and some pills and send you home with instructions? "You've had a heart attack. Take these pills. Get plenty of rest during the next week. If you have further problems, call your doctor." Good luck on that. Henry will get the twenty thousand dollar treatment. I feel sure of that. He's earned it.

On the way home, I have to pull over to the side of the road to let go of my emotions. It's a good release. Pulling out my handkerchief, I blow my nose and clear my head. A few more minutes pass and peace is restored to my soul. Before starting again, I tune in some maniac preacher on the radio proselytizing about the need for more donations to rebuild the Empire of God. His duplicity strikes me as so blatantly transparent that it's good for a real laugh. The temerity of these evangelists! The Empire of God, indeed.

Chapter Eighteen

There's no one home when I arrive, as usual, except for Tiny, who has escaped from the utility room and is contentedly chewing on a couch cushion she has pulled down to the living room floor. A look at the clock on the mantle tells me it's later in the morning than expected. Tiny gets a "bad dog" and scurries away, back to her proper place. She seems to be smiling. I pace around, agitated, then go into the kitchen and make a peanut butter and bacon sandwich, avoiding what has to be done.

Making the phone call to Janette is more upsetting than anticipated and I have to stop a couple of times to compose myself in order to appear to be the calm, reassuring man society prescribes. It doesn't work. Janette is calmer by far. Of course, she hasn't just watched her brother have a heart attack. *Does she even have a brother? I can't remember.*

"I'm going to the hospital," she announces.

"They'll probably have him locked away for awhile."

"I'm going anyway."

"Okay. Do you want me to join you?"

"No, I'll see what's going on and then call you."

"I'll come by to visit him this afternoon."

"What's Mary doing?"

"She's shopping for groceries for Christmas dinner."

"God, what a time to have a heart attack."

"I guess he's been under a lot of stress."

"He never tells me, Harry. He just rants and raves."

"That's Henry..."

There's a brief silence during which we both regain control of ourselves.

"It's not your fault, Janette."

She starts crying. "He doesn't take care of himself. I'm supposed to take care of him. I'm his wife."

"You're a good wife, Janette. And Henry's going to be alright. They said he's doing great. Maybe this is an important message for him. Maybe he'll cut down on the pizza and Tiramisu."

"Maybe he'll learn to relax."

"Right. That's the spirit."

"Maybe he'll quit worrying."

"Absolutely."

"He might even start to enjoy holidays, instead of fuming about them."

"Well, I wouldn't go that far, Janette. He's had a heart attack, not a brain transplant."

She's laughing and crying at the same time. I feel another swell of emotion. Mary comes into the house and sees that something is wrong. Covering the mouthpiece of the phone, I tell her Henry has had a heart attack. She rushes into the kitchen with her groceries and rushes back.

"Is that Janette?" she whispers. I nod. "Let me have her."

"Jesus, Mary. I just got her laughing a little."

"I'm her best friend, Harry. Let me talk to her."

Mary gets the phone.

"Janette?" Mary's voice is full of concern.

You can hear Janette burst into sobs from three feet away.

The hours seem to zip by. The children handle the news well, better than the adults actually. Of course, they're children. Basically, they believe Henry cannot die. It's not so much that he's immortal – they know that's absurd – but that he's invulnerable. Death can't touch him. It's not allowed. They are blithely confident in everyone's ability to continue doing what they do and for everything to remain the same.

❖❖❖❖

The Christmas Curmudgeon

Christmas Eve looms on the horizon like an August moon, large, imposing, prescient. The house is peaceful. Henry progresses well in intensive care, and it looks like the heart attack was a mild one, though they won't know for sure until they probe him. Our afternoon chat tires him. He complains about the change in his diet. The idea of becoming accustomed to it appalls him. All this seems positive compared to yesterday.

On the way back from the visit to the hospital, the perfect gift for Mary comes to mind. It has been there all the time. She mentioned it several times over the course of the last year. Once or twice, anyway. And it's only nine hundred dollars. What's nine hundred dollars to an anti-Christmas card mogul? Nothing! I immediately drive to Office Depot and pick it up.

Normally, the family gathers around the tree on Christmas Eve. After dinner and after imbibing a few heady rums, we would receive Henry and Janette. Their kids come along, and Henry and I hold the Christmas Eve All Out Hot Wheels Spectacular Drag Race Finale. The ultimate in noise and madness. The prizes are enormous. First place receives four nights out on the town, movie and dinner included, with three friends, second place receives three nights out and so on down to fourth place. All the kids win something. The booby-prize winners (two for Christmas Eve) get to clean up the mess and have to perform ridiculous acts that the four main prize winners decide upon in conference. Last year Henry and I were the boobies (as usual), and we had to go up onto his roof and sing "Jingle Bells." This year we had planned to get Mary and Janette involved in the event (maybe they could be the boobies for once). But, this year what I decide – *what Mary decides* – is to postpone the Hot Wheels competition and go to the evening church service.

Late in the afternoon, snow starts falling and in a short time the yard, the streets, the roofs of houses, the sidewalks and shrubbery are covered with several inches of whiteness. It's lovely. A perfect time for a little nap. But Mary has other plans. The kids are outside playing in the snow. Mary wastes no time. She takes me by the hand and leads me upstairs to the bedroom.

"I've got a special Christmas present for you."

When we get there, she puts on some soft piano music by Michael Jones. I receive a complete body rub. This must be a dream. The music and massage transport me into a twilight state between wakefulness and sleep. A vision of The Woman from the Fourth Dimension comes and goes as my eyes open and close. The growing state of relaxation is heavenly. *Close your eyes. Go into the dream state.*

"Harry," she whispers in my ear. She's wearing a light blue metallic slip that glimmers when she moves. Her body is flexible yet taut. She straddles my waist and leans forward to whisper and kiss me. How wonderful it is.

In appearances she's different than Mary, slimmer and more extravagant in her make up and attire. She dresses more like a space alien than Mary. But, in her essence, in the nature of her affection and familiarity, in my comfort with her and my desire for her, she's Mary as I remember her from our first years of marriage.

"Harry," she says. "Are you ready?"

I open my eyes and look at her and see The Woman from the Fourth Dimension dissolve and become Mary. There she is, Mary. It's surprising, actually stunning, yet totally agreeable.

"Ready." I watch as she lifts her slip over her head.

"Let's take off ..."

The nap that follows is one of the best.

◆◆◆◆

For me, attending a church service resembles watching a Walt Disney movie. I don't expect much. The show is mildly entertaining, generally simple-minded, somewhat moralistic, too long to be consistently engaging and appreciated best if you are between five and ten years old. But, it doesn't require much participation except for a modest fee. Actually, I think spiritual practice ought to be part of a daily regimen, an attitude or an approach to life. Organized religion generally impedes progress along these lines. But Mary insists that going to the Christmas Eve service will be beneficial for everyone. So we go, and we all send our prayers out for Henry's recovery.

On the way home, we stop by the park and let the kids out to build a snowman. Willy has been pushing for it all the way. It's one of those perfect winter evenings, still and cold. The last edges of snow fall; individual flakes seems to dangle on thin strings in the air. Since he began his family album, Willy always has his camera with him. He's looking for new scenes, trenchant moments. He's become a little paparazzi. Mary and I sit in the car and watch. They finish the snowman, top his head with Tom's ski cap and Willy takes a few pictures. He convinces Tom to dig a hole through the snowman's head, hide himself to the rear and then stick his arm through and dangle his hand out the snowman's mouth. Now there's a photo.

"What more could you want?"

The kids start throwing snowballs at the car. We ignore them.

"I'm happy," says Mary.

"I'm glad."

"Mr. Gregg wants me to work full time."

"I'm glad, again. Do you know how much we spent this Christmas season?"

"Is it bad?"

The snowballs start coming faster and faster, plastering the windows with blobs of white.

"Well, including the Casio Electronic Synthesizer, the Western Auto remanufactured engine plus labor, the bike, your present and all the rest we're well over five thousand in new debt."

"Five thousand?"

"We invested some in the anti-Christmas cards," I add.

"Harry, you didn't." She punches my arm.

"Yes, I did."

"Are the cards making a profit?"

There's a sudden ominous quiet outside. They're planning an all-out assault.

"Let me put it this way. We learned a lot. Next year will be a really good year."

"For anti-Christmas cards?"

"Absolutely."

"What about this year?"

"This year, it will be a good year for you to work full time at Gregg's Lands Away clothing shop." I punch her back.

Another barrage of snowballs hits the car. In unison, we jump from the car and heave snowballs so fast the kids are overwhelmed. We run in for the attack and bury them alive. At the finish, everyone is covered with snow. We lie on the ground, exhausted. Another photo opportunity for Willy.

༺

Chapter Nineteen

Some families sit around in a circle on Christmas morning and take turns opening presents one at a time. I guess the idea is that each person will receive some sort of apportionment of personal attention and that the gift-giver, also, can reap the benefit of experiencing his or her gift being opened and appreciated. This style of Christmas morning arouses my worst suspicions regarding Americans and the whole human race. These are the same people who label their underwear with the days of the week and have perfectly organized garages and basements. Their furniture may be covered with plastic, their footballs, Frisbees and baseball gloves protected by Saran Wrap.

Our family rapidly dispenses with any attempt at decorum. Willy makes sure everyone is awake and out of bed by seven in the morning. This year, unaware of my rule, he photographs each person at the exact moment of his or her awakening, when their faces are still creased with sleep and their expression as unprepared as possible. Mary manages to brew a pot of coffee, and then we all sit down together in the living room. Tom starts distributing the gifts, and about a third of the way through this process all pretense regarding an orderly procedure is lost. The ribbons and wrapping paper fly.

Mary and I eagerly await Tom's reaction to the synthesizer. It's the third gift he opens. Even Willy senses that something special is about to happen and slows down to watch. Tom unwraps the package and looks at the name-brand label on the box. He can't believe it.

"Whoaah! Wow!!"

Mary and I laugh. I can see there, a tear in her eye. Once Tom gets the machine out of the carton, I can't resist trying to insert a little instructive talk.

"Your mother says if you get this now, Tom, when you're fifteen and older, we can avoid all adolescent difficulties. You will understand that you're so well loved that you won't grow up to be a drug addict or a college drop-out. Is that true?"

"You bet, dad," he answers without thinking. "Man this is the greatest. Joe has been taking drum lessons for a year. Now all we need is a lead guitar and a bass. Man, this is the greatest! Thanks!"

He hasn't heard a word. I should have known better. Mary laughs. We all relax a minute before moving on to the next package. Mary gives Tom a signal and tells Willy to close his eyes. With the heart attack and all, I realize I haven't even thought about assembling Willy's bike. Mary taps me on the shoulder.

"I had Tom do it. He did a professional job, too." she smiles. "No swearing."

Relief. That Tom could do the work on the bike seems impossibly wonderful. And, something very strange is going on. I'm excited to see Willy's bike, more excited than I've been in a long time ...since I got my own new bike once, so many years ago.

Tom enters pushing the bike. Willy jumps up and looks around as if it couldn't possibly be true. The bike he has wanted is real. It's there right in front of him. He's greatly satisfied, even slightly blown away. The day is turning out better than expected.

Mary's gift to me is totally surprising. It's something I've wanted but have deliberately never mentioned since I know we don't need it and can't afford it. How does Mary intuit these things? It's one of the great mysteries of my life.

She hands me a card from beneath the tree. I look it over then open it. The cover of the card is a traditional Christmas scene, a log fire in a cozy living room with stockings hanging from the mantle. The kind of card that Henry despises. Inside, Mary has written a little love note. Also, folded up inside, there's a magazine photograph of a 54" Mitsubishi flat screen television with built in VCR and stereo sound. Virtually a home theater.

"My God."

"It was on sale." Mary sticks her chin out. "Overstock dot com."

This is totally bewildering. I pass the photo to the boys. Feelings of every sort race through my body. Thrills and guilt and fear and happiness and gratitude and anger and affection. The price has got to be in the neighborhood of fifteen hundred dollars. It's dizzying. *Closer to seven grand, now. That's a nice round sum. Maybe you could sell cocaine. Marijuana? One of your kidneys?*

"Alright, Dad!" Tom nods his head repeatedly.

"Can we watch it, too?" asks Willy.

"Only for educational programs."

Willy pushes his lips out to the end of his nose. Tom knows it's a joke and tells him so. Willy smiles with relief.

"When does it get here?" asks Tom.

"Day after tomorrow." Mary holds a shipping notice.

I nudge my special present toward Mary so that she can't avoid it. The kids catch the move and wait to see what Mom will get. She unwraps the package deliberately slowly to tease them and then opens it, covering her mouth and gasping as though her soul might escape if she didn't.

"It's an Apple Power Book!" she shouts.

"Awesome!" Tom's envy is apparent.

Willy turns pale from all the excitement. He stands and starts whirling around in circles. Mary laughs, but to me it seems bizarre, an emotional disturbance of some sort, a primitive behavior that disconnects Willy from the rest of us. I'm suddenly afraid that Willy has gone berserk. He continues twirling around. If he were making a sound like an airplane, it wouldn't be so disturbing, but he silently twirls in some other world. I'm really beginning to think there's something wrong. Then he spins over to me and falls into my lap. I hug him and rub his head. Whatever rapture transported him vanishes as quickly as it came.

Mary leans over and kisses me and rubs my head. It's strangely reassuring. I feel loved and accepted in a way that touches me deeply. For an instant I become completely aware. It's a wonderful moment of feeling totally alive and present in the world. Now, so many years into adulthood, I'm learning to be open again, to be a child, to be real.

Tom receives a beginner's set of tools, a sweater, a computer game on disc and two CD's. Willy gets his own computer game, a set of Junior Classics, a jacket and a baseball glove. I receive two books I've been eager to read and two shirts and ties. Mary gets a bath oil set, a beautiful Lennox vase and a Japanese cookbook. Of course, these are only the larger items. There's much more in the way of smaller gifts – candy, toys, office and house supplies, joke gifts, standard supplies such as underwear and socks and so forth and so on as well as presents that have come in the mail from relatives and friends. All in all, it's not only an extravagant Christmas, but, a day punctuated by strange feelings that I will ponder, no doubt, for many days.

Fixing breakfast without Henry is no fun. I won't make the crepes Suzette without his eggs Benedict. Scrambled eggs and sausage will do, with fresh coffee and whole wheat toast. A host of Christmas feelings devour me. Nearly overcome by guilt, I look out the kitchen window and see a crowd of starving squalid people dressed in rags squatting in the yard, moaning and keening, holding their hands out with hollow pleading eyes. It's a momentary vision, but it nearly knocks me down. Henry is the only one who can understand this kind of experience. I need to tell him, but decide it will have to wait. He would interpret this vision as a message of great import, full of truth and guidance for life.

The Christmas Curmudgeon

◆◆◆◆

During the afternoon on Christmas day I visit Henry. The intensive care unit is modern and very high tech. The glass-walled rooms form a circle around a circular, nursing station in the center of the unit. The place is still, with rocket science concentration, except for the multiple blips and beeps that rise from the machines at the nurses' station and the hushed phone conversations the nurses carry on. Janette left just fifteen minutes earlier and Henry is sleeping. Henry looks okay. I take a seat next to his bed, quite comfortable, and immediately fall off into a pleasant nap.

"Is Christmas over?"

Opening my eyes, I squint into the light. The white glare makes me feel queasy. My brain feels thick with sleep. Henry is on his side, facing me, flicking my ear lobe with a finger. Now that my eyes are open, he gives me a hard one. I sit up, annoyed.

"What the hell! What's wrong with you, Henry? Cut it out." *How can he be so irritating?*

"Shhh," he points out the sliding glass door-wall to the other rooms. "I've had a heart attack." He speaks in a hoarse whisper, laughing lightly.

"Is that what makes you flick my ear?"

"Harry?"

"What?" I'm whispering now, as well.

"Is Christmas over?"

"Well, yes ...I mean no. It's still Christmas day, but the ordeal is over, if that's what you mean."

"Christmas gave me a heart attack, Harry."

"Baloney. Eating Burger King burgers, sausage and eggs, cinnamon rolls, Pecan Sandies and pastries gave you a heart attack."

"Yeah, but Christmas made me have the heart attack."

"What are you up to, Henry?" I'm suspicious of the well-pleased grin on his face. "Is this what you're telling Janette?"

"Yes. Most definitely."

"So, what does she say?"

"She agrees that it's too stressful for me – given my feelings about it and all – and she's agreed to let it go."

"What! She's giving up Christmas? I don't believe it."

"No." He pulls his blanket up to his chin. "Let me explain. Instead of Christmas, we'll take a holiday, a trip, you know. Remember that Raymond Nixon guy? I told her about him, how healthy and happy he looked, how he always went away for Christmas to a beach and rested in the sun. We're going to take a trip next Christmas. We'll still give the kids a few presents, mostly stocking stuffers. We won't be going into debt anymore. We'll just take our vacation at a different time. There will be less stress. If the kids want something, they'll have to earn at least half the cost."

"Geez, Henry. You swindler! I can't believe it. You old donkey!"

"There's more." He bursts into a malicious giggle.

"What?"

"Janette will try to convince Mary to do the same. She's agreed to it. You know ...so you won't have a heart attack. You know how tired you've been lately? That's how I've been feeling, too. That's how it started for me ...before the heart attack."

"I don't think Mary will buy it, Henry."

"Sure she will. The Doc gave Janette all the facts she needs about your odds of having a heart attack."

"Really?"

"It doesn't look good for you, Harry."

"Really?" I don't know what else to say. Suddenly, it seems, the conversation has turned from Christmas or the end of Christmas to my imminent heart attack. And just as quickly my chest feels tight and I'm getting very warm. I'm feeling a little dizzy. My heart seems to be pounding erratically.

"I don't feel so well."

"Of course not," he says. "Look at you. You're a middle-aged, flabby, worried, donkey-man, who works at a desk all day and doesn't exercise. Things have got to change for you, pal. You and me both. Don't worry. Janette will convince Mary. I'm sure of it."

My whole left shoulder feels as though a big block of ice has gotten inside it. My left side feels numb and achy. I think this must a heart attack. *Weird.* It just can't be. *Maybe, its just fear.* I don't know. My breathing feels tight and shallow. *It's just anxiety ...an anxiety attack.*

"Henry, I think I'm having a heart attack."

"Well, you're in the right place for it." He laughs. He flicks my ear again. "It's probably just fear." He watches me. I'm concentrating on my shoulder. The tightness seems to be going away. "Harry ...It's okay. You don't have to have a heart attack. I've done it for both of us. Think of it, Harry! No more Christmas. It's for the best, isn't it?"

The more I think about it, the more I chuckle. This is truly an inspired scheme. Henry nods and laughs along with me. One of the nurses comes by to tell us to quiet down. "There are sick people here," she says. This throws us into another fit of laughter. I can tell that she's about to ask me to leave. I tell her we'll be quiet. It's okay. The discomfort in my shoulder vanishes. It was just tension and stress.

We talk awhile about his heart attack and what he'll have to do to recover. The doctors are very positive. One of them steps in for a consultation and tells Henry about catheterization and taking a look inside his heart. It's very scientific and interesting. Very objective. The doctor leaves. We sit in silence, each of us lost in his own thoughts. It's comfortable for us. We have no need to fill the silence. After awhile, Henry shifts to his back and cranks up his bed with the electric bed adjuster so that he's almost sitting up.

"Harry," he confides. "I owe you an apology."

"About what?"

"You know, for teasing you ...about dem critters."

"Forget it, Henry. You have a right to your own point of view."

"Yes, I know, but you were right. That Virgil fellow did have a strange power. It was like he saw into us or beyond us or something."

"He was quite a person ...that's for sure."

"You know that carving he gave me?"

"Yes."

"He was right. I didn't think it made any sense at the time, but now I do. I thought the first guy was running from the other guy, you know, like a thief running from a store owner ...somebody desperate trying to get away from somebody else. But it you look at it closely, you know what you see?"

"Am I supposed to guess? I saw just what you did, one guy chasing another."

"He's running from himself, Harry. Every little detail of the two men is the same, only their expressions differ. They're the same person. And what's even weirder is that when you look at the expressions on their faces from different angles, they change. Sometimes it's anger being chased by fear, sometimes the other way around. Sometimes its guilt being chased by judgment, sometimes, some other feelings. The thing is amazing."

"It's hard to imagine."

"You have to see it. Once you see it, you get all caught up in it."

"So all this time you've been razzing me, you've been looking at your own little wooden figurine, too?"

"That's right. I just couldn't admit it to you. It's just too damn hokey and New Age for me, Harry."

"You didn't want to admit that it did mean something. Virgil moved you, too." I can't resist making Henry admit it out loud after all he put me through.

"That's right, Harry. Virgil is absolutely right. I'm running away from myself. I've always been running away from myself. I haven't been living what I believe. That's what made me go to the park. I wanted to speak the truth, to live it. That's what this heart attack is all about. I've got to come to terms with myself. I've got to start being more true to myself, Harry, to live according to what I believe."

◆◆◆◆

It's difficult to accept at first, but as Mary and I discuss the idea of changing how we observe Christmas, we come to see Henry's vision. We have gone seven thousand dollars into debt in the space of a few weeks, most of it directly due to Christmas. It's true that our debts enslave us to a spiral of increasing work to pay them, and then we buy more things to counteract the emptiness and loneliness that the debt and work create. It's true that the Christmas season captures and distills this way of life. It's a microcosm of the American way. And reciprocally, the Christmas season is the condensed quintessence of the American marketplace. We the people are caught in this swirling vortex; Christmas and capitalism feed each other in a never-ending spiral of commercialism and consumerism.

America, the American way, has gotten out of control, not just Mary and me. Henry's convinced that it's a corporate and political conspiracy to control the masses. How far the conspiracy extends is a matter for speculation. For the two of us, it's enough to consider how the entire scheme engulfs our family, how it defines our beliefs and controls our behavior.

Henry's truth is that we fear the freedom of defining our lives independently. We fear that freedom more than we fear the slavery of spiraling consumption and debt. Christmas and all the traditions that surround it, all the purchasing and all the debt, make us terribly one-dimensional worker-consumer Americans. It's strange and paradoxical. We're driven by the fear of freedom in the land that cherishes and celebrates freedom. But, we're safe in this definition of ourselves. We do it in the name of love and prosperity, yet we don't venture far from our habits, from buying our toys and losing ourselves on our screens.

Janette has convinced Mary that we should try a few years of non-Christmas and let ourselves explore an alternative way of celebrating our lives and love for each other. As Mary and I continue our discussion, I see that it's in my best interest to allow Mary to convince me in turn. I resist for a while. I'm going to be the devil's advocate, and thereby fortify her position.

"C'mon, Mary. We're at the pinnacle of our buying power. What's a little debt?"

Mary speaks with resolve. "We can get out of debt and stay that way. We can be free. We can have time to relax and pursue some of our creative interests. You can avoid a heart attack. What do you say, Harry?"

We can be free. What an idea.

Janette has done a brilliant, generous and caring thing.

We now know that freedom is having the time and energy to create and define our lives, to live as we want to live. As proof of our commitment, we decide to return the Mitsubishi 54" projection television and the Apple Power Book. It feels right, even righteous. *It's Henry who led the way.*

They release Henry from the hospital after eight days. He's been probed and scoped and he's reasonably healthy. He has to take medication and alter his weight and diet. These are all things he can do. *Well, cutting down on the goodies may not be so easy.* Stopping by to see him on his first day out, I wonder if he's already developing a new scheme. He greets me at the door wearing a bright yellow shirt covered with green, red and blue parrots. He hands me an identical shirt in a plastic bag.

"Merry Christmas, Harry."

"Same to you, Henry. Merry Christmas."

"Next year we'll be wearing these shirts on some island beach. What do you say?"

"I guess we will, Henry. Why not?"

We go inside and sit down in his den. He has been watching football, but he turns the television off. He pulls an envelope out from beside his chair.

"Take a look at that, will you," he says with an attitude of pride.

I open the envelope. Inside, there's a check for four thousand, twenty-four dollars made out to me. Absolutely stunning. Mary and I will definitely appreciate the money. It will go a long way toward finishing off our overblown debt. Where does the money come from? Henry isn't in the business of giving away money. He's a stockbroker, after all.

"What the heck?"

Henry mocks my bewildered expression.

"Card number three did very well." He slaps his knee and grins.

"Card number three? Which one was that?"

"The one you liked. You know, a traditional Santa on the cover saying 'Remember...' Then inside it says, 'Nothing is better than debt!'"

"That was a good one. It made that much?"

"It did very well. The nasty ones helped, too, but they didn't do nearly as well. They did sell though ...probably enough to indicate a sizable market out there."

"The hardcore cynics and emotionally challenged?"

"Ha! Yes, probably. Guys in touch with the dark humor, sickness and absurdity of their lives."

"Guys like you and me."

"Yeah," agrees Henry, smiling warmly. "Guys like you and me."

◆◆◆◆

Back home, where the post-Christmas solitude stretches toward infinity, the warmth inside the cold devouring the world, Mary sleeps with Tiny by her side. In the den, Willy has his photo scrapbook out on a table. Melanie, Tom and Viv look on as he flips the

The Christmas Curmudgeon

pages. Observing from the doorway, I stand unnoticed.

"Here's one of dad dragging the mangled tree into the living room."

"He looks crazy."

"Not as crazy as our dad." Viv seems proud of Henry's madness. "Did you get any photos of that?"

"I wasn't there, you know, but I did get some photos. I went down to the newspaper building, and there was a guy there who said he had some extra pictures, even some that weren't in the paper. He gave them to me."

Tip-toeing a little closer, I can see over their shoulders. Tom and Mel look back and nod. Willy turns the page. There's Henry shouting at the crowd. Then, there's one of him being dragged away by two policemen. Apparently, this photographer had been at the scene from the start. Another shows me accosting the police. Finally, a couple more show us on the ground being handcuffed. These along with the two pictures clipped from the newspaper complete the arrangement.

"I'm going to write stuff on the pages like great grandma did." Willy looks around, pleased with the idea.

"That's good." Tom gives Willy a head rub.

It will certainly be something special, a wonderful photo album. The grandchildren will laugh, whenever we have grandchildren. Willy has the sense of what's important. It's not the big events, though they're interesting. It's the snowman he and Tom built, then the same with Tom's arm dangling from its mouth, several shots of the two families at the table, Uncle Henry holding up the worm he just pulled from his mouth, an exaggerated look of shock and disgust on his face, Tiny chasing a squirrel, a shot of Willy with his arms in casts, Mary and Janette talking at the kitchen table, Mary and me in a hug, Janette and Mel in the exact same dress, one Tom took of Willy riding his bike on Christmas day and many more.

He's put more that forty pictures into the book,

along with Christmas cards, sprigs of Christmas tree and pieces of wrapping paper and ribbon, Christmas related headlines and stories cut from newspapers and magazines and, on the cover, a close-up of the hideous Santa head with the broken tooth on the front door. On the first page, Willy has printed in large font, "Ho, ho, ho and a Merry Christmas!"

No doubt, the rest of his written entries will show his wit and warmth. He takes after his great grandmother and that's a wonderful and pleasing thing. The connection there is real, though he never saw her alive. The character is the same, somehow passed on to him through the generations. We're a line, a lineage, a family that has a history and a present life driven by that history with a strength that will carry.

Epilogue

Henry and I have begun taking walks around town each day. As a result, I've been feeling more energetic, and he has regained some confidence in his body. It's both exercise and relaxation and we enjoy the time. A number of neighbors whom neither of us knew before have become acquaintances. They wave or shout hello as we pass.

We're regulars now at Joanie's Digital Diner on Main Street, downtown. Joanie is a hippie type in her forties with long blond hair who has embraced health food and fitness. Her veggie deluxe sandwich on sunflower bread is out of this world. After a Saturday morning walk on a remarkably warm spring day, we're seated at Joanie's diner having salad and fish for lunch with hot tea. Henry introduces his latest scheme.

"I've got an idea," he says calmly.

"I don't think I'm ready for a new idea, Henry. If you don't mind."

"I guarantee you'll like this idea."

"Okay, let's hear it. But I'm telling you right now, I'm not going to do it. No matter what."

"Fine." Henry, smiles, confident he will change my mind. He waits a moment, looking at me. I sip my coffee, wondering when he'll begin. He continues smiling then gazes around the diner with a diffident look. It seems as though he's distracted.

"What? I told you I would listen."

"You know ...I was just thinking about them Critzers."

"Oh?"

"Wouldn't it be great if we could do something for them?"

"Doesn't seem likely, Henry. Those people live

The Christmas Curmudgeon

in a different world from us. What could we do?"

"We could help them start a little business."

I lean back and look at him. For a minute, it seems that the Critzers are a sidetrack, a little reminiscence before he launches the main idea. Then it becomes clear that he has been sucking me into his scheme all along.

"What kind of little business, Henry – a hillbilly cappuccino stand?"

"How you talk. No, I was thinking more along the line of a flower business. Janette and Mary could run the shop and the Critzers could grow the flowers ...like they said they were going to."

It's an astonishingly practical and caring idea. Henry takes a bite from his sandwich and relaxes. *Mr. Smug.* He gives me plenty of time to think. Joanie comes by and asks if we want anything else. We've become her favorite regulars. Henry likes the way she treats us. He tries to sell her some Sysco stock on a margin while I think about the flower shop idea. Apparently, Joanie is perfectly satisfied running the Digital Diner and doesn't really need the Sysco stock. She leaves shaking her head.

"Let's do it," I say.

"You see." Henry smiles. "He who speaks without knowing says nothing."

We leave the diner, making plans to go visit the Critzers later in the afternoon. Having accepted the idea, I'm excited to go, eager mostly to see how the Critzers are doing. Both Janette and Mary are enthusiastic about Henry's idea. They want very much to join the ranks of women entrepreneurs.

Henry and I head out around two in the afternoon. The day is gorgeous, a clear blue sky, sun and a promise of increasing warmth in the air. Some of the dogwoods are beginning to bloom. Maybe we'll have an early spring.

We drive out Hastings County Road into New Hope Valley. It's beginning to green and there are farmers out in the fields. But there are still patches in the shadows where snow sits, waiting for the ground to gather warmth. Some big yellow road graders, bulldozers and backhoes are working along the side of Bear Creek Road. A woman in a hard hat and an orange day-glo vest directs us over a new culvert. The road is in bad shape, rutted and eroded. We make slow progress up the hill toward the Critzers.

We find the house easily. At first glance, it looks about the same. The weeds have sprouted some tiny blue flowers. The wood on the porch seems drier and grayer in appearance. Otherwise, it looks the same, except now the windows look dark and empty. The place suddenly looks and feels as though it has been abandoned. I go up on the porch and knock on the door while Henry looks around the yard.

"Morgan! Are you there? Virgil? Is anybody home?"

No one answers.

The door is ajar and I open it and look inside. The front room is empty except for a few chairs and wooden crates. There are no shoes or clothes in sight. The room is bare. No signs of life. Running my finger along the windowsill, I check for evidence of any cleaning. To tell the truth, I can't remember whether the place was this dirty and neglected before. A thick grimy paste made of oily dust comes off the wood. It's perplexing. Every surface in the place is covered with dust and the rooms smell dank and musty. Masses of cobwebs catch the light and seem to float like wisps of smoke coming down from the ceiling. A mouse skitters along the edge of the wall and disappears into the kitchen. I turn around and stand in the doorway, looking out.

"There's no one here, Henry."

Henry looks up at me from the yard. He has been puttering around out there, looking over the side lot and the fields in back to evaluate their value for cultivation.

"Well, they're probably out in the woods or something."

"I don't think so. This is really weird, Henry. There's no one here. Nobody lives here. The place is empty."

"You joking around with me, Harry?"

"No ...if I didn't know better, I'd say nobody has lived in this place for quite some time."

Henry climbs up on the porch, gives me a scornful look of disbelief and looks inside. He walks around the living room, looks into the kitchen, and then looks at me as if I had traded his car for two tickets to a symposium on UFO's.

"This can't be."

"Maybe they moved."

"Moved?" says Henry. "This place hasn't been occupied in years. Something strange is going on, I'll tell you that."

Nothing is impossible. Who knows? We're both rational men, most of the time. We like to think we can solve most problems, figure out and analyze what bothers us. But, this place, now that we have seen it, seems beyond comprehension. It's dilapidated and overgrown, without a trace of any recent occupancy. There's a sense of mystery here that confounds us both. We sit on the porch and look out over the yard. A sense of being in a completely alien place surrounds us. I don't know how long we sit there on the porch, lost in our thoughts, separately trying to come to terms with what is beyond the boundaries of our normal experience. Time shifts in this place; it does not run around the clock.

"Yoo hoo ...oh, yoo hoo."

We look out to the road where an old woman, perhaps in her seventies, stands and waves at us. She's wearing a colorful scarf on her head. The rest of her clothing is brown and simple; a long peasant dress, a pale tan blouse and a dark sweater. She continues waving.

"Yoo hoo!"

Henry gets up and walks out to see what she wants. I watch him go. Something looks familiar about

The Christmas Curmudgeon

the woman, though I've never seen her before. There's something unusual about her appearance. She seems safe and kind, unusually kind. There's no sense of danger. Then, I feel pushed into a distance, as though viewing Henry through a lens, as you might look in on the activity of some small forest creature, a bird or a squirrel, through a high-powered scope. In this absolutely silent and absorbed state of mind, while sitting on the porch, at least a hundred yards from the road, I can see and hear everything as though standing right there next to Henry and the old woman.

"Hello, young man," the old woman greets Henry as he steps through the weeds down to the road.

"Hello."

"Are you interested in this place?"

"Well, yes. We, uh, we recently met the people who live here and we were actually coming by to talk with them."

"Ahhh." She nods her head.

"Do you know where they are?" asks Henry. "It looks as though they moved out."

"You mean the Critzers, do you?"

"Yes. We met them just before Christmas."

"Oh, I see," says the woman. "You know, you're not the first."

"What?" Henry stands back, clearly baffled by her statement.

"The Critzers haven't lived here for years."

"Well, that can't be, Ma'am. With all respect, we just saw two of them, Virgil and Morgan, just a few months ago, just before Christmas."

"That's how it usually is. Did you look inside?"

"Yes, I did."

She points at the house. "No one has lived there for years. There was that unfortunate accident that killed Wyatt ...that was a long time back. Then the old man died. The mother and the two boys you mention lived on there for a good piece. Then they just up and moved out – all at once – over the mountains, to

The Christmas Curmudgeon

Tennessee, I think." She shakes her head. "I heard they died in a car accident. Terrible thing. They were fine people."

Henry turns and looks back at me. He looks as though he's literally caught in an absurdity. He's realized an impossibility. He's seeking deliverance.

But, a strange peacefulness permeates this place and this moment.

It's possible to experience the world directly, without thought or meaning, to see the rich and fruitful life of the trees, to feel the slow rotation of the earth. Beyond Henry, in the sky, the clouds drift away. There's a mass of them drifting toward the horizon. That the earth is curved is apparent, that the rotation of the earth and the movement of the clouds are of a piece, a harmony of utter magnificence, is real. Raising my hands in the air, raising my eyebrows, I try to signal Henry to return. There is no explanation, there is no way to understand. We might as well accept it.

Henry turns back to the woman, but she has started walking uphill on the road. Henry doesn't say anything; he just watches her go. Something about the way she moves reminds me of an earlier time; a time when people gathered in warm rooms by crackling fires, spoke softly, made gifts for each other and laughed easily. Standing on the porch, I look up the road after her, but it's getting dark now and my eyes are uncertain. She walks into the shadows under the oaks and maples farther up the hill. Henry remains, standing there, looking up the road. He looks back at me. I wave at him to come back to the porch.

We sit on the porch steps until dusk. Neither of us says what he thinks. Neither of us can put it into words. The moon is nearly full. A couple of crows fly by and settle in a tree across the road. "Caw," goes one. "Caw, Caw," goes the other. They seem to be talking. Every now and then, Henry shakes his head and laughs. At one point, he starts laughing and can't stop. His laughter builds and shakes his body. He slams his hand on the porch. He whoops and hollers, releasing an internal tension greater than warranted by the moment. I sit beside him and enjoy his release but remain quiet. The deep sky opens and the stars seem to swirl. The shadows around us twitch and stretch. The moon slowly rises. Everything is in motion, yet the world is silent, so utterly silent and real.